TIME FALL

Jaclyn Belmay

TIME FALL

DOUBLE DRAGON

A DOUBLE DRAGON PAPERBACK

CHAPTER 1

It happened decades ago on a sunny Easter Sunday morning. My witchy black-spider aunt Regina led me down the cliffside walk to her beach, where she stood me against several bales of hay, casually nocked an arrow to the string on her longbow, stretched it taut, and aimed it at my heart. I was six years old. My grandmother Jenny saved my life, and years later, when she died, she willed me everything she owned. Regina—her daughter— killed her, and now Regina, that self-same human cockroach, is coming after me again.

I am told I have great powers, but I know less than I should about what they might be. And my time is running out.

I work in the motion picture industry as a stunt lady. I know what I am doing and I do not take unnecessary risks, so it is not as dangerous as you might imagine. I was at my agent Sumner Blinker's office in mid-Wilshire just east of Beverly Hills when I had my first hint that my life was about to change. I heard a ring tone and reached for my cell phone.

What I heard was an old blues song:

It ain't necessarily so/It ain't necessarily so

The things that you're liable/To read in the Bible

Ain't necessarily so...

I did not recognize the caller ID. Still, answering the phone is something automatic with me. The phone is a lifeline in my business. *Ignore at your own risk.* But when I flicked it on, there was nobody there. And yet I was still hearing *It ain't necessarily so*... Then a woman's voice came on the line and said, "It's Blu Baxter! Hey, girl, may I come on in?"

I replied with a sharp *"No!"* with some degree of attitude. I hate cold calls, people wanting to clean your air ducts or sell you solar panels. There was no click or anything, just dead air, so I guessed the person went away.

Sumner gave me a funny look.

"You okay?"

"Of course I'm okay. It's just my damn phone."

"You took a pretty bad tumble up there on Mulholland."

"Sumner, I did not fall on my head."

Maybe I was a little too sharp with him. He was not on my favorites list at that time. He was supposed to be my agent, always in my corner, always there for me. But I was suspecting that had recently not been the case, and he was acting more than a little guilty.

"Okay, *okay!*" He threw up his hands, gave me a disgusted look, and turned his attention out the nearest window where absolutely nothing was going on. He was being even weirder than usual, and that only fueled my suspicions.

I have premonitions. A lot of people do, but with my family history I tend to pay attention to the little things. In a way I am just a beginner at the important things in my life. I guess you could call me a raw apprentice, a sort of witch in training. I am not all that old (as in *old hag*) but it takes a century or two to begin to *master* the craft, if such a thing is possible. So I am just a kid at this game. And worse luck, I do not have anybody training me. My grandmother, so the old family story goes, dated William Shakespeare. But maybe she was not born back in that time. There is another way to do that. But I am getting ahead of myself here. I promise, I *will* explain.

Anyway, I am in no way your old-school definition of a magical person. I have not memorized any spells or incantations. Not yet, at least, though I have been tempted, and I *do* have a book of special mixings, chants, and "mind pushes," and I have been fooling around with a curse or two (without much success). My little not-prayer book was handed down to me by my mother, though I doubt she ever read a line of it herself. My mom was sure those ancient scribblings in old dead languages were the work of the devil. Maybe they are. It depends on your definition of what a devil might actually be.

So, clearly I can be expected to have no recipes for eye of newt and wing of bat, no heavy black cauldron that I have to lug around, and I can say that most of the common prattle you hear about witches is superstitious nonsense or badly misleading and if I were you I would not worry about it.

You hear crazy stories about *women with powers* and you have to realize those are just ways to explain things that are impossible to understand, even with the general public's current awareness of parts of the universe known as dark matter, or as some of us refer to it, *the dark side*. A person appears out of thin air, helps you or zaps you to a cinder, and then disappears. They must have come from Mars, thank you, Orson Welles. *How else do you explain it?* You have a hot dream, the best, most fantastic sex ever and you wake up to realize you are alone in your own totally messed-up bed. Oh God, just another wet dream. Or was it?

If people only knew one way or another for sure, they probably would not come up with the superstitious stuff, or all that crazy, outdated sci-fi stuff, either. No, there are no canals with water on Mars. Of course, if you took away fantasy, then I guess nobody would watch *The Wizard of Oz* anymore, and I for one would miss the part where Dorothy gives the Tin Man that quizzical look, *What the heck are you, anyway?* As often as not when I see that shiny fellow, I start wondering how all his parts work, but let me admit that is just ordinary oversexed me, and if you are lucky in that way, maybe you are a bit of the same. Seriously, have you ever wondered how it would be if the tin guy had actually been a tin *lady*? Think about it. Every time you had to take a leak, you would risk a rusty butt, and what sort of life would that be? *Keep the oil can handy, gal.*

Sumner kept ignoring me, and then my phone rang again. Or maybe not—hard to figure out what was happening with it. All I knew was I heard another ring tone from somewhere close by and I picked up again. There was a sound of drunken laughter, and I had the feeling I was trapped in a bar in Munich during Oktoberfest and a merry band was chanting

Ist das nicht ein Schnitzelbank?
Ja, das ist ein Schnitzelbank!

The ring tone cut out and a cheerful woman's

voice said. "Juniper Warner, it's Tillie Noonschnapper!"

Nobody I knew. "Go away," I said out loud.

Those Germans sounded like they were having a great time, but I certainly did not know anybody named Tillie, much less with the ridiculous last name Noonschnapper. Sounded like she was hanging out in a happy beer hall. I bet she was getting her share of fine Teutonic romance and good lovings, to boot. Okay, so I was jealous of a person I did not know in a place I had never been. Nobody is perfect.

I was on pain meds for my knee at the time and so I was feeling a *drowsy mean,* so to speak, and my mind started to drift. I could not remember the last time I had gone for some really great affectionate intimacy. I do not know why it has to be so difficult. There is nothing even remotely mysterious about the rules for how to have wonderful sex, or of cosmic physics, for that matter. You give me five minutes and I can dispel a lot of silly old beliefs about sauerkraut making you impotent and pickles making you horny. Actually, it is a bit of the other way around, particularly if you are talking about those tiny little green gherkins. Now there is a turnoff for you. As for modern science, no, Pope Urban VIII, sorry, but these days nobody follows your declaration that the sun revolves around the sun. After all, since Einstein and Hawking figured out a few bits of the space-time continuum, anyone can see how a person like me (and maybe you) might be able to bend time a little, or raise or lower your body density so you could punch like Iron Man or disappear through a solid brick wall. You see

9

how drifty I was.

I can only guess why I am bringing up a lot of doubts and concerns here, but believe me, ladies with powers are basically just ordinary people with wants and desires and plenty of faults, and they are just as confused about the meaning of life as anybody else. And since we are talking about superpowers, sooner or later you are bound to ask, and the answer is no, I have not yet found a guy with a rod like iron who can go all night without chemical additives. That does not mean I have stopped looking. Hope springs eternal, if you will pardon the pun.

And in the next moment there was a *third* ring tone! This time I heard an old Harry Belafonte ballad:

Love, oh love, oh careless love/Love, oh love, oh careless love
You've broken the heart of many a poor guy
But you'll never/break this heart of mine!

An ancient voice came on and said her name was Margotha—those cold callers will try anything, but it was going to take more than a pitiful old lady to scam me—I screamed a silent *Go away!* and shook my head and slipped the phone back in the pocket of my jeans. That seemed to take care of it.

Still, I had to reflect that an unusual number of little weird things had been happening lately. The other night I had the odd notion a spider on the wall in my apartment was trying to talk to me. And for the last few days Scamperdoodle, the damn black cat that lives in the bushes next to my front door, has been dashing across the sidewalk in front of me every time I leave my apartment. It is something

10

more than the old wives' tale about the black cat curse, I am sure of it. He stops for a moment and gives me the gimp eye and then moves on with a grave, measured step. And another thing. My super-dependable motor scooter, Putt-Putt, has been running rough as a cob. And now my cell phone is acting up. Maybe I *am* going crazy, but I do not think so. Something is up and I am pretty sure it involves me.

No, I am not being stupid or paranoid. Really. I have to pay attention to the little things. People like me can live a long time—hundreds of years, actually—but usually we do not. Over the centuries, we seem to lead awkwardly dangerous lives, and we are just too impetuous for our own good. Rashness is bred into us like an unlucky charm. *Born to die and no reason why,* at least no real reason that I can see, other than maybe if we were a bit less wild and carefree we would be on top of the world.

When I was very young, my own mother and father disappeared while on a questionable venture they thought of as a charity mission. Supposedly, while they were flying to a remote village, their plane crashed in the green jungles of Borneo. I was barely six years old, just about the time Auntie Regina tried to nail me with an arrow, come to think of it. To this day I do not know for sure whether Mom and Pop actually died back then, but if they did, I doubt it was in so mundane a fashion. Think about it. Why would my mom need any sort of airplane to go anywhere? And she could bring Pops along, no trouble at all. How? I will explain later.

Anyway, when I was a young girl you might have described me as timid. Okay, that is the exact opposite of "impetuous," but there were reasons why I became a scaredy-cat for a while. For one thing, the loss of my parents made me hesitate before taking a step in any direction. I tried to think about what I was doing, to at least try to control the impetuous nature Regina assured me was mine. Timid at the start of things. And yet look at me now: I turned out to be an attractive (if not totally luscious) Hollywood stunt girl.

My name is Juniper Warner. *Juniper.* It is not a common name and some of the kids in early grade school called me Loony Joonie, Ju-Ju Bird, or Juicy. My uncle Alfred called me Jouse, his own bemused putdown, a combination of my real name and "mouse."

The irony was that I turned out to make my way with a fairly risky job. I am not an amateur; I am a Hollywood professional. I make my living, such as it is, as a member of the Screen Actors Guild, and I have been in the Stuntwomen's Association of Motion Pictures for the last dozen years or so and I have performed various rides, skids, jumps, and falls in twenty-two pictures. And although I do not look it, I am something past thirty, as I keep reminding my agent. He does not believe me, or maybe that is just his latest excuse. As I may have said before, we witchy ladies do not show our age much. If you had been keeping score you might have realized I am way over twice the age I have said. And yet, just an infant in the witching biz.

Still, show biz for me has been a lot of hard rides with my fair share of bumps and thumps and scrapes and bruises. A girl's knees should not ache at my age, should they? Or maybe a wiser question

12

might be *Should not a girl who expects to live a long, long time be a little more careful?* Whatever. I am at the stage where I am thinking it is time to move on to a more stable profession, like directing. But when I talk about it, my agent, shifty old Sumner Blinker, does his song and dance, shuffles the papers on his cluttered desk, and looks out the window.

I can talk about the subject of witches with some authority. You see, as far back as anyone can remember, most of the women I know of in my family have had more than their fair share of mysterious powers. And from what I have seen, many of them have lived sad and wasted lives.

Romance for us is a complicated business. For instance, suppose you might pick some rock-studly fellow to be your *life mate*, and your love is true for maybe a half century or so but then his magic wand begins to wilt while you are still longing for young lust. Okay, so it is not all just about heat underneath the sheets, but suppose it was you, look at the situation: the ultimate May/December tragic romance begins when you are born in 1702 (the start of Queen Anne's War, the second French & Indian War) and even though you marry a young rake in 1752 (total population in the American colonies was estimated at something over a million people, so you get something of a choice). But by the time 1802 rolls around... Thomas Jefferson is President of the sixteen United States and your beloved is more interested in bocce ball than your (still) tender and (still) young nipples. This is actually nobody's fault, as far as I can see, but why are there not more man witches to spread around?

Maybe because they are even more impetuous than us girls and impetuosity is our doom? Could be.

Another problem: You think being able to read men like an open book is the answer to personal fulfillment? How is knowing every time you get cheated on going to secure a lasting relationship? Or how traveling back in time makes you a better person? Or being able to disappear even when you are still standing right there—how is that going to strengthen your bond with a lover who cannot do the same? How do you even explain it?

It is hard enough for the ordinary person to find happiness. It is nearly impossible to find a life that is even somewhat balanced and fulfilled when your unearthly abilities make you that much different from everybody else.

Perhaps the one exception was Grandma Jenny. Jenny somehow found a way that seemed to work for her, and it gave me hope that I someday might do the same.

I loved my grandmother, but I had not thought much about her in years. That was why it was so unexpected when I found out she had bequeathed me all her worldly possessions and a couple of unworldly ones as well. I inherited everything she had, and all that good fortune just about killed me. Of course, by the time she actually *did* die, I was under the impression she had been dead for years. Life is full of surprises.

This happened that same day I got the odd phone calls that proved to not actually be phone calls at all. As I may have mentioned, I was limping around with a knee brace and an ankle swollen twice normal size due to a bike stunt gone wrong on one of those car chase movies where the hero gets in a rage and zooms away in his cherry red Mustang and the hot girlfriend—that's me, at least that was the starlet I was doubling for—anyway, she takes off after him on her big motorcycle to warn him he has no brakes. Only *she* has no brakes, either. This is often the kind of thing you see in movies a few months after three or four morons are sitting around in a huge office with framed movie posters on the walls trying to justify their big paychecks. There is the director, two producer types, and one of the producers' wanna-be starlet girlfriends, and these idiots are trying to do the writer one better by "fixing" his screenplay. As in, *Here, you poor fool, let me fix that for you.* Ah, Hollywood!

Anyway, sorry for the digression. The thing is, my last stunt was a high-speed spill on a winding stretch of Mulholland Drive. High speed in stunting means something a little over thirty miles per hour. Maybe you are thinking *really* high speed should be more than twice that, but believe me, all I am wearing under that string bikini is a thin, skin-colored Mylar body suit. Thirty is plenty fast enough and they can always fool around with it in post-production. My rented Husqvarna was supposed to skid on a curve and then the scene would cut to angles of the bike and to a dummy in slo-mo going over the edge and tumbling down the hill. Except we did not have to do any pickup shots because this time the bike did not skid to a halt in time and the dummy was me.

I was in freefall for what felt like eternity but was actually only about four seconds before I did a tuck-and-roll and continued bouncing and bumping my way to finally come to an uneasy rest a hundred feet below. I would have tumbled and thumped the rest of my sorry-assed way on down the hill, except for the scraggly little tree trunk that snagged my right leg and stopped me just short of flying over a switchback cut that loomed directly below. There was no room to spare; my arms were actually over the edge of the forty-foot straight-down drop when I was brought to a jerking halt. We can agree that was the lucky part.

A few members of the cast and crew peered over the steep edge and clapped and cheered, but the producer, who had overruled my objections to this particular bend in the highway (and was now glaringly aware of the possibilities of long hospital stays and expensive lawsuits), had personally scrambled over the edge and was gingerly making his way down to *save the stunt girl*, a role he actually accomplished, snatching me by the left ankle just as the tree root holding my right leg gave way.

The upshot was, I had to go on the disabled list and I missed a fight in a biker bar, a nude scene in an exploding waterbed, a crash through some splintering sugar-glass, and a naked-girl fall off a forty-story building. You may be starting to get the idea that I specialize in *nakedness and nudity.* That is not precisely accurate, as I am always wearing something skin colored, but it is as close to nude as the producer can get without his or her film being pinned with an R rating, or worse, a naughty X.

Still, whether I am bundled up to the max or naked as a jaybird, no producer in their right mind wants to take a chance on a gimped-up stunt girl. At least that was what Sumner was saying for the fourth or fifth time. There I was, grumping around in his second-floor office while he tried to keep the conversation light and inconsequential. *What a thieving, conniving scoundrel he is!*

For years, Sumner rented a converted two-bedroom condo in a mid-century ex-apartment complex just off Olympic and Wilshire. His establishment was freshened up with ancient movie posters from *Sorcerer* (Billy Friedkin's failed remake of the French classic *Wages of Fear*), *Herbie Goes Bananas* (Disney's tired three-quel that chugged onscreen after the original *Herbie* and *Herbie Goes to Monaco*), and a cardboard theater lobby stand-up of Shaft pretending he is some sort of angry black James Bond.

Sumner himself was a horny middle-aged fellow with his head shaved bald like his hero David Carradine played in the *Kung Fu* TV series, except that Sumner was middle aged (describing him kindly) and he had a wide face that peered out at an unjust world over his vastly expanded waistline. He wore huge glasses with big plastic rims, as did his father and many other powerful old Hollywood dudes in the 1970s.

Sumner was in a running verbal war with Janie, his worn-down-by-life secretary, who thought the movie memorabilia should be junked in favor of travel posters of the Bahamas that might uplift her spirits. But that was not going to happen. Sumner *knew* to the bottom of his scheming black heart that his movie posters were timeless. No one would ever be able to convince him otherwise. His dad, Seymour Blinker, was a top agent before him, so of

17

course Sumner knew *everything* by Tinseltown osmosis. He reverently talked about the glory years when his dad represented guys like Rock Hudson and James Cagney, and he earnestly believed that the classic Hollywood of many decades ago was still alive. It had to be, with the slam-bam spirit of his legendary dad now coursing through his own veins.

On a practical level, Sumner enjoyed the fact that my more or less steady stream of gigs contributed if only on a minor level to his cost of living, and he had claimed for the last four years that he was trying to get me a shot as a film director. On my end I had been trying to get him to invest in a newer computer with a little more zip than his antique Apple IIE, and maybe invest in a smart phone or two, and—most important to me—get out there and pound the pavement a bit more on my behalf. Sumner still used cell phones that weighed about two pounds and were as big as twelve-inch Subway sandwiches. Timeless classics, he called them. A few weeks previous he caught Janie trying to sell them on eBay.

Anyway, I was hanging out in his office and moaning about lost opportunities while he had his feet up on his desk and stared out the window. He was filing his nails with an emery board, and occasionally he would grunt to assure me he was still listening.

"What does it take to fall off a balcony?" I said. "I jump off and gravity does the rest."

He looked up from the serious touch-up he was applying to the nail above his gigantic imitation blood diamond pinkie ring.

18

"You're busted up something fierce, kiddo."

"Just a sprained ACL."

"And an ankle the size of a grandioso prize-winning coconut."

"I could do the trick."

"No way. Think about it. You were supposed to double for a hot chick in a halter and cutoff shorts. How are they going to shoot around that *mungonious* black knee brace you're wearing?"

That was Sumner. He could never just say "big." Everything in his world was *fantastico, stellarific, marveloso, cracker-jacker-smacker-packer*...hyperbolic words he thought show biz people actually said, and I guess they did in his own mind's eye, in the world as seen by *Blinquez the Magnifico*.

"They could write something like that in the script."

"Why would they do that?"

There was no answer for that one. I could not think of a single reason. There were at least a dozen hot chick stunters ready and eager to replace me at the drop of a cue card.

"Well, they could cut around it."

"Oh, yeah. With no master shot. How's that gonna work?"

In stunting, the master shot is everything, and we both knew it. All I could do was shrug, ceding the point. You would have thought that would settle him down, but it did not. Sumner kept yammering away, probably thinking he was on a roll. It was getting to where I wished for another weird ring tone.

19

"Another thing, and here I virtuously repeat myself, they said they want a *true-ly-oso hot-err-ific babe*. But you, Ju-Ju Bird, oh no, you keep turning down the boob job. Hell, my offer stands. I'll go in for fifty percent; you could double my commission until I get my dime back."

"A generous offer," I said. "Boob equity."

With that I had run out of snappy things to say. *Could I really get more work with a bigger set of girls?* But Sumner, who was never one to let silence fill an empty space, was already yammering about something else.

"*Speedaroo* guy called to pass on his gratitude to you for saving the cat."

Sumner was talking about Harlow Wallace, the producer-director of *Speedaroo*. Wallace was the motion picture demigod who had sent me skidding over the edge of Mulholland Drive, and now was trying his best to get in my pants for a variety of reasons, not the least of which was that I was known around the biz as a great piece of ass. But I did not get the rest of what Sumner was saying.

"There was no cat in the shot."

"Actually, it looked like maybe a woodchuck. Or a *gaul-diferous* gopher."

"I get the reference, but…"

Save The Cat was the title of a book that had been a recent *fare de jour* with Hollywood scriptwriters. The Cat Rule—and in Tinseltown, the herd always follows such proclamations—was that somewhere in the opening scenes of your movie, the hero or heroine has to show empathy by saving some deserving person or animal. Maybe this happens by rescuing an old hound dog from a raging river flood or saving a cute hamster from a deadly spin in a clothes dryer. The so-called cat could even be a bug or some crippled but lovable uncle with big ears, bowlegs, crossed eyes, and a wart on his nose. Anything, as long as the critter is worthy of *empathy*. And believe me, I am not knocking it; the guy who came up with that new golden rule made a ton of money.

But Sumner was still flapping his spacious jaws.

"You went off a cliff, soared like a *splendiferous* eagle and banged yourself up to save a lousy, stinking no-go gopher."

"I did not! That would be unprofessional! I skidded on a sandy patch on the road! End of story!"

Do not get me wrong. I am not one of those holier-than-thou animal-rights fanatics. There is no sign on any of my motor vehicles saying I brake for squirrels or old ladies or anything else on the road. I know that any time my front wheel smacks into anything unpredictable as a skunk or a turtle, a thousand things could—and probably would—go bad. So I believe my instinct would be to run over the cat to avoid something worse from happening.

Beyond that, the truth was, I did not remember exactly. There was some remote chance I might have swerved to avoid this little critter, one of the thousands of split-second decisions stunt people make all the time. Still, it was not anything worthy of a medal. If I did it, chances are it was to save my own precious skin.

"You swerved and they got the proof. On slo-mo, even. Front rubber missed him by about an itty-

21

bitty half inch. Poor little bucktooth critter has his tiny little gopher mouth open in wide-eyed terror, and you pull his *fartiguous* fat out of the fire."

"Well, it was an accident. And 'fartiguous' is not even a word."

"*Well*, it should be. Butt fat is near where gophers fart…I think. Hey, take the joy, pal. You not only saved a day's shoot, but Meg Sparks came off looking *glorifically em*-pathetic, instead of just pathetic, if you can believe it."

And then my cell phone actually *did* ring. I knew it was a genuine call because the ring tone was my own snarky Groucho Marx ring tone. You know, that sniggery *gnark, gnark, gnark* of his. And this time my phone lit up. It had to be a real call.

"Am I speaking," a crisp male voice asked when I answered, "to Juniper Warner?"

"Yes. That is me for sure," I said.

"Jennifer Warner is your grandmother?"

"Was," I said. "She died years ago, when I was a kid."

"How do you know that?"

"She left me her old Hudson Hornet in her will. Hey, who is this, anyway?"

"Did you ever see that will?"

"No, but I have the car."

"Doesn't mean anything. It's just a car."

"A very special car!"

The stranger on the other end of the phone harrumphed, a sound meant to say I was certainly, absolutely one hundred percent wrong, regardless.

"Your grandmother Jennifer Warner is currently in critical but stable condition here at Cedars-Sinai Medical Center, and you are listed as her closest relative. To be contacted in case of an emergency, you see."

"But I do *not* see."

It was beyond credulity. Grandma Jenny was supposed to have died years ago. How had she lived for decades without my knowing it? That would have meant that both of my parents *and* my aunt and uncle had lied to me. Aunt Regina I could understand; she was born to tell the convenient non-truth. But Uncle Alfred was not at all that way. Well, he might lie if a business deal was involved, but he thought that was different. *Say anything to make the deal work*, you know? And as for my parents, they were dead, but when alive they had been a pair of holier-than-thous who always preached that the sin of not telling the truth was among the blackest, least forgivable acts. Hard memories, them yelling at me for fibbing about putting my finger in the yummy vanilla cake frosting. How could they possibly have lied to me about my dear, special, and only remaining grandmother's death? Maybe the rule was *Never lie about anything small.*

Still, at first blush I could not believe it.

"No, there must be a mistake," I said. "Warner is a common name."

"What's going on, Juniper?" Sumner chimed in from the background. He could be an annoying putz, but he had a sincere streak and an at least imitation gold-plated heart.

I shrugged my shoulders in his direction as the calm voice from my cell phone harrumphed again and then continued.

"Your grandmother, Jennifer Carey Warner, has listed you as her closest relative. I have performed my obligation in contacting you."

"She asked for me?"

"Ms. Warner is unconscious and not expected to live." There was a pause on the other end of the line. "Pardon me. There seems to be some mistake here. Her form says she is one hundred and thirty-five years old."

I knew better than to say anything. Any honest answer would have raised a firestorm of questions. I did not know the entire story about my family, but I knew enough to keep quiet around strangers.

"Well, then, I can write down that you have been informed and are not coming?"

"Yes, and no," I said. "You can write whatever you want, but I will be there as soon as I can."

I clicked off and Sumner gave me a sheepish, apologetic look.

"Sorry. I didn't mean to interrupt."

I was already limping toward the door.

"My grandmother. She was supposed to have died years ago. But they say she is in the hospital."

"What, Cedars? You want I should schlep you over there?"

"No, I am on Putt-Putt."

I was riding my classic cream-colored Vespa. Gnarly Duke, my racing green Ducati, was on hold for a week or two until my aches and bruises subsided. And I had stored Grandma Jenny's gift to me, the beautiful sky-blue Hudson with the classic white convertible top and big whitewall tires, the lovely vehicle that I called Horny Hudson, with a prop house that cared for him and rented him out for

24

cushy shoots where there would be no possibility of dings or dents. Yes, *Horny Hudson*. I think every machine deserves a name and a sexual identity. After all, they drive us around, pull us up to Starbucks for vente lattes, and try their best to get us home safe and sound when the wrap party has lingered into the wee hours.

Anyway, this time Putt-Putt started right up without any trouble and I was on my way. Street traffic was heavy, but Sumner's office was near Beverly Hills, really just a dropkick from the hospital. Putt-Putt darted in and out of the lanes, and with us accepting a few honks and me passing along a casual finger or two, we pulled up to the sweeping drop-off area in front of Cedars in ten minutes flat.

I locked up my Vespa and managed a painful jog into the main building, where a silver-haired lady exuding a strong scent of rose water and gussied up in a maroon pantsuit directed me to a bank of elevators. I was whisked up to the critical care floor, and there, a solemn young man in dark-green scrubs ushered me into a quiet room with subdued lighting, and to the side of an unconscious elderly woman. She was banged up and bruised a hundred times worse than I was. Her face was so damaged that anybody else might not have recognized her. Yet, somehow, with one quick look I knew in my heart that this was the lady who had been my favorite person. Impossible, but true. It was my grandmother Jenny.

I was horrified. I found my voice, but it was barely above a whisper.

"Who did this to her?"

"The doctors do not think it was a beating. And there are no stab or puncture wounds of any kind."

"But…then how?"

"She was found on the sidewalk in front of her bungalow. The police said she probably fell off her roof."

"Old ladies do not climb on roofs."

The intern shrugged and stiffened a little behind his kindness. "Sorry. We don't do crime scene investigations here."

"Has she said anything?"

"Sadly, she has not. And the doctors do not expect her to. She is on life support. Have you seen enough?"

"Yes, thank you. I will wait here."

He gave me a doubtful look.

"It could take hours, the night, even."

"No one should die alone. And this is my grandmother."

He nodded and a brief smile reeled in most of his distanced manner.

"I'll get you a chair. She left a consent form. She wants to be let go. When it is time, we'll let you know. I'm afraid you get to say when to pull the plug."

"Me?"

"Yes. She seemed to be waiting for something or somebody. Maybe it's you. I mean, that's not a medical opinion. It's just that after being around here for a while, you get a sense of things. Maybe she knew you would be coming."

He left me alone in the semi-darkness, listening to the slight hiss of oxygen and a steady mechanical beep from a heart monitor.

The intern had treated me decently. I can be bristly when I am upset and he had a tough job. It had to be difficult for him to be quiet and calm while an endless flow of agitated people like me came into his particular bend in the river from which many did not return. He left me, only to return a few moments later with two orderlies who rolled in a light recliner chair.

"It has a section so you can put your leg up," the intern said.

"Do I look that bad?"

"You wince every time you take a step. And the huge black brace is a giveaway."

He showed me the lever on the side of the chair that made the leg support pop up so the chair became a recliner. As he was about to leave, he handed me a rather large old handbag. It was tightly woven in an intricate wool design, one of those catch-carries-everything bags you see in the Central American goods stalls over on Olivera Street in downtown LA.

"I nearly forgot," he said. "This was hers. She was unconscious when they brought her in here, but the on-call medic in Emergency said they had to pry this old carry clutch from her fists."

I took the ornately woven bag and thanked him and they left me alone in the room. Jenny's face was puffed up and she had deep maroon-and-black bruises around her eyes and cheeks, and her arms and legs showed bruises everywhere. I could only guess at the unseen trauma under her white gown. Her short, snow-white hair alone seemed untouched as it formed a light crown around her face. I knew a good bit about bumps, bruises, and scrapes. To me, it looked like my grandmother had fallen from a lot higher than the roof of a house, improbable as that might seem.

When Grandma Jenny was younger, her hair had been slightly curled and strawberry blond like mine. And she wore it short like I did. She always encouraged the tomboy in me, from climbing trees to kicking whatever ball was handy to riding my first two-wheeler no hands. I know I told you I was timid, and I still think of myself that way. But even extreme worriers can push themselves to try new things, and Jenny brought out that in me.

From the little I knew, she herself had lived an adventuresome life. She loved to hike alone in the hilly woods of upper Michigan where she had a cabin, and she had insisted her husband, John, teach her to fly his airplane. After he died (and there was more than a little mystery about that) she had moved to Los Angeles, and had supposedly passed away years before I myself moved from Chicago to California. I had adored her, and looking back, I could see there was something about her independent streak that I had subconsciously tried to imitate.

Now I watched her slow and steady breathing while I tried to rest my knee, marveling that she was actually here, in this room. I had not seen her in more than twenty years, but I had wonderful memories from that long-ago time when I was just a little girl. She used to sing me old Irish ballads in a lilting high, sweet voice and tell me wonderful stories of fierce, brave women, dangerous high cliffs, and magical strangers from another land where there lived sea monsters, wicked high priests, and roving bandits.

That was before the family breakup that changed everything for me. At one point when I was still little, we were all living in Aunt Regina and Uncle Alfred's big country mansion next to Lake Michigan in Winnetka, a suburb north of Chicago. There had been a tremendous argument about something or other, and after that, Grandma Jenny was simply gone. The rest of the family tried to stay quiet about it, but I missed my grandma and kept asking questions until finally my mother and father sat me down and told me she had died. I wanted to know, the way kids do, how that could have been possible. Kids find it hard to believe people can simply remove themselves from our lives like that and we never see them again. But the older people just shrugged and went about their business. There were things little people should not snoop into, I was told, and as far as they were concerned, that was that.

Even back then I would have had to have been deaf, dumb, and blind not to realize that my family, small as it was, did not get along. Aside from Grandma Jenny, there was only my mother and father, and Aunt Regina and her husband, grumpy Uncle Alfred. Jenny's husband, my grandfather, had died under mysterious circumstances that were never discussed, and even less was said about his ending than my grandmother's.

I told you my parents were not the garden-variety mom and pop. My aunt and uncle laughed about their pious ways when they were not around, which was most of the time. Mother and Father (as

29

they insisted I call them) had devoted their lives to the care of the less fortunate. At least, my father had, and Mother trailed along wherever he went. She was a thin wisp of a woman, but tough and unrelenting in her own beliefs, which when it came to me were mostly about enforcing grammatical precision. I cannot (can't) tell you how many times that grim and pale figure stood over me while I washed my mouth out with soap for using evil verbal contractions. Maybe everybody is fanatical about something, but the gleam of her light blue eyes haunts my restless nights.

From what I picked up through Regina and Alfred, Father was well intentioned but rigid in his beliefs, which were fundamental Lutheran. They were supported by a trust fund set up by my grandfather, the John Warner Family Trust. This was an arrangement for which my uncle and aunt were openly grateful, because it meant Mom and Pop were never serious candidates for handouts from them.

So grandfather John Warner, the pioneer aviator, had made enough money to provide for the generation that followed, and yet nobody knew, or if they did know, would say nothing about the circumstances of his passing.

And in my own growing up until they were reported missing and presumed dead, these religiously propelled parents of mine had been mostly out of touch with me. While I was skinning my knees in soccer and tumbling off my bike or roller skates or skateboard, Father was scuffing up his life by scurrying about in various third-world countries with his dutiful wife scurrying behind him like some grim and tattered fairy lady.

I know you are probably thinking: *What kind of parents would run all over the world and leave their kid behind to grow up like a wild thing?* But that was the way they were. Duty came first, and I was left behind with stiff and disapproving evil Auntie Regina and weirdly uncaring Uncle Alfred. And then, of course, a few years later my parents also died and, as they used to say in the old silver-screen potboilers, *the plot thickened.*

It is a fact that Aunt Regina and I did not get along since the day I came to live with them. Exasperated with everything about me, Regina began our relationship by "helping" me fall down a stairway. Luckily, I proved to be a good tumbler and did not end up crippled or dead. I am not making this up or imagining things, because that calculated first shove was not her only attempt. I tried to get even with a wild roundhouse swing. Imagine, I was only four or five but my kiddy punch somehow accidentally connected with her nose, an unfortunate hit that bloodied her up a touch and caused me to eat alone in the kitchen for six weeks until I could return to the *respectable people's table.*

Need another example? She actually set out to murder me, tried to do me in one Easter Sunday, a few years after my historic punch connected with the end of her somewhat sharp and classic witchy nose. Sounds awful even to me, when I think about it after all these years. It is like some story that pouty little girls might make up out of their too-vivid imaginations. But it was true, and she had even admitted it to me later when she was in one of her huffy snits. For my own good, she said. *Trying to kill me had been for my own good.* Figure that one out.

No, I will tell you some more from what I remember about it. It was one sunny Sunday morning in the balmy Midwestern springtime, and she tried to shoot me dead with an arrow through my then-innocent little heart. I have not mentioned it, but Regina had this rare and unexpected skill: She was an ace shot with a long bow even though she hardly ever practiced, and that morning she set out to drill me through the heart with an iron-tipped wooden shaft like I was some silly rabbit, and she was the evil sure-shot daughter of Robin Hood. Storybook stuff. I could not have been more than six at the time, but I remember like it happened five minutes ago. Believe me, so would you.

We had come back from an Easter egg hunt on the Winnetka village green. I was tired and happy, not a care in the world. Caught off-guard, you see. I was wearing my new pink pinafore and a big white bow in my hair, white stockings halfway up to my knees and white shoes that I had scuffed a little bit in the mad scurry for my fair share of those multi-colored plastic eggs with the Tootsie Rolls and chocolate Kisses inside. Regina said she had a special surprise for me and we should take the cliff steps down to the beach. She insisted I put down my basket of plastic eggs. It was Easter Sunday. I picked up the tattered prayer book my mother had given me and I kept with me. I had misgivings. I did not want to go. I did not trust her, even at that early age. Silly me, because even with all my fears and reservations I was *actually not afraid enough*. I should have run and locked myself in the bathroom.

Everybody gets to be young once, so you know how kids think sometimes. You are just trying to be good so you worry about every little thing, and you miss the really big thing that is right there in front of you. For a moment I thought Regina would be furious about the grass stains on my shoes, but she smiled in that watchful and somehow superior way of hers and said it really did not matter, she wanted to show me this important thing but we had to walk down the beachside cliff to our little patch of private and deserted Lake Michigan beach. She said I was to say good-bye to Alfred, and I did so but he was in his favorite chair in the study, deep into *The Chicago Tribune* Sunday funnies, and muttered something I could not make out from behind the pages. I was naturally tagging some distance behind because my new bad thought was that she was going to give me a big shove down the steep stone steps that led to the sandy two hundred feet or so strip of beach that the Winnetka Warners called their own.

Regina was in the lead and kept nagging me along, talking over her shoulder, and when we got to the flat level stretch of sand I was surprised to see she had stacked two bales of hay with a target stuck on it against the brushy cliff face. I stood there like a little witless wonder in my pink Easter pinafore while she casually shouldered an old-fashioned wooden bow and nocked an arrow, and at the next moment she turned to point that ugly medieval killing device with its iron metal tip directly in my face. She shifted her aim a little until the shaft was lined up directly in line with my chest. No way she could miss; she was standing practically right on top of me.

"The heart shot is the best," she said, in a tone made to seem like she might be trying to comfort me. "The little fawn never feels a thing."

Actually, I knew to the bottom of my bones that her soothing tone was exactly what it sounded like. It said that she did not want me running away because that would be a tougher shot and things could get messy.

She pulled the bow a bit more, still pointing directly at me. There was a glare on her face, and yet I thought she was afraid of something, God in heaven only knew what, but it was a look I had never seen from her before.

"You're lucky, little Juniper. You'll never experience the horrible things I have had to endure."

"What bad things?" I said. My voice was trembling a little. I was just a kid. Kids that age do not really believe they can actually die. At that moment I was not angry or even afraid. I guess I was numb. Yes, that had to be it. I was frozen with the realization that she had so easily and neatly trapped me. Still, as much as anything else, there was this question, this burning curiosity. Something inside me wanted to know why she would do this to me. *What bad things had she endured?*

Only fifteen feet separated us. There was no way she could miss, and in the next second she let loose her arrow. For some reason I unthinkingly held the prayer book out in front of me with both hands, and lucky me, the arrow struck the center of that little book. The force of it knocked me back on

34

my little girl panties on the cold damp sand. The arrow penetrated the pages, stopping when the shaft was halfway through and the point a bare inch away from my quivering chest.

I was in shock. I stood up and dropped the bleached leather–covered book with the dark gray iron arrowhead pierced through it. My upper lip trembled and I started to cry. My aunt had an entire quiver full of arrows leaning against the hay bales. She angrily reached for another arrow, but at that moment, someone—or some*thing*—called from the top of the cliff. There was the sharp, piercing cry of a diving hawk, and I looked up to catch a glimpse of Grandma Jenny! At least, I thought it was her. But part of me also realized there was no possible way my grandmother could have appeared like that. This was after she was banished from Regina's house and I was told she was dead.

The screaming person, whoever it was, was dressed in a flowing (or raggedy, I could not be sure) black robe. One shrill cry came from her mouth and then she pointed two fingers of her right hand to her own eyes and thrust them like a pitchfork down at us. Well, more to the point, at my aunt. Regina froze where she stood and then fell to the ground in a crumpled mess. She was close to the water's edge and a foamy wavelet rushed in to soak her. That woke her up.

Regina hated to be messy. She shook her head in some desperate attempt to clear her rattled brain and in the next moment she was frantically looking around for her bow. It was lying on the ground next to her, but it was broken in half.

Next, she unsteadily lurched to her feet. Her spitting rage was something to see. I thought she was about to explode. She never gave me another glance. Instead, she ran down the beach away from me. I looked up at the top of the cliff, but whoever had been there was gone.

Regina was not the only person shaken to the core on that day. In shock, I picked up my prayer book with the arrow still stuck in it and slowly trudged back up the steps and across the lawn to the house. As I walked past Alfred, I noticed he had progressed past the front page of the funny papers and was into the adventures of Brenda Starr on the inner-page back side.

My brain was churning on idle. For no real reason I wondered if Brenda's friend with the black eye patch had found his cure. It had something to do with a strange flower called the black orchid.

Alfred spoke from behind his newspaper. "I told you so."

I guessed he thought he was talking to his wife.

"It is Juniper," I said. "Regina shot my prayer book."

He set down his newspaper and appraised my frightened look. "What happened after that?"

"Grandma came out of nowhere and gave her a thing with her fingers. Like this." I jabbed in his direction like I had seen Jenny do.

That seemed to make him uncomfortable and he moved aside a little as if there might be some force in my gesture. He pushed my hand away and nodded.

"That would do it," he said. He reached for the prayer book. It had the arrow still sticking through it. "Here, give it to me."

With some effort he snapped the shaft and pulled it from the book and gave the book back to me. He sniffed the metal tip and frowned, then carefully placed both halves of the arrow in his wastebasket. He pointed to the book in my hands, now punctured with a hole through the middle.

"It is not a prayer book. Your aunt wouldn't allow anything like that in the house."

He was right about the book. It was full of hand-drawn diagrams and notes in a language I could not read. I still have it, and I still cannot read much of it, though from time to time I try. I have the feeling it is something I really should not ignore any more. Regardless, that was the last time Regina tried to get rid of me, at least with the direct and open approach. No more shoves from the top of steps or from the edge of the lakeside cliff, either.

Believe it or not, as the years went by, my aunt somehow patched up the stories about those *unfortunate little incidents* with anyone who asked, explaining I was just blathering storytelling nonsense. She had a gift—she always got away with her not-so-little lies.

Nonetheless, with my own aunt stalking me, you can understand why I grew up with quick reflexes. Helpful for the stunt trade. Still, back then I was too young to run away and join the circus or whatever little kids thought they could do. In those days I knew I had no choice but to live in that large and fashionable house in Winnetka where there was a dangerous marble staircase and a steep cliff close by at the edge of a big empty backyard.

After I became a teenager, I no longer stayed in the house itself; my aunt and I would have found that impossible. From my freshman year in high school on I lived alone in the carriage house, a little one-bedroom brick building at the edge of their property, and I lived there until our final blowup after I had finished college.

Waiting for hours in a semi-darkened room at Cedars-Sinai and listening to the steady hissing intake and expulsion of oxygen from the silent figure of my unconscious grandmother started me reflecting on a past that I had tried to forget. I sat in the brown vinyl reclining chair the hospital had provided me, sat stiffly with my injured leg up, and the hours passed with the steady beeps and the quiet hum of Grandma Jenny's life support machine.

As the slow hands on my big black shockproof wristwatch moved toward dinner time, a cheery young candy striper volunteer brought me a tray of hospital food for dinner. It was bland and lukewarm, but I was grateful for it as I had not eaten since breakfast. I finished the beef-and-noodles, slurped the lemon Jell-O, and sipped the warm tea. I fiddled with the lever on the recliner, trying to adjust my leg into a position as comfortable as possible and I finally drifted off into sleep.

I dreamed about a story Jenny had told me. It was the last story she had been allowed to tell me, and, more than anything else, it was a legend that I believed her telling me had somehow caused my parents to ban her from the house. I remember the arguments and my mother shouting, but I had never understood what all the clamor and commotion was about.

"Never, never, *never*!" my mother shrieked. "I gave it up, I gave it all up forever, and that includes my daughter!"

"You can't do that, dear," Grandma Jenny said. "You are not your daughter."

"Then I forbid you from talking to her about that subject—and particularly that story!" That was my father bellowing in his deep bass imitation-preacher's voice.

"Forbidden! Do you hear us? It's just stupid old wives' nonsense! It is nothing for little children's ears!" That last, the echo of my mother's shrill voice chiming in on top of my father's outrage.

As for the story itself, it came back to me in my dream as I heard in my mind once again the light lilting brogue of my favorite grown person, Grandma Jenny, the one I knew always loved me best.

CHAPTER 2

The tale Jenny told...

My dear loving little girlie-child, I want you to know that this was a long, long time ago on the island that today is sweet green Ireland, a beautiful place far, far away, across the cold, dark waters of the wide Atlantic Ocean. And our story starts with a fierce and unearthly war in the clouds. At least, what we know about it did start that way.

There is almost everything we do not know about that strange war itself, who won and who lost and what it was that they fought over. We do not know because it was not our own troubles. Not of this world, you see. Yes, there are other worlds. I have seen them with my own eyes, and the wonder of those other places is nearly beyond imagination, and so someday perhaps will you see them as well. But the first to learn anything about this war that might be of importance to humans was a tall young woman named Aidana, which translated means *the fiery one*. I will tell you what she knew, and as you will see, being only human like us, she could just gather in so much as a human from that time could know.

Even before the adventure that changed her destiny, this special girl Aidana showed signs she was not just an ordinary girl. She could be spotted at a distance by her long dark hair, for it had glints of red that shone on it when the sunlight was bright in the heart of the day. Some said it even glowed at night with a strange glistening, though none spoke of that to her face, and certainly not after she *became unto herself*, as it was softly and somewhat fearfully said of her.

Her early days knew bad times, but Aidana had a grace all her own, and a proud spirit that would not bow to anyone. In days of trouble—and in that time and place there was always trouble, with wandering bandits and the raiders from the sea—she was absolutely fearless, and was even said to be reckless. Of course, nobody paid much attention to her. After all, she was *just a woman*, and it was *just words* she was saying. Words are always known to be easy and cheap, and women…well, women can be easily underestimated.

The village where she lived was on top of the western sea cliffs in what today are known as the foreboding cliffs of Moher. Life was hard, and the struggle to survive and help those less fortunate than she was occupied much of her time. She had never paid much attention to the distant warring gods. Their commotion in the faraway heavens might be a real conflict or it might be a thunderstorm out over the western seas, but she knew ordinary life went on for ordinary humans and she felt she had to be there to help as best she could. There were berries to be picked and rabbits to be trapped for food. The aged and the sick had to be tended to, and Aidana was a healer taught well by her grandmother, and she knew many secrets such as the herbs to cure sour stomach and the potions boiled to bind a wound without fester, and where the cool salve healer leaves could be gathered.

Still, even if it was better not to dwell on such remote matters, it was easy to guess when the sky-gods were angry. Anybody could tell their displeasure when the storms came in the winter, or when there was a bad summer of too little rain that meant creatures of all sort would go hungry and babies unlucky to be born then would almost surely die.

But this time, with this strange unearthly war in the clouds, this *noisy conflagration of the high mists* was different. Aidana saw more of it than most because she liked to get away from the village to the cliffs, away from the mean huts where she was born, that sad place of piled stone walls and straw over driftwood roofs, the place where generations had huddled in fear of the unknown while they scratched out a mean living from the thin and rocky soil.

The villagers had known bad times, so many that nobody could remember, but at this particular time their lives were as wretched or worse than they had ever been. There had been a score or more of miserable years piled one on top of another until now the village itself appeared to be dying, and everybody stumbled about with pale cheeks, hopeless eyes, and dread in their hearts. Less than two hundred men, women, and children were left after the red spot plague, and now with the crops failing again and no fish from the sea, their end was clear in sight. Soon the last of the goat herd would be gone, roasted over meager fires so their owners might live a few more days or weeks and perhaps make it to the new year.

Just about everyone accepted their fate and huddled inside their huts, dreading the day when there would be no more scraps of food or bits of wild grain. Until those very last days, they had their sacrifices and their hopeless prayers to the sky-gods.

Everyone had given up all hope—everyone, that is, except Aidana. She was openly scornful of their despair. *You are just waiting to die*, she would tell anyone who would listen. She was the only one who believed they should pack up their few possessions and either put out to sea or begin a trek south and east to where the land was more generous, with forests and trees and wild game. But nobody listened to her. The men believed fierce tribes had to live in those lands to the south and east because they were so promising. They argued that to move there was too dangerous. And the sea, they said, was crowded with monsters.

So while they fidgeted and cursed and made excuses, when she was not gathering herbs for medicines or tending to the sick, Aidana went alone to the ocean's edge, to the sheer cliff edges of the land where she could ponder her own thoughts while she looked out to sea. She would often scratch images of farm animals and sea serpents with chalky stone on the slab walls of the gray-green marble cliffs. This pleased her for she knew that people's lives were short, but these pictures would remain after she was gone, some little sign that she had been here.

The able-bodied men, whose job it was supposed to be to care for the village, did not give any importance to what she did. If she went to the cliffs or if she were to simply fall off one of the dangerous ledges and disappear forever, that would be of no mind for them. Sometimes she would bring back a few crabs or a string of small fish, so they assumed she had found her own path from the high grassy ground down to the edge of the sea. *So little nourishment for such a foolish climb!* No one else had ever found it, but since the men had decided it was too dangerous, no one else ever really tried.

Aidana was looked on jokingly as a mutterer and a self-talker; in short, they saw her as a crazy woman. She lived on her own with no children and no responsibilities, and the villagers decided it was just as well, for the girl was as foolish as a mad-head goat and should she have a child, who would care for it?

Now as to Aidana herself, when the light was right, she looked pretty in an unkempt, wild-haired sort of way, attractive enough that one or another of the young bucks would occasionally lie in wait to see if they might have their way with her. But Aidana was surprisingly strong, and of her own mind about her favors. One fine young lad lost an ear, another an eye, and a third who had blithely bragged he would accept her little challenge later said he had fallen down and accidentally broken his arm. And yet another had no excuses for the deep purple bruises around his groin. Lately, the few young swaggers left in the village had taken the clear warnings to heart and were limiting their advances toward the lasses of the age who were more willing to accept their advances.

Aidana was the first of the powerful women in our family's old Irish legends, now mostly long buried in the past. It is true to say that if Aidana had not done as she had, most if not all of the strange series of events that followed would not have happened. But how can you blame a mere mortal woman who, no matter how unwittingly, chose to enjoy forbidden friendship with a demigod? Of course, forbidden. The priestly ones even back then had whispered that there were rules against it. Or, at least, they said there should be, and who knows, perhaps such learned old robes were right. Perhaps. The history is not clear, for few of us have lived full and happy lives...not even me. But let me not get ahead of myself.

This was in a place called Connemara, centuries before the Romans came to neighboring England. It was a time when events were not written on parchment, but handed down from certain mothers to certain daughters, for the most part unbeknown, of course, to their menfolk, and only suspected by the holy robes.

And know you well that, over the centuries, much of this hard-gained wisdom has been lost, and the few scraps that remain have been badly misunderstood. Women of a certain purpose have here and there been called witches. Pah! Nonsense! These foolish tongues do not even have the beginnings of the truth of what a witch is or what she might be able to do! Of course, over the generations the less crafty, the unfortunate, and the more impulsive women of power have always burned in roaring bonfires with wine-drenched lunatics cheering and know-nothing fools dancing about. Such women have been stoned to death for choosing their own path, boiled in black pots for the misunderstood and presumed practice of the dark arts. They have been tied to trees in the woods and left to be torn apart by hungry wolves. This I swear to you is true for I have seen it with my own eyes.

Juniper, you will hear much nonsense. Believe

none of it, particularly not from your prattling mother and father. Pretending-to-be-wise old robes sometimes try to spin the yarn that no one is at fault for this, that our troubles necessarily begin and end with us outsider women ourselves. You must be warned, there is the reverse side, a known evil habit about the clannish lukewarm porridge that makes up so much of humanity. These evil weak ones need everyone else to be ordinary, like themselves. Consider *Jesu Christi*, if you need an example. About all being *different* earns outsiders like us is a cross nailing for the trouble. But let me save judgment for another day. It is not my place. And, after all, there is the story to tell.

In this remote and ancient land that I am describing to you, in the cliffside village where Aidana lived, there was only the clan, the little scratch-patch of humans attempting to hunt and farm and fish the rocky green coastal valleys and even venture a few throws out to sea, and there existed no more of value except for the beauty of the earth and the sky and the wind, and common poor people were too busy scraping together a living to see anything of worth in that!

And beyond their weary hopeless ways, they were afraid! Almost none of the men dared launch more than a hundred feet or so into the wild salt seas where fish were abundant, because everyone knew there were also fierce muggery water beasties and giant scaled serpents flopping about out there, and the village men swore oaths to each other that their boats were too tiny and frail to be venturing more than a stone's throw into the evil currents of the deep cold-water bay.

So life was harsh and simple. When the sky-god was good, there was just about enough food to go around. When he was not, the village leaders chided the old Druid priest to offer up a young virgin girl for a sacrifice, and if that did not satisfy, they would present another and yet still another for the bloody stone altar. That was the way it had always been. Nobody really liked that mean and grisly business, but they accepted it as a necessary cruelty and tried to keep it out of their minds. That is, everybody did except for our Aidana.

The useless and foolish offerings of young virgin girls made her furious, and in this time of great trouble she saw that it was happening again. The fish, the meat, and the grain had all failed them at the same time, and beyond these signs, the sky-gods were clearly at war. There were flashes of light and mighty booming noises from the heavens. These were no natural bolts of lightning but bursts of raw energy that met with strange creatures of the sky in huge blasts that ended in flaring splinters and sharp bits of smoking objects that came whistling or floating to the earth. There were no fish to be had. What villager in his right mind would venture off the shore with the sky-god conflict going on? They would not even go out on a clear day. No rabbits or mice, either, or if there were, the men were too timid to go after them. One of the men had dared step into the nearby woods the week before, and nothing of him was left but one bloody shoe. Wolves, or more likely a dragon. No rain, no grain. Yes, the sky-gods were in a fury and would have to be appeased!

Aidana watched with flashing, resentful eyes as

47

their wrinkled old Druid robe droned on over a shivering girl who had been roped naked on a grayish-green rock slab altar. Yesterday, this young sprite had been playing with her friends, trying to milk the thirsty dry goats, helping her mother prepare a skimpy evening meal. Today, she was the chosen blood sacrifice.

The cadence of the unholy chanting went on for over an hour until it was finally reduced to brainless mumbling from the old crones and impatient yells from the rest of the gathering to get on with it. The chosen one had been carefully examined and proven to be of virtue worthy of the sky-god. Although the girl was bound, the weak old robe was anticipating trouble, and ordered the nearest village men to straddle her and hold with a firm grip on her outstretched arms and legs. They jerked her head back by yanking her long dark braids and forced a gourd full of mead down her gagging throat. The drink was laced with sleeping herbs, and after some moments she no longer struggled against the bindings around her bloody wrists. The long flint knife trembled as the wrinkled old robe raised it over his head. The ceremonial blade gleamed in the firelight.

Aidana could stand it no longer. She ran forward. Her thought was to grab the knife. Something, anything to stop this wickedness!

"No!" she said. "This is wrong! This one did nothing to offend your stupid gods! You should sacrifice the bumbling and weak hunters who bring us no food!"

The village leaders raised their voices.

"Stop the mad woman!"

"Beat her to the ground!"

"Smash her with a rock!"

It took five or six of the men, but with stones and wooden clubs they managed to drive her off into the darkness.

Aidana heard one lost, lorn shriek from the savaged innocent as the knife sank squarely between the young girl's heaving breasts. Aidana forced herself to watch as the old man jabbed and ripped at her thin chest.

Aidana trembled violently in her rage. The ancient robed one was feeble, too old for the physical part of his ritual and clearly making a mess of it. He sawed and hacked and pounded and finally was able to push his hands inside the girl's shuddering chest. He unsteadily raised a dripping red heart that still throbbed in the open air.

Aidana yelled from the darkness. "Murderers!"

The gray-faced old robe looked as stunned by what he had done as any of the shabby bunch of onlookers. The small crowd muttered and mumbled things like *Glad that's over with*. They made religious signs in the air, and began to shuffle back to their huts. But Aidana was not finished cursing them.

"This isn't prayer! This is the evil of cowards! Of desperate, soft baby-men who have forgotten how to fish or hunt! As if they ever even knew how! So you say the gods are angry? To solve this menace, you kill little girls! I agree, the gods are angry—with *you!* Why not eat her heart, too, you bloody cannibals!"

After that she ran off into the darkness of night, yelling at the top of her lungs. The men were

49

furious for the way she humiliated them, but they did not dare to chase after her, not after Aidana The Fierce One. Not one of them was brave enough or fool enough to leave the firelight and go after her in the dark.

The next morning, little remained of the sacrificial maiden but a dark blood stain on the slab of stone and a few smoldering bones in the now-dying fire. And, of course, the villagers' shame. That would remain their entire lives, Aidana would see to that!

All that horror, suffering, and sacrifice, and the omens still would not turn to the good. Brooding cloudbanks hung far out to the west over the restless seas. Flashes of light and stuttered battle chatter came from within the dark cloud-masses. Aidana saw all that and yet she was not afraid. That morning, she walked swiftly in the direction of the gray-green marble cliff faces, heading toward the place where, with slow precision, she had been scratching the outline of a horse dancing over the sun. She had a talent for drawing pictures, a skill the villagers took for near magic. The aged, wrinkled robe, cowed by Aidana's unpredictability, had long ago declared there was a religious significance to her efforts, though now he was reconsidering his tolerance.

She passed a dozen or so of the village men. They were returning early, probably from another abandoned fishing expedition that never got started.

"Catch anything, oh timid, tiny-hearted little fishermen?" she said.

They said nothing in return as they passed her in a sullen clump of male fury. No one made any remarks or tried to fondle her breasts. She recognized from their defeated look that something extraordinarily unpleasant must have happened, something to silence their usual empty bravado.

That evening the men built a huge driftwood fire in the center of town. They sat in a circle around the blazing flames and showed none of their usual brag and boast. Most of the women figured it was simply because their men had caught nothing to flavor the rank onion and grass soup that would be their supper. Aidana knew it was something more.

As the men folks retired in a surly mood to the blackness of the men's cave, she saw many were bruised. One had a broken leg bandaged with a splint, and several of the village men were simply missing.

The burly man who had recently claimed dominance over the others was not pleased at her scornful disdain as she eyed his dispirited troop of followers.

"Looking for a little warmth in the night?" he said, grabbing her by the arm. She struggled to get free, but he was too strong. She sagged against him, pretending to give in, but he didn't loosen his grip.

"We make fierce love, like two proud boars!" he said.

She howled her rage and struggled, but the men clapped their hands and bet a few seashells on the outcome. The hairy fellow threw her to the ground and dove on top of her, but at the last moment she twisted her body and found his groin with one knee. That took the joy out of him, and it was all over before it had begun. He rose unsteadily to his feet and angrily ordered the women to their huts in his great, bawling voice. He gave Aidana a surly glare as he limped after his fellows to join them in their men's cave.

There had been some sort of an encounter earlier in the day. Aidana was sure of it, and equally sure that the village men had come away defeated. Demons, maybe, or monsters or wolves.

Aidana herself was fearless. She resolved to find out for herself. She waited until the men were inside, safely blocked in their dark den with a blazing fire roaring at the front opening while the women were left to keep the dying embers of the earlier bonfire smoldering and fend for themselves. She knew the men of the village would not again discover what was left of their bravery until dawn returned.

She walked to a nearby stream to wash herself. Then she set out on her own, easily reading their clumsy back trail, intent on discovering what could have turned such self-proclaimed brave fighter-hunters into a bunch of frightened little rodents.

And she found the source of their defeat. It was a single being, a strange, profoundly *otherly* man with flashes of fire under skin dark as night. This one had taken refuge in a small hollow near the last mossy hill before the land gave way to the jagged cliffs. This place he had found seemed darker as if by magic, blacker even than the rest of the moonless night. She saw the broken, still bodies of several of the missing village men scattered about. And then she turned her attention to the stranger.

His breath came in gasps and his dark blood oozed from a dozen wounds. He looked to be human, but he was of such a strange appearance that

52

he was not like any other she had ever seen. And more, he was barely alive—she knew that, too. He had been badly wounded, though even while terribly battered and slashed he looked to be a creature of great power. His wounds had to be the result of forces other than what might be inflicted by the puny efforts of the village men. She came closer to this man-thing and knew instantly that he was not of her world.

"Help me," the thing that was a man and yet not a man said.

"Who are you?"

"Help me," he repeated.

"Yes. Yes, I will help you."

This wondrous creature was beyond her experience. In the dark he seemed little more than a mass of black on black, his form given definition by fiery shapes that raced and flickered under his translucent skin and zig-zagged across his head like submerged lightning. But then, perhaps sensing her uncertainty, or perhaps she had not seen clearly in the dim light, the creature stopped wavering and wobbling and took more the shape of an individual man, though one who was dark and yet glowing.

"Who are you?" she said.

"You are not afraid?"

She knew he must be a god, for he rumbled the words in her head like thunder. And yet she was more curious than afraid.

"I am Aidana, who draws stone figures for the sky-gods."

The dark man paused, as if searching for words, and then replied, "I am one such."

She took a hesitant step forward.

53

"You, a sky-god? Then I have nothing to fear."

"I suppose I seem somewhat god-like to you, maybe."

"A god of some sort. But not very powerful at the moment."

"You come to laugh at me. To joke at my passing."

"No."

"To take joy in my death."

"No! You idiot! I already said I would help you!"

She gathered her courage and stepped even closer to him. *This was a true wonder—magic did exist in the world after all!* He was a thing to marvel—she was sure it was a "he"—and his face was perfect, the god-man she had dreamed about in a thousand dreams. It did not matter that his features, his very soul, seemed luminescent blackness, the glowing pitch-heart of dark itself.

"Tell me what to do," she said.

"I am nearly…extinguished. You can help, if you dare. But it will cost you."

As he spoke, his voice took on such an impersonal tone that Aidana felt she was being unfairly judged. *How like a man!* She threw back her long, dark hair in a gesture of defiance. She remembered her mother's encouraging words: *Plunge forward, always plunge forward!*

"The real sky-gods will protect me."

"No, your heavenly gods will not protect you."

"Who are you to say these things to me?"

"No insult meant. It is something other…a rule. We take, we give. But help must be freely given. You must give it freely. This is a sacred code older

54

than the ground on which you stand."

She had little notion of what his codes and rules might be and so she also had no way to understand what he was saying. Still, Aidana's past allegiances meant nothing to her, and she broke them without a second thought. Her instinct was to help this wondrous creature, and she knew how to give a true oath. She put one hand over her heart and reached with the other for a small pouch of healing herbs from around her waist.

"Then I freely give my help. So I say it; so it is. Where are your wounds?"

Words rumbled from the dark thing.

"Enemies cut me adrift. I fell for a long time, alone. My ship crashed on the other side of this world. Now I need the raw emotion of life itself. I must have it or die. Grant me this and…you and your female descendants, for all time, will lose some judgment."

Aidana tossed her head impatiently. "I do not know what that means."

There was a glint of humor in his fading smile.

"They will be even more impulsive than you."

Again, she did not see how that mattered, and now she was really angry. *Who was this person? Who was it in the entire universe who could measure human will power and courage and charity like little weights? Surely, no one!*

"And?" she said. "You are not being very clear."

"And in return for my life, I will give you a fair trade. I will grant you some few powers that your ordinary human companions do not have. Do you understand?"

55

Aidana could see he was weakening visibly, his wondrous image wavering before her eyes. In truth, she did not truly understand anything of what he was saying, but she knew he was dying while they talked, and if she did not do something, and do it soon, he would die.

"No," she said, "but I will help you anyway."

Aidana felt his glowing presence reach for her, first caressing the wave of black hair that had fallen across her face, and then gently moving light fingertips, tracing the line of her nose and her full lips, "We will have to co-mingle fates."

"Yes," she said, feeling a sudden yearning for him as she had never before in her life wanted anything.

"You and your line will never be the same."

"I will have no line. The priests have cursed me. I cannot bear children."

"I think you can."

Before the night was over, Aidana believed there was a god and that she loved him. The joy of their co-mingling and the pleasure she felt was too unimaginable to be real. They lay together, alternately tender and passionate, on a soft cloud of mist he gathered for her in some magical way. They were dry and warm though the northwest wind picked up and icy rain spattered all around them. It was as if they had a roof over their heads and a steady fire in a fireplace and warm walls all around them.

An hour before dawn, she knew he was healed, and that he had to go. She felt small and grateful, and also sad that this part of her life had ended so soon.

"Will I ever see you again?"

"Once again. I will come for you. I promise it."

"Tell me one thing. Are you good or evil?"

His great, booming laugh roared in her head, but then he saw that he had frightened her. "I'm sorry, dear precious human girl. Things are complicated, and I have not been asked that question for…well, let us just say, a long time."

But Aidana was, if nothing else, stubborn, and insisted on an answer to her question.

"Which are you, then?"

"I am what your people a few hundred or thousand years from now may call a demigod. Or maybe *an outsider*. A stranger from another world. Beyond that, it does not matter to anybody but the two of us what I am. And I will always be good to you, for you have saved my life."

The dark being reached out and gently caressed her cheek. He took a lock of her hair, which had turned bright reddish gold, between his fingers.

"The real question, the important question for you, Aidana, since you cannot peer into tomorrow and thus still possess the delicious and strange lack of knowledge known as freedom of choice, the real question is—are *you* good or evil?"

She had no answer for that. They held hands, accepting each other, standing together on the cliff overlooking the sea. He gathered her in his arms in one last powerful embrace, all the while with a stern glance out to the water.

"My enemies are coming for me, you must know this."

"But you said you were healed."

"Yes, I am, thanks to you. But they are many,

57

and they have found my trace. I must go."

"Will you be safe?"

"Yes, I will. And one of the gifts you have earned," he said. "I will show you now."

"Is it a good thing?"

"Like most presents given in life, it is part good and part bad. But you can learn to control it, and with time it may even save your life."

He kissed her lips, her forehead, and her hand. And then he leaped straight and far off the cliff. He plunged down and down like a fallen angel, but years later Aidana would swear to her daughter that his body never struck cliff, nor sandy beach, nor lapping waves.

The legends tell us Aidana of the newly red-gold hair lived a long and full life. She had the strength of ten warriors and never lost a battle. She never married, yet had the one child, born nine months to the day after her god-man flew from the cliffs of Connemara. Through the years, Aidana only realized a small fraction of her powers. But it was enough to ban the bloodthirsty Druid rites and for her to assume the role of high robe priestess for the village people, who learned to conquer their fears of sea monsters and grew into a prosperous seafaring community under her rule.

And she did not again feel the dark fire of her god-lover until the day she died. As she was going to meet the sky-gods who she believed would determine her final fate, she saw him, clear as day and black as night, standing before her cot. She raised herself on one arm and spoke to him in a voice tremulous with old age, "Still for you, just the one question, god-love—was I good or evil?"

He cradled her gently in his star-flecked, ebony expanse, and told her she would be coming with him now, and she was very, very good, indeed.

When Grandma Jenny first told me this story, I was filled with childish wonder. Now, remembering that time, it seemed there might have been something more than reverence for what had happened. There was a note of sadness and sympathy for Aidana, and one other thing I thought I sensed: a hint of skepticism, a warning that there might be much more to the story that was missing.

CHAPTER 3

I woke to find Grandma Jenny watching me. Her eyes were kindly and there was a small proud smile on her lips.

"Grandma!"

She put a finger to her lips.

"Shush, now," she said. "I have to talk to you, my dear sweet girl, and I do not think we want the night nurses interrupting. No, we don't want that at all, now do we, dear girl?"

"But Granny, what—how? —who did this outrage to you?"

The old lady continued to give me the quiet smile I remembered so well. But there was a glint of steel in her eyes as she spoke.

"My own daughter, dark Regina, and some few of her followers did this to me. Who else? It was quite a fight, a *battle royale*, as the poets say, and she needed all the help she could muster. We fought in the sky over my bungalow—your place now, if you want the old heap. My own offspring, if you can imagine. The greedy foolish little bitch caught me by surprise, which was all on me because by that time I certainly was aware she was poison. Even so, if I were a bit younger, a bit stronger, I do think they might not have bested me."

"But why? How?"

"Young Juniper, I am and I will be fine. It is you we have to worry about."

"Oh, Granny, compared to you, I am in top shape. I just banged up my leg a little bit."

"That is the least of your problems, Juniper Rose. You have inherited a great and dangerous

60

enemy. You are in grave and serious trouble, and it is entirely my fault."

"Granny, no, you have to rest."

She raised one hand to interrupt whatever I was about to say.

"My time is brief, dear child. Listen carefully. Your Aunt Regina is one of the rare dark spider-ladies. One of us, yes, but gone terribly wrong. She does not fight broom-to-broom. And for her kind there can only be one female in her line."

"I know that Aunt Regina hates me."

"Yes, and your empty-headed parents never should have left you with her."

"I am never going back there."

"That is wise. But you are not out of danger. You know too much about her."

"She cannot hurt me. She is back in Chicago."

"Space means little to her and time even less. She is everywhere she wants to be. You were meant to go off that cliff on your husky-whatever, that motor bicycle with the funny name. You were supposed to die there, Juniper Rose. Regina set it up."

Juniper Rose. I could feel the tears starting in the corners of my eyes. I had not been called that since I last saw my grandmother.

"I have not been to visit Regina in five or six years."

"She has been watching you."

"But why?"

"It is an old custom among her kind. The spider-ladies' saying is *Kill the young before they kill you.*"

"But that's horrible!"

61

"My fault, my fault. According to the old-book way, once I suspected she was foul-born, I was supposed to get rid of her, but I just could not. Sometimes a person has to tempt fate and free themselves from the old ways. I tried to find a new path, and as you see, in the end it killed me."

"How could any decent human do anything different, Granny?"

"Yes, maybe, could be... But I have left you with a terrible problem. You are all that is left in our line that is any good, and she certainly is motivated to come after you."

"But what can I do? I do not know how to do anything special."

"You have powers. Great, unimaginable, fantastic abilities. You have the ability to do far more than you know. That motion picture tumble you took should have killed you."

I understood at least that part of what she was saying. In the rough business of stunting, I was something of a golden girl. I was not getting rich and I was not even in the AMA Motorcycle Hall of Fame, but I was known as the young stunter who could survive the improbable and make it look good on the screen. I was a *lucky choice*, and casting directors believe in voodoo and charms nearly as much as witches do.

"But...those are not actual powers."

"Well, some would say they are. And you would do well with a little more patience here. We live a long, long time. You will grow into yourself, into what you will become. I believe you can. I believe you will."

"What should I do?"

"Stay wary. Your aunt is greedy for power, and now she thinks she has found a way to get it."

"I do not understand what you are saying."

"Your aunt, the foul Regina, wishes to be the ruler of this world."

"But that is crazy…I mean, in this day and age?"

"No, Juniper Rose. There are powerful forces the wisest people on Earth know little about. And Regina in her greed and ignorance has been experimenting where our kind has been warned never to go."

"So the family stories I was told were lies?"

"Are true," she said. "Listen to me. You have allies. My three old friends will help. There's Blu and Tillie and ancient Margotha."

"I think they tried to call me."

"Trust my old friends, dear child. They can help you."

Her words faded into a quiet hum. After a few seconds, a half-dozen nurses and orderlies rushed in, and in that moment I came to the painful awareness that I had been dreaming all along.

Now finally awake, I saw that hum was the sound of Grandma Jenny's heart monitor. My grandmother's body had given out in spite of the bank of instruments dedicated to keeping her lungs and heart operating. And the recording log indicated, despite what I thought had been my last talk with Jenny, that there had been no signs of brain activity for hours. I guess with all our modern machinery we still do not know how to chart the human spirit. Maybe we never will.

The sun was barely over the horizon, shining between the distant towers of downtown LA, when I limped out of the hospital, Granny's embroidered bag in hand, and made my slow progress toward the enclosed parking lot where I had chain-strapped and locked Putt-Putt to the backside of a handy newspaper rack.

Without warning, someone in a heavy gray hoodie rushed out of some nearby ornamental shrubs at me. Instinct kicked in and without thinking I dropped to the floor and rolled sideways.

My burly attacker gave out a weird, high-pitched *ki-yi-yi!* scream and to me it sounded like a girl's voice, though maybe it was just one of those battle cries you hear in the kung-fu movies. What was more, the voice sounded vaguely familiar. I decided it was a girl, a tough, squirmy little bitch trying to disguise herself. She scratched and clawed and tried to bite me. She was wearing a white breathing mask, and that was her undoing, because as she tried to grab Granny's bag, I pulled the mask up over her eyes and hit her in the throat with the flat edge of my hand. She gave a gargling cough, lurched to her feet, and staggered away. Maybe I should have hit her harder, but that strike was an emergency move that could have crushed her windpipe, and I did not want to kill anybody, not even a punk bitch thief.

I stood up and looked around. The parking structure was busy with a steady line of cars coming and going, but nobody seemed to have noticed that I had been attacked by a mugger. Funny how that happens in big cities. Everybody is rushing around minding their own business and nobody is paying attention to what is happening to anybody else, even when it happens right under their nose. I shrugged it off, thinking *No harm, no foul.*

There was a bandana left on the ground in front of me. It was black with a yellow lightning-strike pattern. *Aha! A clue!* I thought to myself, my mind wandering off as if I were a player in a Nancy Drew mystery novel. *Right, and I was Juniper Rose Warner, girl super stunter and detective!*

But in my heart I knew that was textbook silly. I could have fingerprints and videotape of the entire attack, but I had been in Los Angeles long enough to know there was nothing the police could or would do for me. My mugger was nowhere in sight, and she had not gotten away with anything. In my mind's eye I could see the officer they would send hours after the fact with me waiting there as the day got hotter and I grew angrier. He would give me that weary cop look. *What's your beef, lady?* And that would be it.

I unwound the cable from around the metal post securing my trusty Vespa to the newspaper rack, started up Putt-Putt and pointed my handlebars over Laurel Canyon Boulevard to my hillside apartment.

About a decade before, when I first settled in Los Angeles, I had rented an inexpensive one bedroom in Studio City. It still suited my needs. It was the lowest of four such hillside apartments, each stacked up and a bit set back from the one before. Sometimes Scamperdoodle, the semi-wild black cat who roamed the local hills, slept on my patio where I put out a bowl of milk and some cat food for him. My apartment fronted on a steep and narrow street, and my small patio peeped through some trees and past the bulk of a commercial building to a view of the black cube of the Universal building and part of one of the hotels located next to the Universal Studios tour. *Ah, Hollywood.*

I drove Putt-Putt into her parking slot under my apartment. She shared the parking space with my Ducati, appropriately named Duke, or Sir Duke in times after he gave me a particularly invigorating ride. He could go over 130 miles an hour on the freeway.

After my recent experience thwarting my lady mugger, I made sure both my bikes were locked down. With my knee stiffening up, the dozen steep and crooked steps to the side door leading into my apartment were something of a struggle. Thank the goddess for the handrail! Once inside, I decided I would take a couple of Tylenols and lie down for a bit. But I no sooner had entered my living room when the phone in the kitchen began to ring.

It was the funeral home calling to go over arrangements. They said they were located in old Hollywood, off Melrose a mile or so east of Paramount Studios. The somber voice on the phone informed me that my grandmother had made all arrangements, everything was paid for, I was expected to attend and, should I wish, to give a small farewell address. And, the voice continued in an apologetic tone, although it might seem a little rushed, the simple gathering would be held that afternoon at four.

I hung up and went to the bathroom for a Vicodin, the stunt lady's friend. Then I dragged myself over to the fridge for a bag of ice and made my way to the couch. With my aching knee and ankle propped with soft pillows and my head resting on the curved back of my couch, I was ready to drift off for a nap when Jenny's big handbag caught my eye. I reached over and snagged it, and dumped the contents on my lap.

There was a worn old wallet done in soft red leather. Apparently, my grandmother had not driven a car in a half century; her identification, issued in Chicago, was dated in the 1930s. That seemed quaint and otherworldly, but the ID also said she was born in 1880. I guess nobody could figure out when she was born. Or maybe she wanted it that way. My eyelids were getting heavy, with the pain pill starting to take effect.

There was a small folded-over packet of worn one- and two-dollar bills and three odd nickels with a big "V" on the back. I set the money aside. The bag also contained two ladies' outfits—old clothing, the kind you might find on hangers at the back of an antique shop. There was a flapper's dress in shiny royal blue satin and a more businesslike dress of similar vintage in gray linen, and filmy old lady's undergarments and stockings definitely from a bygone age, and a black bobbed wig. There was also a soft-bristled hairbrush and a makeup kit, both in a mottled honey and black turtle shell. Not only that, I found a pair of beautiful old leather shoes with medium heels, in excellent condition, fashionable and yet sensible. And another pair, sleek silver satin dancing shoes. And way at the bottom of the handbag was an ornate clutch purse with a primitive silver and black embroidered design. I recognized it as Jenny's purse because the embroidery was of a horse leaping over the sun—it had to be the same beautiful beaded purse she had shown me when I was a little girl.

I opened the intricately designed pocketbook, not expecting to find anything. But I was wrong. There was a single heavy gold coin, a ten-dollar Indian head gold piece dated 1932.

The contents started me wondering. Everything in the bag was way more than eighty years old. The bag itself, though beautifully hand woven, was showing similar signs of age. Not that my grandmother should not cherish her old memories, but why would Jenny choose to carry a bag filled with her own things from nearly a century ago? And then I remembered Regina had a similar travel bag. Hers was of a classic French designer's make, though I was fairly certain it had to be a clever copy made in Hong Kong or Bangkok. What was going on? Was there some unknown league of powerful ladies who had abilities beyond the ordinary senses?

And a question that hit closer to home: Was my wicked aunt actually going to come after me after all this time? Why could not Aunt Regina just leave me alone to live my own life? All questions for which I had no answers.

The pain pill was finally working its magic. My knee and ankle were throbbing less, and I found myself thinking back to the last time I had seen Regina, just before I had moved to Los Angeles. By then she had come to the realization I was not going to allow myself to be shot with an arrow or pushed to my death. Yes, in addition to the tumble down the stairway, she had also tried to push me off the edge of the steep slope in their backyard—

"accidentally," of course. After that, I would not go anywhere near that cliff edge when she was around. I had started to avoid her, the way friends of a family shy from a brother or uncle they know to be crazy and unstable. For her part, my aunt would not stop telling everybody how clumsy I was.

But when those direct attempts to put an end to me failed, she worked up a more sophisticated approach—she developed a plan to marry me off to George, the disgustingly shallow rich kid who lived next door.

CHAPTER 4

Regina's plan to submerge me into a sort of cheaply manufactured marital bliss surfaced after I had graduated from nearby Northwestern University and was, as they say, at loose ends about what to do with the rest of my life. At the time, I was still living in the small carriage house in Winnetka. I was bummed out because for some years I had been fooling around with local motorbike trials, gradually improving my riding skills until I thought I was becoming more than just a promotion gag, a *girly biker*. I had a few wins on the smaller tracks and had applied for a job with a motorcycle racing team on the European circuit. It was because of an ad I found in *Motorcyclist* magazine, but I actually thought I had made it until I found out the Italians were talking about me posing naked straddling a bike painted in their colors.

When I received that smarmy offer by email, I felt like I had reached the lowest point in my life. I had nowhere else to go. The eager manipulators and fixer-uppers of the world like my aunt love a vacuum, and Regina moved right in on me just about then, shuffling and adjusting and fitting the bits until it looked like she was finally going to solve the problem of me once and for all. I had nothing better to do, so I went along with the matchup.

Early on the morning of my wedding, Regina came out to check up on me. I was lying on my back on a flat roller a few inches up from the cold concrete floor in Uncle Alfred's garage, working away under my good old Horny Hudson. My aunt

70

was looking ageless and pretty, even though dawn's first golden light and the surface water sparkle off the lake were barely peeping through the trees in our backyard.

As far back as I could remember, Regina had made a point of looking fresh and perfect, and this morning was no exception. She was nibbling on half a bagel that had a thin veneer of pineapple cream cheese on it, and sipping a cup of her favorite Yorkshire tea. That maneuver would have been awkward for anybody else in the known universe, what with the Aynsley antique pink teacup and saucer, but my aunt was not like anybody else, and she handled her morning's repast on the fly with her usual flawless grace and that air of calm superiority I found both annoying and admirable.

You may have noticed I said, "antique pink," not "pink antique." That's your clue; as a self-made socialite up from Chicago's tattered old near-south inner city, as a matter of social preservation Regina had spent a great deal of time and effort carefully sculpting who she was. She made sure any and all her social acquaintances understood and looked up to the *design* of her. It was a complete tip-to-toe image presentation.

Her French country house—she had designed it—with its mansard roof and pulled brick individually hand-selected by herself was a showpiece of architecture, but it was also a clever blend that mixed the real with the reproduction. Those bricks were not imported from France; they came from the clay pits of northern Illinois. Make no mistake, the lady had a great sense of design, and she did know the difference. Only Alfred, who unflinchingly paid the bills, and I, who had been steeped in her many deceptive layers since I was a little girl, were in on her secrets, both tiny and enormous. Beyond what my uncle and aunt's business guests and social acquaintances knew for certain they may have had their own suspicions, but none ever dared to voice them. If anyone had the nerve, Regina would casually slap them back with her beautifully turned untruths. My aunt was an easy, accomplished, habitual liar. *This old bit of porcelain?*   *Early eighteenth century, my dear. Left to me by my Warner cousins in London.*

And that brings us to the Warner family. My aunt traced that lineage back to the Domesday Book in 1086, and even a bit further back to 1066, when the Earl of Warner and his buddy William, the Duke of Normandy, crossed the English Channel to end the Dark Ages and start up a proper medieval monarchy in Jolly Olde England.

Maybe you get the picture. I was down there, checking the brakes under my car and Regina standing nearby up there, probably gazing at her long string of ancestors on the back wall of the garage. She did not have to study it. She knew it by heart, the dendritic drainage system of her ancestry leading up to the photographic age and ending with black and white photographs like the one of Grandpa John Warner in a dark suit and tie, standing proudly next to his rare and precious Curtiss Robin airplane, probably in the middle of some ordinary sunny day in the 1930s.

So much for the English. Regina had tacked up what she referred to as the trash Irish side of her family off in one neglected corner. And Alfred's ancestry was entirely ignored except for a four-by-six notecard tacked high in the remotest corner that said simply "Schotenheimer, Alfred and Rudy, brothers." That made a sort of sense because before she would agree to marry him, she had insisted Alfred take her family name, and he had shrugged and said, "Okay, but I'm gonna need some new business cards."

On this morning, like any other, Regina looked her normal perfect self, made up to the Max Factor and imperially slim in one of the expensive outfits she picked up from Marshall Fields in Chicago or from one of her expensive forays to Fifth Avenue in New York City. You could be sure she was not happy she had been forced to trek the few paces to the elegant *motorcar garage* to discuss matters with me, but there she was.

Horny, my sky-blue Hudson, had been spit-shined and waxed and all, but sadly enough he would not be going to the wedding. A shame, too; he was the Brougham model and I had been visualizing pulling up in front of the steps at St. Patrick's with Horny's big shiny whitewall tires gleaming and his white top down and me all silky and stunningly beautiful with the wind fluttering through my reddish-blond hair and freshening my white veil just a bit.

But that was not to be. Regina and Alfred had set their foot down. Well, at least Regina had. I was to be driven to the wedding in a long black Cadillac limo. You see, this was going to be my wedding, but so far it had been her choice of groom, dress, church, reception hall, guest list—more than two hundred of Chicago's finest—and marriage motor vehicle, this last being a black Cadillac stretch limo no doubt more often rented by the local Midwestern mafia, still trying hard to keep up appearances for old times' sake.

At the rehearsal, I barely recognized any of the bridesmaids, except they were eligible debs all, nubile and conniving young sluts I had casually rubbed elbows with at the cotillion dances where eager damsels of prominence met a selection of nimrod galahads among which, it was presumed, there would blossom a serious garden of prosperity.

I pretty much had figured out that Regina was frowning, holding her teacup and saucer and bagel and looking down at my grease-stained Air Jordans sticking out from under my car. I could just make out one of her impatiently tapping pumps. She was probably communing with the spirit of Grandpa and his cherished Curtiss Robin, sending him thoughts like *Johnny boy, if you only knew the things I have to put up with!*

An hour before I had carefully driven Horny up on foot-high blocks, but even so, a Hudson is a low-slung automobile and I was feeling a little tight under there. I sensed a slight tremor—evil Auntie Reggie testing to see how steady the blocks were, no doubt tempted to have at it with one great shove and get the matter of me over with once and for all.

I rolled out from under Horny and grinned up at the woman who had put up with me for nearly two decades, reveling in her annoyance and hoping my true feelings did not show too much.

"Hey, Regina!" I said, chirpy and daring her to try anything. "Over a half-century old and only sixty thou on the speedometer! Not you, the car.

You've got a lot more miles on you."

"Juniper, you will get all smudgy!"

By way of response, I belted out a happy lyric:

"Daddy don't 'low no stinkin' dirt in here!
Daddy don't 'low no stinking' dirt in here!"

I was in high spirits and that was my whimsical take on an old song, "Momma don't 'low no banjo playin' in here," but it was also true. As the breadwinner in the family, her husband Alfred was the momma of this here place, and he was a mighty finicky fellow. You could practically eat off the floor in his five-car garage—that is, if you could move the cars out of the way.

There was his little jewel, a candy apple red 1956 Alfa Romeo Tipo 750E with "138" painted in white on the hood. And his royal blue '67 Boss Mustang parked next to Regina's hot bronze Pontiac Firebird. And a few Bultacos, Harleys, and Putt-Putt, my humble Vespa—machines that would never dare to shed a drop of Pennzoil on that floor. And last but not least, my own treasured Hudson Hornet that Grandma Jenny had left me. Sweet Jenny with her Irish lullabies to lull the baby me to sleep in the long ago and far away. Maybe she was trash Irish to Regina, but she was precious memories to me.

However, Regina was not having any of my foolishness. Not on this day of days.

"Well, Juniper, you might break a nail or something."

What could I say to that? I had been pampered and fluffed and clipped and preened for weeks now. As a special punishment, she had selected a gown accentuating the lines of a lady much thinner than I

75

was, and put me on a diet to squeeze into it. She had hired a regular prenup army and assigned them to spruce me up for the big moment, the celebration of my upcoming marital bliss.

Later today, Auntie and Uncle would be handing me off to George, the banker's son who lived in the Tudor manse just north of our digs. Well, actually, George's parents lived there. George was turning twenty-four and he already rented a *très cher* one-bedroom apartment in a high rise in Manhattan. Everything was too easy for him. George had never been tested by real life. True, he was a luscious fellow, but he had a suspiciously too-pleasant smile under dimpled cheeks. He had curly black hair and an enviable job with a big investment firm in New York City. At least his pals from the good old times at New Trier High all envied what he seemed to have *gathered unto himself*, and I guess that was supposed to include me.

Georgie-Porgie and I had been an on-and-off item through our high school and college years, mostly on in the summers and off during the school seasons, though we would see each other on holidays, and once he flew me back East for the big homecoming weekend at Harvard. I suppose he wanted to see how I stacked up against the Ivy League babes. I do not think they were impressed; I know I felt the same. I had turned down intense pressure from my aunt to join that self-same *East Coast Snot-nose Mob*. Not my style. In those days I was busy working on my own mixed-bag degree of literature and design at Northwestern, just down the street from where we lived, plus moonlighting the dirt bike circuit, and I did not give much of a hoot

76

what George did when I was not around. At least, that was what I told myself.

Now the carefully laid-out plan was for me to marry the promising young lord of finance, load up my stuff, and head for the Big Apple. George had been suggesting, one level short of demanding, that I sell Horny as soon as possible. He said his high-rise digs featured a workout room and a swimming pool, but no garage parking. *Sorry, babes; Manhattan, you know, and with the price we'll get for that classic old cow, well, there's the honeymoon trip to Venice right there!*

This morning Regina was on edge, and anybody could see The Big Day was making her twice as nitpicky as her ordinary unpleasant self. A bad case of what I called her *nattery snits* was in the air. I had to admit, when my aunt set out to do something, she was a force to be reckoned with, and at this time, on this day, things were coming right down to the wire. She was so close to her victory that she could taste it, savor it along with every little bite of her breakfast. In short, she could not help it. She was going to do whatever it took to nip her prize filly's butt across that finish line and get me hooked up permanently to that great financial prospect next door.

"You should probably take a beauty nap, dear," she said.

"Re-*gee*-na, it is seven thirty in the morning."

She glowered at me, but I rolled back under huggable Horny and finished checking the brake lines. It only took thirty seconds and then I pushed myself out from under and grinned up at her. Actually, I did not trust her, or I would have stayed

77

under longer and checked a few more things.

I got to my feet and stretched, then launched a sudden high kick at the heavy bag hanging next to the Irish trash corner of the wall. My foot caught the bag midway with a satisfying thump.

Regina was not expecting that and she jumped back and let out a little yip.

"Oh, Jousie, that is so unladylike!"

I grinned and leapt toward her like a ballet dancer, ending with a light twirl. I had not done that since I was fourteen. It surprised me that I could still almost get up on my toes, even in sneakers, even after all that time.

Regina sighed. My aunt had the sense of humor of a Puritan minister, a thought not far off the mark as she claimed one of our first crossing ancestors had *most probably* been on the good ship *Mayflower*. Now her voice took on the light whine of a frustrated mosquito.

"You could be with the New York Ballet Company right now."

"Oh Reggie, I have too much across the hips, and you know it. And look at the bright side. Yes, I could be flopping my way through *Swan Lake*, but then—oh no! —I could not be here to marry Georgie-Porgie Pudding Pie."

"I wish you would not call him that. It is disrespectful to call him that."

"Like you call your sweetie 'Alfie'?"

You can see by this time I was pretty good at baiting the tigress.

Regina bit her lip, wanting to say much more but knowing it would lead us off in a bad direction. It always did. I was so *common* and *useless*. I was the detested tomboy with scratches on my knees from soccer and lacrosse. I was the most graceful dancer the cotillion teacher had ever seen (Mrs. Miller, the teacher, said so herself). Once I heard that, I went to the practice sessions as little as possible. *Just being the nasty, obstreperous little brat that you are*, Regina said. She was right, I had to give her that one.

I learned to care for my own grimy dirt bike. And then after New Trier High, I committed the mortal sin of attending the plebian Northwestern instead of journeying East to join that *haut* girly gang of Seven Sisters lamebrains. And somewhere along the way I had committed a mortal sin by deserting ballet for karate. Holy moley, in those days, every normal kid in Winnetka—yes, there was such a phenomenon—wanted to be a kickboxer. *Hah! Boot to the head!* Just because I was a girl could not change that, at least not in my own mind.

I gave Horny's light blue finish and shining white convertible top one last fond inspection that ended with a little honk on the horn.

"He sure is pretty."

That displeased Regina as well—of course—and a frown showed itself through her makeup.

"Don't be silly, Juniper. It is just a car. Cars are not pretty, girls are pretty."

Before I could reply, she was off in another direction.

"Oh, Jousy-dear, now you've gone and smeared *grease* on your cheek!"

You would have thought I was mortally wounded.

"Auntie, it is just grease!"

79

I rubbed my cheek with a clean-up rag, making the mess a bit worse.

"No. Here, let me," she said.

She set down her breakfast and spit on a linen handkerchief that had magically appeared from somewhere on her fastidious personage and carefully dabbed at my face. Then she stood back and gave me a critical appraisal.

"There. No real damage."

I let her pat my cheek. I even managed a smile.

"Thank you, Regina. You are up so early. And look at you, all made up and everything for my special day!"

"You had better get going, young lady."

"Plenty of time, auntie dear. All the time in the world."

"Not really, Juniper. Not really."

There it was again, the last word.

Regina had been planning my wedding for over two years. Maybe longer. For all I knew, she could have been plotting to hook me up with the rich kid next door since my early high school days. You might say I had tried him out and he did not seem like anything special, at least not to me.

"Let's go in. I'll help with your makeup," she said.

"Actually, I am going out for coffee. You want anything?"

"You're going off the property like *that*?"

I was wearing a pair of worn but appropriately sexy cutoff jeans and a red tank top. I guess she thought pink would have been better, maybe something pert and flouncy that showed less skin. Young Winnetka ladies did not advertise their wares in flame-red wraparounds.

"Would an overcoat and a pair of galoshes help?" I asked.

"I am serious! You most certainly could do better than running around town on the morning of your wedding."

I could see her point of view, but my aunt was not going to have her way with me entirely on this day of days. I went for light ridicule as my weapon of choice.

"Naughty young lady has last wild fling at the coffee shop. All of Winnetka is agog."

Regina pouted her disapproval, but said nothing more. She did manage a last petulant little stamp with one foot, but that was the only sign she was boiling inside.

I slid onto the smooth ivory leather of Horny's soft front seat. I turned the key. The big straight six gave a throaty cough and then settled into a contented purr while my aunt favored me with a disapproving glare.

"See you later, Reggie," I said as I carefully backed Horny out through the open garage door. I did not say how much later.

But for all that smart talk, I was not that sure of myself or my intentions. Yes, I was about to be confined like the proverbial bird in the gilded cage, but there was no sense of relief in knowing my future was going to be provided for. George might not care for me with sincere feelings and passion of true love, but he was a hard worker, and if he strayed from his matrimonial vows I could always take him to the cleaners in divorce court. Not, I reflected, a great way to start a wedding by considering alternate endings. Still, the doubt lingered. *What was I about to do with my life?*

It was a beautiful day in the neighborhood, as that television personality used to sing in that light tenor of his, way back in the long ago and far away. A beautiful day in early May. I had my dual degree in fine arts and humanities from Northwestern and a few hundred dollars in my pocket from my summer art-directing job at a downtown ad agency. I gave Horny Hudson a drink of high grade at the local Chevron station. Horny's whitewalled tires rolled smoothly south along North Shore Drive as I headed toward downtown Chicago.

It had rained the night before and water drops sparkled on the new green leaves of the maple trees as I passed my alma mater. I drove on until I was heartened by a beautiful watery landscape on my left, a few distant white sails, and the sunlight dancing over the waves on Lake Michigan, while in front of me the downtown skyscrapers loomed tall against a brilliant blue sky. Traffic was light as I did a nostalgic tour of Randolph and Clark and Lake and Wabash and Michigan Avenue. Horny purred with renewed energy as I hit the freeway, heading south and west across the suburbs. It was nearly noon when I rolled into an old-fashioned A&W root beer drive in Joliet.

By then poor old George might have still been standing at the altar, or maybe sitting in a front pew talking on his cell phone, complaining to his buddies I was always late or (if he had already figured things out) wondering if he could get an afternoon tee time at his parents' country club, while for her part, Regina would be working herself into a full-blown rage. A small part of me was wondering if I should be suffering any pangs of guilt, but all I felt was an overwhelming sense of relief. I ordered a black cow and spooned in a chunk of vanilla ice cream while I wondered if the society page of the *Tribune* would print a retraction, with a headline like "Winnetka Girl Decides Not To Get Married After All."

If Regina wanted so desperately to make this ceremony happen, she should have divorced her darling Alfie and married Georgie-Porgie herself. From the naked selfies I had semi-accidentally found in her purse barely a week ago, she certainly knew our brash young neighbor well enough.

I eventually phoned from the El Rancho Hotel in Gallup, New Mexico, and was lucky enough to catch Uncle Alfred at a moment when Regina was out and he was not calling Brazil or yelling at one of the gardeners, none of whom could understand English and did not know the difference between a daisy and a flowering ragweed. He sounded busy as usual, and maybe a little tired. He probably had somebody long distance waiting on the other line.

"No, Jousie, I'm not angry about the wedding. It's been a good year and I could use a big tax write-off. It was your aunt's idea, anyway, pushing for sooner rather than later."

"How is she taking it, Alfie?"

"Well, there was the initial uproar, and that was followed by the mandatory upwelling of tears, but she seems to have calmed down since then."

"Wish I had been there to see it."

"That's not nice."

The way he said it I knew he was grinning. She

had to be out of the house or he would never have said that. To my experience, Alfred had never dared talk even the slightest bit in jest about his wife. It had to be hard for him to live in that house. After that tiny slip, I heard his long-distance sound, a sort of moaning hum as he tightened up the old emotional belt, and then he was back to being gruff old Alfred.

"Um…bottom line, she'll be all right. Your aunt's a survivor. She has tickets to a Bette Midler concert, and since I've got to catch a plane to Miami, she's going to try to apologize to George, ease the poor boy's pain."

"She is good at that."

"What do you mean?"

I was a little too close to the edge with that last remark. Alfred was not only terrified of his wife, there were times when he was insanely jealous. I quickly retreated into neutral territory.

"She always knows the right things to say."

He accepted that.

"Well, I guess…what now for you?"

"I think I'll take Horny on a spin to the West Coast. Give things a chance to settle down. After that, if my rooms are still open at your place?"

He paused before he spoke again.

"You know they always are, Jousie."

You had to know the Warner family language. That slight hesitation was his way of saying my cushy old life at home no longer was an option. Just another motivation for me to get on with my new life.

CHAPTER 5

Awake and back in the present in my hillside apartment in North Hollywood, I rode my stationary bike for ten minutes to loosen my knee joint, but that proved to be a move in the wrong direction. My gimp knee protested until it finally locked up, and it took a half hour soaking in a tub of hot water before it loosened and I could bend it again. If I did not heal fast I was going to have to get more serious about finding a new profession.

I got into my only black dress, suitably somber except for the short skirt, and called a taxi to take me to Grandma Jenny's funeral. Well, actually, I had them take me to Car Props, where I limped over to my Hudson and drove myself to the service. I did not know why I did it that way; it just seemed appropriate. It was right that Jenny's old pal Horny showed up for her funeral.

The services were held at a funeral home that I had not even known existed. Not knowing it was there did not strike me as odd at the time. After all, the only time you go looking for a mortuary is when you need one.

Edward & Friendly was located in old Hollywood near Paramount Studios. It was an out-of-the-way place on a quiet street, three left turns that backended a couple blocks off Melrose. It was an establishment that logically should not have been there, but there it was. In outward appearance, the building looked like one of those faux Tudor-front manses that rich and successful show biz people went for in a big way back in the golden age of silent movies. It was set back from the street in a thick grove of dark green cypress trees, and you could only reach it by taking a gravel walkway. They did not look busy.

I parked on the otherwise deserted street right in front of the mortuary. I checked my makeup and locked the car. Good luck with that last gesture. One slit in the white canvas convertible top and any car thief would have Horny hot-wired in about thirty seconds, and then on down the freeway to a car-parts shop in West Covina. I tossed a pox on the hood, something Regina used to do with her bronze Firebird. Of course it was a joke, but nobody ever messed with my aunt's car, not even the traffic ticket lady. So it was only a half-joke, the gag being that I did not have the faintest idea how to do a pox, if such a thing actually existed. I was hoping maybe it was an automatic thing, like using a credit card. You stuck it in the cash machine and money poured out, but you never really have to know how all that robot stuff inside makes the magic happen.

I left Horny and made my way through a heavy front door into a quiet reception room. I thought I was fifteen minutes early, but as I entered the high-ceilinged room, three spry old ladies moved forward to greet me.

"Blu Baxter," the first one said. She was nearly wide as she was tall, though the top of her head barely came up to my chin. She had mahogany-colored skin and kinky black hair braided in corn rows, and a wide grin that lightened the room. She was dressed in an expensive navy blue pantsuit and she spoke with a warm and friendly New Orleans accent.

"Why honey child, imagine, Jenny's granddaughter!"

She brushed right past my outstretched hand and gathered me in an enthusiastic hug.

"Let me get a piece of that," the second woman said. She was six inches shorter than Blu Baxter, which made her less than five feet tall, but her eyes sparkled and she seemed to radiate energy.

"I'm Tillie Noonschnapper, your grandma's best friend."

Tillie was dressed like a German barmaid, her dirndl trimmed in black with lilies embroidered in her white blouse.

"No," Blu said. "*I'm* her best friend."

"Will you two old gabbers refrain?" the third lady said. She was hunched over and looked incredibly old, I thought more wrinkled and bent over than the oldest person I had ever seen, but when she straightened to bark at her friends she was taller than me. She was unkempt and wild-eyed with the appearance of a large and shaggy gray Irish wolfhound. "I am Margotha Swillwell. I would hug you, but I have the mange."

Tillie pushed her forward. "Don't be silly, Margotha. What you got is old age, and that isn't catching."

The old lady accepted my tentative hug. I felt impressions of stiff manners and the strength of a kindly ancient giant. She brushed a cold cheek against my face, and then held me at arm's length.

"My dear Jennifer's granddaughter," she said.

"Margotha is Aidana's great-granddaughter," Tillie said.

Aidana from the story that Jenny told me? I looked from her to Blu and then back to the tall and spare ancient woman, who still had me in her appraising glance.

"It's true," she said. Of course that could hardly be true, as it would mean Margotha Swillwell was hundreds of years older than anyone I had ever met.

"Family hug," Blu said, and the four of us bonded together in a small but comforting quartet, arms laced around each other's waists.

I knew nothing about them but apparently my grandmother had talked to them about me, and for no exact reason I could think of I knew in every fabric of my being that we were family.

They said sympathetic and kind things about my loss, and they were appropriately dressed in black. Their dresses, while clean and carefully pressed, looked as out of fashion as those I had found in Jenny's handbag, different and yet elegant and proper in a timeless way. I found myself wishing I owned a longer skirt, but they seemed to accept me as I was. Margotha wore what I guess you could call the classic witch hat, an ancient cone with a bent visor that circled the base, and she wore a black lace veil. Tillie's hat was more a crisp Teutonic military cap, but it seemed to work with her dirndl. Blu had a black turban. At first glance I thought it was studded with sequins, but on closer inspection the sequins proved to be gems of some kind that sparkled against the ebony fabric.

Each lady wore a similar diamond ring featuring one large square diamond cut with a few facets, a cut I had never seen. The stones looked dark as coal until they caught the light and then there was an unexpectedly brilliant flash.

Margotha, who was clearly their leader, took a ring identical to theirs from a gray purse of dimpled ostrich skin leather and held it out to me with trembling fingers.

"Jenny wished this for you, little chicklet."

"Oh..."

"Do you accept this ring?"

"Yes, I do accept it," I said.

It slipped easily over the ring finger on my right hand.

"I was not sure it would fit."

"Nonsense, girl. Of course it fits," Tillie said.

The other ladies smiled and nodded.

Margotha pointed to the way we had to go.

"Buck up now, me fine bitches."

We went in together through the heavy wooden doors and were solemnly greeted by a stiff old man in a dark gray suit. He was the grayest man I had ever seen. I mean, he had skin as gray as a mule's fur. And his long silver hair was combed straight back on his head. His striking, somber complexion was only a few shades lighter than his suit.

"I am Benjamin Perkins," he said, and he led us into a chapel room with a closed coffin in the center on a long wooden table. "I was Jenny's...err, butler, for lack of a better word."

I wondered what the proper word was, but under the circumstances I did not think it right to ask. The high-ceilinged chapel was lined with tall and stained-glass windows. These were filled with vague and misty figures that seemed to twist and writhe with the movement of the soft afternoon sunlight that filtered in through the thick pine branches. We stood silently around the closed ebony-dark lid of an ornately carved coffin.

"A right fine place of rest," Blu said. "For a life filled with a right fine mess of complications."

"What do you mean?" I said.

Tillie patted my shoulder and scowled at her friend. "Don't mind her, mine little one. The voodoo princess thinks our sweet Jenny had too soft a heart."

"Say it like it is," Blu said. Her voice softened to a whisper. "If I had been there, this would have turned out different."

Margotha placed a sprig of red-berried holly on the dark wood.

"She lived good. Those under her prospered. Too soon, she went to her reward."

"Never. You are forgotten never."

"We ain't gonna forget you, honey."

"Vengeance we promise you, dear sweet Jennifer," Margotha said.

"Just a few words from you, dear girl," Tillie said.

"But…I don't know what to say."

"Oh, you go on ahead, child," Blu said. "Whatever comes to mind."

"Yes. You start, and it will come to you," Tillie encouraged me.

I was startled to see the gray presence of Benjamin Perkins at my side.

"I thought you had left the room."

"No, young madam," he whispered with the ghost of a smile. "Take this rites tome. I have marked the appropriate page."

I accepted the worn and tattered booklet and in the next moment I was startled to find myself whisked out of my normal existence. It was impossible, it was too strange, and it was some sort of magic, and so many times in my own life I had questioned whether real magic actually existed!

The solid walls of the chapel dissolved and the three ladies and Benjamin and I were outdoors. We were still standing around the dark coffin but we were perched on a high cliff overlooking a cold gray sea. Lightning flashed in the distance and an icy rain pelted our faces. In seconds we were soaked to the skin. But that did not seem to matter in the slightest to us. We were lost and found in the moment, and the moment was everything. I opened the booklet to the page Benjamin had marked and read sentences that illuminated themselves in glowing green letters.

"Time is a river," I said.

"*Dam it up or let it flow,*" the three ladies murmured.

"Time is a river," I repeated.

"*Twist and turn, but let it go,*" they said.

"Time is a river," I said once more.

"*Softly tending, never ending, where next doth go we never know.*"

"Farewell, dear one."

"*Let her go, let it flow.*"

The ladies each blessed themselves with the sign of the cross, but done at an angle like an "X," and without thinking I did the same.

And with that simple gesture the cliffside scene faded, the wind died, and we were once more in the chapel at the funeral home. The moisture swiftly dissipated from our clothing and in a few seconds we were dry, but the smooth surface of the black coffin remained beaded with moisture. Benjamin gave me the slightest smile and a nod of approval.

"Well done!" Tillie said.

"That damn Celtic rain gets more icy every time," Blu said.

"Should be used to it. You've been around since the Ice Age," Tillie said.

"Hush, bitches," Margotha said, lightly tapping Tillie with a half-rebuking little poke. The three of them shared a sad smile.

Benjamin took me by the arm and had us step back from the coffin. I had no idea what to expect, but in the next moment six gray-faced men in frocked shirts, black tights, and elegant medieval pantaloons with bulging codpieces entered the room. They took up standing positions, three on each side of the casket. They looked like sextuplets, and it was impossible to see any difference in their similarity to Benjamin, except they wore identical puffy satin hats while he was bareheaded. Their faces were grim and with their pallor I thought they belonged in a movie about the living dead, which I found out later was not a bad guess. One of them gave a brief command and they grasped rails of darkly burnished brass on either side of the casket and marched out through wide doors that opened for them. They made their way along a gravel drive at the rear of the funeral home.

We watched through panes of leaded glass as the six gray men loaded the casket into a black carriage that was trimmed in burnished brass metal ornamentation. Four white horses stood patiently while the casket was secured with ropes of corded black silk.

"I hope they realize they are headed into heavy traffic," I said, trying to imagine how they would manage the bustling impatience and rudeness of the frenetic Los Angeles drivetime freeways. "A horse-drawn carriage making its way downtown is going to be a honkfest."

"Oh, they will not have any trouble," Benjamin assured me.

Blu touched her right thumb to her tongue, touched it to the palm of her left hand, balled her right fist and smacked it into the same open hand.

"Luck," she said.

The other women nodded and each performed the same little ritual.

Tillie looked at me.

"White horses. You lick-spit them. For good luck."

Okay. I went through the simple gesture, touching my thumb to my tongue, wetting the palm of my hand and stamping it with the other. It seemed the right thing to do. The three ladies nodded.

The funeral carriage moved away with the men walking double file behind it. They rounded a corner and then they were out of sight.

It was not five seconds later that my evil Aunt Regina burst into the room, pushing her way through the door where we had first entered. It was Regina in a full rage, a sight to see! Her fury was beyond the one I imagined she had worked up all those years ago when I skipped out on Georgie-Porgie. But if she looked a sight, my grandmother's three old friends were a grand spectacle. They reared back like wildcats ready to strike.

"Low, crawling spawn of Satan!" Blu hissed.

"Get out of here, you wicked bad evil pond scum!" Tillie said.

But Margotha topped them all with her low growl.

"Foul clit. Mother of vile waste. Get thee gone, stinkpot!"

Regina took a step back, and then collected herself.

"I claim blood right!" she shouted, ignoring the aged women to fix her glare directly on me.

"Where is the casket?" my aunt shouted at the top of her lungs. "The casket!"

Tillie moved in front of me.

"You're too late, Regina. You have missed her."

My aunt pushed Tillie aside, and again looked directly at me.

"The body!" my aunt shrieked. "I must see the body!"

"To steal her power?" Tillie said. "To snatch her ring? To take her charm book?"

"Too late for any of that," Blu said. "Maybe you shoulda taken an earlier flight."

My aunt ignored them all, focusing her anger on me.

"Jousie! Little foolish stupid Jousie! You get out of here right this minute! You have no right to be here! This is none of your concern!"

Her gaze fell on the ring on my finger. The look on her face morphed into one of uncontrollable fury and her voice rose to a horrible shriek.

94

"The diamond! Jenny's diamond! *My* diamond! Give it to me! I am her daughter! It belongs to *me!* Come now to ruin *you!*"

She grabbed my hand in an iron grip and tried to rip the ring from my finger. But it would not move.

I pulled back, sickened with a sudden realization of what this woman must have done.

"No! *You* killed Grandma Jenny! You murdered your own mother!"

We were all stunned by the horror of her inhuman deed, all its ugly nakedness spoken loud and so revealed in the light of day.

No matter how vicious her attack on my hand, the ring stayed on my finger. It seemed to have a mind of its own, and it would not budge.

Regina tried another grab at the ring, but this time, instead of pulling back, I felt my own rage growing and words poured out of me that until that time I did not know I possessed.

"Mother-murderer! You evil, foul, wicked person! I no longer know you! You are not welcome! Get out of here!"

With my declaration a dark fog seemed to settle over my aunt. It was as if she had no other choice but to let go of my hand and step away from me. Even so, she retreated one step at a time, spitting her words at us like the deadly black-spider lady I knew she was.

"You'll be sorry! Yes, you will! I curse you to ruin, foolish stupid little Mousie Jousie-girl!"

After that display of verbal fireworks, I expected her to disappear in a puff of smoke, but instead, she did her usual Regina cloudburst and stormed out of the room in tears.

"Whew," Blu said. "What a drama queen! This girl plenty glad that be over!"

"You hear her try to pull the old 'come to ruin' curse on Juniper?" Tillie said. "Old school, don't you think?"

"That *flim flam flather* will not blaze," Margotha said. "If she truly possessed overpower, she would have crisped us in the moment."

"Couldn't take us all on at once. But look out, you, Juniper Rose."

Margotha nodded. She put one arm on my shoulder and gave me a stern look.

"She will be avenging in your direction. Be lax not for a moment. Let not down thy guard."

CHAPTER 6

We stood in a small, awkward foursome on the sidewalk in front of the funeral home. Once we were outside the building, my three new friends were increasingly nervous, as jittery as frightened sparrows. They must have known something I did not. For my part, I felt drained and empty, thanks to this latest encounter with my evil crazy aunt, and I was grimly uncertain as well as to where my future might lead. The last half hour had torn apart my relatively safe day-to-day world that consisted of stunt assignments, wrap parties, shallow sex in cheap location motels, and on to the next gig.

Something caught the corner of my eye. I looked up and saw a small moving spot high overhead. No way to know how high or what it was, but only that it was moving toward us, fast, and growing larger.

"You see that?" I said.

Tillie looked up. "Oh, yeah," she said. "Regina's harpies. We all heard the rumors."

"Her *what?*"

"Harpies. They're not real witches. But they can do real damage."

Blu, Tillie, and Margotha gathered in a tight circle surrounding me.

"Worry not," Margotha said. "We shall nail the little sluts before they cause thee harm."

The flying spot grew closer until it became five objects flying in a "V" formation. I heard distant screeches and then the flying wedge was diving straight toward us. I could make out five young women, and they were riding on flying ultralights

97

that were half wings and half sleek lightweight motorbikes.

When they were within a hundred yards, my three friends raised forked fingers in their direction and gave answering cries to the approaching group. In response, there was a series of muffled shock waves high overhead and four of the fliers veered away. The remaining one wobbled down to crash into one of the lower limbs of a nearby cypress. The rider flopped to the ground in front of us, an embarrassing display of a young lady in what looked like an awful khaki-green gown that was up around her hips, her tangled hair around her face, her lipstick and heavy eyeliner smeared and messed up. She groaned and sat up.

She did not look like she had broken any bones, though she had taken a terrible tumble. And impossible and out of place as it seemed to me at the time, I recognized her.

"Debbie Waterman?" I said.

Debbie Waterman had been in cotillion dance classes with me, one of the young ladies being groomed for our place in high Chicago social circles.

"You bloody bitch!" she hissed at me.

"Debbie, what the hell are you doing here?"

Even shaken as she was, her glare at me was one of total fury.

"You didn't marry your Georgie-Porgie, so in the end I had to!"

"Regina's idea, right?"

"I don't want to talk about it.

"And how did that turn out for you?"

98

"Not good, you bitch!" she said, lunging for me.

I did a sidestep and sent her flying with the energy of her own velocity.

"Bravo," Tillie said.

Debbie staggered to her feet, shook her head, and sprinted to her flying machine, which she pulled out of the tree branches. She gave it a running start and managed to escape with the smoking bikeplane sputtering and not quite managing to take off. She ran through a bush and knocked over a garbage can before she disappeared around a corner. We heard the roar of an engine as she managed to get airborne.

"That was Debbie Waterman," I said, still shaking my head.

"We knew Regina couldn't have overcome your grandmother all by herself," Blu said.

"She's gone rogue crone for sure," Tillie said with a nod, looking after the wobbling dot in the sky struggling to catch up with the rest of the retreating formation.

"From now on, we all needs be more careful. That means you, especially, young witch lady," Margotha said.

"Witch code be always broom-to-broom," Blu said. "But when Regina sends a flock of harpies..."

You could say I was waking up to my adult life. I had been cursed and I had been warned, and what I had experienced was not just a scene from a movie or a chapter in a novel.

The ladies nervously eyed the sky. I did not like the thought that we were about to go our separate ways and I had no idea when I might see them again.

"Can I give you a ride? I've got Jenny's old Hudson."

"Oh, dear girl, we thought you'd never ask!"

"Wonderful, that muttering old beast of Jenny's."

"Can we make it so the top will go down?"

"Of course," I said.

They were all suddenly animated, everybody talking at once.

"We have so much to tell you!"

"You must be careful, honey child! Regina, she gonna come after you again, sure as sin and purgatory!"

"You must not worry too much that it consumes your life!"

"But you gotta be vigilant, girl!"

"You must not let her get the best of you!"

We were ten feet or so from the car when the first earthquake struck. It was one of those sharp temblors, the ones that jerk the ground out from under you and then just as quickly put it back again so that you are not thrown off your feet, but your senses reel and you look around a bit because that is just the first one and you are quite convinced more are about to come.

The ladies looked at each other, shaking their heads.

"No, she couldn't—"

"No, she *wouldn't*—"

"I think she just did."

Their mood changed to one of grim determination. Tillie took my arm.

"Schista kaufen!"

"What does that mean?"

She grinned at me.

"Shit. Shit on everything. And that means change of plans, dear girl. There is less time than we thought. There is much you need to know, but now there's no time at all!"

"We gotta go! I gotta get back to my swamp shack!"

"Bitch mates, we must leave at once," Margotha said, her voice edgy and sharp.

"No. Jist one more thing, for Jenny's sake!" Blu said. "Juniper, you gotta know: dat river we talk about can never be stopped! An' one more thing you gotta know: it should never be tampered wit'!"

Margotha nodded. "Yes. Know this clear, my dear young bitch witch: There exist junctures, moments in balance, all things can go up or down, heaven or hell, bliss or perdition."

Blu looked around in wide-eyed worry and spoke hurriedly.

"People like us, we been warned over and over, *Never tamper!* But looks to me like your nasty Aunt Regina now be breakin' the prime rule!"

Margotha grimaced and shook her ancient mop of white hair. "The vile clit proposes to bend time itself to her perversity."

"Perversity? What does she want?"

Tillie shook her head and made a clucking sound.

"Your crazy aunt wishes to be the queen of the world."

"What?"

There was another tremble, and this time I felt a difference—this was no ordinary shaker! Instead of a simple tremor from side to side or up and down, it felt as if everything I knew was suffering a warped shifting, a pull, a twist of the fabric of being itself.

"Holy verity!" Margotha said, blessing herself with the crosswise gesture.

"Dat vile bitch done found a juncture!"

"Oh, now it is so much harder—who can stop her now?"

"What is it?" I asked, alarmed. "What is she doing?"

"We do not know where the vile bitch is! She could be anywhere in the past!"

"She be back der, somewhere in lost history, reshapin' the here an' now!"

"Wicked, foul, evil, pernicious…"

Tillie patted my shoulder.

"Juniper, you had better go to Jenny's bungalow! Get inside. You should be safe for a while. Maybe you can figure out what Regina is up to."

Right there in front of me on the sidewalk on the quiet side street in old Hollywood, the three old ladies began to disappear like quick fades in a movie, and in a few seconds they were gone. I turned to look back at the Victorian funeral home, but it too had disappeared, leaving nothing but an empty cypress grove with the tree branches quivering in an uncertain wind.

Okay. As if I was not already confused, as I climbed into Horny Hudson and sat there for a moment wondering how I could possibly find my grandmother's bungalow since everything in her bag had an address in Chicago back in the 1930s, my cell phone rang.

"She's gone!" a familiar voice wailed in my ear.

It was Uncle Alfred and he was sobbing like he would never stop. I sighed, guessing how Regina's absence had gone down with him. Alfred had that breathless little-boy-lost tone in his voice that I remembered from my childhood, that tone so over the top it always made me question, if only for the moment, how sincere he was.

"It's Regina! She's missing. Gone. I've looked everywhere!"

How much did Alfred know about Regina's secret life as an evil sorceress? Was I supposed to tell him his wife had just popped in on her mother's funeral out here on the West Coast? Or that Jenny, who everybody had been saying died years ago, had not died after all, but had recently been murdered by her daughter, who happened to be his wife?

It was a good idea to calm my uncle down or he would be calling me back every five minutes, and now was really not the time for that. Under almost any other circumstances, Regina's sudden absence would not be unusual. She went where she wanted. Once or twice a year without giving any notice, my imperious aunt would take off for points unknown, or at least, to places she did not announce before she left. When she came back, she always had her reasons; a diamond brooch she had seen in *Vogue* that was so attractive she just had to have it, a new silk shawl you could only get in Manhattan, or even an outfit she had brought back from a fashion show in Milan. She kept a travel bag packed in the foyer closet. An odd travel bag, I might add, as I had seen what was in it.

Hey, you would peek, too. My aunt was always going through my things like she had every right to do so, so when she was at the hairdressers or the nail salon or the spa, I returned the favor by pawing through her things, and what she packed in her travel bag gave me the impression she was at least mildly off her rocker. In some ways, her travel stuff reminded me of the contents in Jenny's handbag. But now was not the time to get into that. Right now, I had to do something about my uncle, who was still making snuffling noises on the phone.

"Calm down, Alfred. When is the last time you saw her?"

"We were in the garage. Last night. I was polishing my sports car—you know, the red one."

"The Alfa?"

He had been dickering to buy a 1956 Alfa Romeo Sprint Veloce just about the time I was copping out of my wedding. It was the only one of his toys I had not had a chance to take out for a spin.

"Yes, that one. And Regina came in like she always does and it was a minute or two before I even realized she was there."

"Well, that is her way."

"She was looking at that chart she made of all her ancestors."

"She always does that. She has a fixation."

"I wasn't paying much attention, Jousie. One moment she was right there, holding her glass of Chablis with the three ice cubes, dressed like she was ready to go to a nightclub or something."

"Exactly where was she sitting?"

"Well, that was a little unusual. She was perched on top of our stepladder, for dramatic effect, I suppose. You know Regina. She likes to make a statement."

"What time of night was this?"

"After ten. I didn't think anything of it. Regina likes to dress up any time of the day or night."

"What exactly was she wearing?"

There was a pause, with Alfred thinking about it. I heard a clink of ice over the phone, and realized he was taking a sip from one of his heavy cut-glass tumblers. It was early afternoon back in the Midwest, but that would not mean anything to Alfred. He often said that, as an international traveler, he could drink in any time zone. As if a functioning alcoholic needed a reason.

"Something fancy. I don't know. I never saw it before. Something you might see in an old photograph of a wedding or something."

Something clicked in my mind. *She had been wearing one of the gowns from her travel bag.* But this was no time to start a conversation about that with my uncle. That definitely would give him a heart attack.

"Maybe me skipping out on my wedding with Georgie finally pushed her over the edge?"

"Come on, Jousie-girl, that was years ago, and Regina has never been even close to any edge. She is steady as a rock."

I bit my tongue, hard. What do you say when you know the lady he shared his bed with was a foul creature who had murdered her own mother? I was torn. This was my uncle who provided a home for me when I was a kid. And life with Regina must have been difficult for him as well. Like living with Lady Macbeth.

"You are probably right…but can you be sure she has taken off for somewhere?" I asked.

"I tell you, Ju-Ju, one moment she was sitting right there and we were talking and I asked her a question and when she didn't answer I turned around and she was gone!"

"What exactly were you talking about, Alfie?"

When she was out of sorts, Regina referred to her husband as "Alfie," in a scoffing, belittling way. I did, too, but only when he started in with "Jousie" or "Ju-Ju." We had been doing it for years, and I do not believe he ever caught on; the man had a deaf ear for everything but the clink of money or ice in a whiskey tumbler. There was a pause in the conversation and then he dismissed whatever he was thinking with a snort.

"It was just nonsense. She was looking at that old picture of her father with his airplane and she wanted to know how far he could fly on a tank of gas." Alfred blew out an exasperated breath. "Like I would know."

It is hard to describe the feeling of dread that swarmed over me. I had no idea what her plans were, but whatever they were, she was most certainly behind those earth tremors. My new friends would have said it was *dangerous mischief.* Trouble for me. Trouble for the whole world.

What did I know about Regina? She would not run off half-cocked. She had always been very careful about planning her little escapes. Regina had once said Grandpa John had disappeared in May

106

1939. Was that the juncture the three old ladies were talking about? How could that even be possible? It felt like a very thin trail, but if it was so, I needed to know so much more before I could make any sense out of what was happening. And what if it was nothing? What if I was completely wrong? Maybe I was imagining things because earlier, on my way to the funeral home, I thought I had caught a glimpse of a Curtiss Robin like my grandpa's flying low overhead. That in itself was odd because fewer than eight hundred of those airplanes had ever been made, and most of them had been scrapped for metal in the early days of World War II. And what could that mean, anyway?

Alfred's sobbing halfway across the country brought me back to the moment. His being upset was not good news. My uncle was always joking about his bad heart.

"Come on, Alfie. Buck up. It's not like she has never done anything like this before. What about her travel bag?"

"Missing."

So Regina had left in a hurry. She had killed Jenny, she had come out to steal what she believed was hers, and having failed at that, she had her secondary plans. I knew Alfred suspected she was unfaithful to him, and for years I had figured she must be living another life somewhere else, probably in Manhattan.

If Regina had left their home in Winnetka last night, and she showed up at Jenny's funeral this afternoon, the simple explanation would be she had caught a flight from Chicago to Los Angeles. I stopped myself before I spoke. Alfred knew nothing about the funeral, or he would have said something. What a mess!

"Alfred? Are you still on the line? Where are you, exactly?"

"In our bedroom. Sitting at her dressing table. She has a notebook. Lots of comments but nothing makes any sense."

That was unusual. The most I had ever seen my aunt write was her name on a check when she was buying something she did not need.

"Like what?"

"Sheer nonsense. Here's one: *Don't forget panties. When brooming a lady wears the right clothes.*"

More tumblers clicked in my head. My aunt had some sort of powers, all right. But what was "brooming"? I could not visualize the perfectly made-up Regina picking bugs from her teeth as she rode the wind on her favorite straw broom, cutting in front of regular passenger planes on her way to LAX. But Alfred was sobbing again and I had to say something to straighten him out.

"Alfred, you have to calm down. She probably meant 'grooming'."

In my heart I knew that was another lie. But what was one more fib in that house of lies? She had meant "brooming". Riding the broom, whatever the hell that was.

Alfred was beginning to show his usual impatience with life in general and me in particular. My uncle was a *Let's-get-things-done* guy. He was probably wondering why he had called me in the first place.

"I don't know, Jousie! That's why I'm asking

108

you. How about this one? She scribbled 'Gold. Double-check dates.' Or, this one: 'Show no fear. Ride, ride, ride.'"

That last one gave me the cold shivers.

"Maybe we should contact the police," I said.

"But I'm supposed to fly down to South America for two weeks."

At last I thought I saw a way out of the immediate problem.

"I think you have to set all this aside and go."

"Really? You think that would be okay?"

"Look, Alfred, I am sure Regina will turn up. And when she does, you do not want to be mad at her because you lost some business."

"Well, yeah, that would piss me off. This one could be worth close to a million buckaroos."

That was what he wanted to do, catch a jet for somewhere and make a deal. In a way he had called to get my permission. I figured the best way to deal with his anxiety was to give him what he wanted.

"Yeah, you had better go ahead, Alfie."

"You'll stay in touch?"

"Yes, I will."

I clicked off my phone and sighed.

"Life certainly can be complicated, can it not?" a voice said. It was Benjamin, standing on the sidewalk near Horny, looking down at me in his solemn slate-gray way.

"Benjamin! You startled me."

"I am sorry, young madam. Margotha said I am to direct you to Jenny's place, if I may."

"Well, yes, of course. Get in."

He inspected the door handle and then opened the door and slid into the passenger seat.

109

"This is a wonderful motor vehicle," he said. "I have always admired it."

"You and Jenny—?"

"Are very old friends."

As we went along, he pointed out where I was to turn. Shortly after going north up Vine Street, we got on the freeway and headed north up the Cahuenga Pass.

When I was not scanning the sky for harpies, I found myself watching him out of the corner of my eye.

"I knew those harpies when they were just ordinary girls. Well, not ordinary. They were up-and-coming Winnetka socialites. But now they are different."

"Yes. But only through Regina. She is their power source."

"You...you are not like a zombie, are you?"

"Well, no." He paused to think about it. "Well, actually, yes and no. Though mostly no."

"That is confusing."

"Allow me to explain. I worked in a mortuary, a long time ago. Everybody is afraid of dying, but me perhaps more so. In my case, the more of death I saw, the more frightened I became. And when my time came, I was given a choice."

"By whom?"

"Your grandmother."

"Oh. I think I understand, sort of. And are there a lot of you?"

"Not so many. You met six at the funeral service."

"How come ordinary people know about you?"

"About gray people? Well, look."

He faded to invisibility, and then back again. It seemed to be a common trick. Blu, Tillie, and Margotha all knew it.

"I hope I live long enough to learn how to do that."

"You should hope you never are in such danger that you have to use it."

"Not likely, the way things are going."

No flying legions of harpies reappeared, and under Benjamin's direction we got off the freeway at Barham. I was surprised when he had me turn up Fredonia, the steep road that passed by my apartment.

"But this is the street where I live!"

"Well, yes. Just a coincidence. Jenny's place is further up the hill. Near the top, actually."

I doubted *coincidence*. Grandma Jenny had probably been keeping her eye on me all the time I lived there. As I drove past my place, I glanced over to make sure both Putt-Putt and Duke were securely locked up the way I had left them. Benjamin pointed us onward and we climbed higher and deeper into Hollywood Hills.

"How old was Jenny, anyway?"

"I'm not sure. Older than me. Shakespeare courted her."

"William Shakespeare? No way!"

"Well, maybe that does not count."

"What do you mean?"

"I am not allowed to say. You will find out for yourself."

"There seem to be a lot of rules."

"Yes. In any society. It is how people get along."

We had now arrived at a small California Craftsman-style bungalow set back in the shadows of a stand of gnarled old cedar pines. The view was wonderful. Below and to the southwest, the webwork of Los Angeles streets stretched away to end at the curved rim of the Pacific Ocean. To the northeast, the San Gabriel mountains jutted up toward towering scoops of bright clouds. I pulled into the driveway and parked in front of an attached one-car garage. There was a brisk breeze, so I pulled the top up.

When I finished, I saw Benjamin looking out at the spectacular view.

"Humans love flying like birds," he said, pointing across the road to the steep precipice where two kids, one with a red hang glider and another with a white one, had just launched themselves into the evening air. I found myself scanning the sky for harpies. And then my thoughts wandered back to my strange new friend.

"But—you are still human."

"Sort of... But sometimes I do not feel that way."

"How do you feel?"

"Maybe like Frankenstein. Or Jesus."

"Why Jesus?"

"I have no good answer for that. I have not figured out much of this. I suppose you think I must be stupid, me having all the time in the world. Jesus was supposed to have come back from the dead. But rumor has it that then he could not stand earthly life anymore, and he went on to heaven. Gray people like me do not seem to have that choice."

The flying pair of hang gliders dipped out of

112

our view.

"Wait a minute, I will show you around," he said.

Benjamin walked down to the mailbox and returned with a handful of colorful flyers and a few bills. He pointed out a small house a few hundred feet farther up the hill behind Jenny's bungalow. I squinted and was able to make out a small Spanish-style stucco house with solar panels on a red tile roof.

"That is my place," he said. "That is, if you will allow it."

Both houses had to be on the same piece of land. "Of course I allow it!"

He nodded in his grave gray-man way.

"Thank you. I will, in turn, be at your service. It is but yours to ask."

"Grandma did not go solar?"

"No, she said it was always cool in her bungalow. Me, in the summers I used to spend a fortune on electricity. The money was no problem, but the pesky greenies were always after me. I finally put in so much solar they do not bother me anymore."

"Problems of the living dead."

"May I point out 'living dead' is probably the ultimate oxymoron?"

I could see why Jenny had gotten along well with this strange creature with his quiet sense of humor.

"You do not seem as worried as Blu, Tillie, and Margotha."

"Age has a pecking order," he corrected me. "Thus, it should be Margotha, Tillie, and Blu."

113

"Tillie is older than Blu?"

"By about a hundred and twenty years. And I currently have little reason for concern about my demise. If the world were to come to grief, the gray men could well be the last beings standing."

"How is it that you live, anyway?"

He pointed to the solar panels on his roof.

"Like those things do. I have researched it. The best I can tell, the secret of my success is that I am a living solar device."

"So you do not worry about food?"

"Or oxygen."

"Must be nice."

"Maybe you think so. There are times when I would die for a hamburger and some French fries from Bob's Big Boy." He wrinkled his face, thinking about what he had just said. "But I cannot, you see. Can *not* die, and can *not* have the burger, either."

He selected a few of the bills from the mail he said were his own and handed the rest to me. As he did so, there was another shake and the small stack of mail fell from my grasp to the old and somewhat crumbling asphalt driveway.

"Regina continues," Benjamin said as he helped me pick up Jenny's mail.

When he handed them to me, my attention was drawn to a flyer on the top. It was promoting the Van Nuys Air Show and the front panel featured a photo of a familiar airplane.

"Benjamin, this is my grandfather's plane!"

"You mean the same make?"

"No, the same aircraft! I recognize the numbers on the tail!"

114

"It is some kind of trap," he said.

"I have to go see!"

"I will go with you tomorrow."

"The air show closes today. I have to go now!"

"Here, this may come in handy," he said. And he handed me Grandma Jenny's knit travel bag.

"For luck, right?" I grinned at him. I was beginning to understand that the bag was part of my brooming journey.

"For luck," he agreed.

I hopped back into Horny and rumbled down the hill to my apartment, where I traded the chubby Hudson for Putt-Putt, figuring I might be able to get on runway apron more easily with a little Vespa mobility. The trip to Van Nuys airport took twenty minutes, and I was able to use my official stuntman credentials to move Putt-Putt behind the regular air show to the hangars.

CHAPTER 7

John Warner's Curtiss Robin was sitting halfway out of a dark hangar when I got there. I maneuvered my Vespa as close as I could get while still leaving myself enough room to skid around and head the other way. The old aircraft was painted lime green with pale yellow trim, and looked like a pretty little bird that was ready to take off into the clear morning air.

A gruff voice spoke from the dark interior of the hangar.

"Hey, girlie. What you want, schnooping around here like you are?"

I thought I heard a hint of a Dutch or German accent. I should have taken the opportunity to drive away, but curiosity has killed lots of cats smarter than me. I hit the kickstand, slung Granny's bag around my shoulder, and walked toward the front end of the airplane to see what I could see. I had done my research on the old black and white John Warner photo, and I knew his plane was outfitted with a radial engine, as was this one. Although Curtiss made more than seven hundred Robins, only about fifty were outfitted with radial engines. And there it was right on the tail, the early identification number NC6H.

"I—I like your airplane. My grandpa had one just like it."

The man had thick arms and a wide chest overlooking an even wider stomach. But I would not say he was fat, or that he had a pot belly. Rather, he looked like one of those thick fellows who worked a lot, ate a lot, and could shake off a cannon ball to the midsection and walk away, an old circus trick that went out of favor when some grim jokester dumped too much gunpowder in the cannon. His voice was deep and resonant and I would be willing to bet he spoke Low German like Uncle Alfred.

"I have a very serious doubt of that, missy. This here ancient monoplane is a genuine Curtiss Robin. They only made but a few hundred of them, and most was flown to death or melted down in the war. World War Deuce, that is, the one against the Nazis, well before your time."

"Well, my grandpa had one. His name was John Warner."

He gave me a hard stare that made me feel uncomfortable.

"Zat is not possible! *My* name is John Warner, and I am hardly old enough to be grandparent to anybody old as you. Now just what is the game you play, missy?"

Awkward silence filled the air between us. I was really sorry I had put that much distance between myself and Putt-Putt. I did not have any answer for his belligerent question. I wanted to run away, start up my scooter, and scoot on out of there. But it was too late for that. The man strolled out of the shadows and looked me over. He was right; he did not look anything like my grandpa John Warner, who I remembered being told as standing upright with a somewhat aristocratic air. This fellow was a big middle-aged guy with a stooped-over posture. He had a nose slightly bent to the right and a Baron von Bismarck mustache that covered much of his weather-beaten and tanned face.

117

"I guess both John and Warner are common-enough names," he said.

The skeptical look on my face must have showed. *Two* John Warners with *two* Curtiss Robins? "Well, I will not bother you any further," I said.

But as I tried to leave, he moved between me and Putt-Putt. He scuffed the ground with one of his tattered old motorcycle boots, as if that might put me at ease.

"I fly out of an airport near Trenton, New Jersey," he said. "You probably never heard of it."

I was overcome with a sudden rush of panic, the fear collecting like rough gravel in the pit of my stomach. I was pretty sure Regina had said my grandfather's home airport was in New Jersey.

"I really should go."

But now his tone turned conversational.

"Actually, my name used to be something else, but I changed it to Warner."

That was so unbelievable that I snapped out the first thing that came to mind.

"What was it, Schotenheimer?"

He looked at me in stunned amazement and then his face darkened. *Oh Ju-Ju Bird, why can you never learn to shut your mouth and mask your true emotions like your dear clever evil auntie?*

"Need any help, Rudy?" a voice from the hangar said.

That was when a half-dozen young punks hustled out and surrounded me. They were notable for their jailhouse tats. One even sported a black swastika on the crown of his bald head.

"Yes, Schotenheimer," said the man who not a

118

moment ago had claimed he was John Warner. "Rudy Schotenheimer."

"But that was my uncle Alfred's name," I blurted out.

"So Alfred Schotenheimer could become a Warner, but his older brother could not? Come on, missy, let's you and me go for a ride."

I tried to back away, but found myself ringed by Rudy's gang of thugs. Now I know actor Tom Laughlin kicked and punched down a whole swarm of bikers in the movie *Born Losers*, but I am just an ordinary stunt girl with a gimp leg, so what can you expect from me?

They hustled me over to the plane and two of the goons happily boosted my butt into the passenger seat, a bench seat that normally held two people sitting side by side. Rudy was right behind them. He must have guessed I was thinking of making a run for it.

"Don't vorry. I vill teach you to fly," he said, the accent suddenly becoming thicker. "It is easy for someone like you."

There was an old leather jacket on the seat. I eyed it.

"Am I supposed to put this on?"

"Suit yourself."

And with that, Rudy climbed into the pilot's seat in front of me. His gang of tattoo-embossed thugs gave me no more time to think about my escape. Effortlessly, they lifted the tail of the monoplane and turned the light aircraft in a half circle, pointing it toward the runway.

The Curtiss Robin sports an overhead wing, which is great for visibility, assuming there is anything below that you are actually interested in seeing. To me it looked something like an early-model Piper Cub with an enclosed cockpit, the main difference being the big radial engine up front. I am saying "enclosed," but the window panels were out and the side doors were low and loose like those on a carnival tilt-a-whirl. There was the side-by-side passenger seat I was sitting on, but this stunt girl was not very happy about getting in there. I was pretty good with bikes and cars, and even boats, but I had yet to do any "perils of Pauline" maneuvers in an airplane.

"What about a parachute?" I yelled over the sound of the engine.

"You von't need one."

"I do not think I should be doing this!"

"When you're afraid of something you chust have to go forward."

Chust. Now that we were taking off, this guy's German accent was coming out strong. Yelling as we were, it was hard to communicate, but I felt I had to keep trying.

"My real mother used to say that, you know, *Always go forward*, but saying it does not make it any easier."

"Your *real* mother? You got a fake mother, too?"

"Yes, my real mother died…in a plane crash."

That seemed to register with him, but not in a way that made him more considerate of my feelings. He gave me a crafty look.

"All right, how about *zis*? I will give you one good flying lesson. Free. There is nothing really hard about it. It is the fun. And it will take your

120

mind off your problem, *vich* is entirely of the mentals."

The situation was past arguing, so I simply nodded. He revved the motor and the Robin lifted easily off the runway and soared up and away from Van Nuys. I could figure out we were heading north because the freeway below began winding through the mountains and I recognized it as the freeway called "the Grapevine," the nickname for the main route from Los Angeles to California's Central Valley. And the truth was, I was happy to put on that dusty old leather jacket because it was surprisingly chilly up there a dozen thousand feet in the air, or however high it was. I tried to forget how little I trusted this man, which was to say, not at all.

"You promised you would show me how to fly!" I said quickly, hoping to distract him from what I suspected were his plans against me.

Rudy was true to his word, showing me with gestures and pointing out the way the pilot could click a little stick on the panel in front of him and the Robin went up and down. He showed me how to turn and how to go a little faster. It was pretty simple, and I was interested as I always am about anything mechanical, and I had the fundamentals down before we were halfway across the mountains.

I was starting to scheme how I might take over the plane and get myself safely back to the ground. But it did not look like I was going to get the chance to pull off a mutiny, as my lesson came to an abrupt end before I could think of anything I could do in that direction. We were shouting at each other over the roar of the wind and the clatter of the radial engine.

"There!" he said. "I have liffed up to my part of the bargain! Now it is your turn, little missy!"

He set the plane curving to the left in a tight circle. I no longer needed to peer over the side; I could see the pine-covered slopes and dry creek washes of Southern California straight down below us.

"My turn? To do what?"

"To show me you know how to fly. Regina says she does not think you can."

He had shifted sideways in the pilot's seat and was grinning back at me in a toothy, vulpine way. And in his free hand he held a luger, one of those old German pistols you see in World War II movies.

"That's not a—"

"Oh, *zis* is real, all right, young missy. *Zis* was my father's brother's sidearm in the war. *Vould* you care for a demonstration?"

"No. Why? You can't..."

"Oh yes, I can." He gestured with the pistol and his voice got hard and flat.

"You. Out. Now!"

He fired the big ugly pistol without waiting for an answer. The bullet missed me by inches, but even over the clatter of the Robin's engine and the roar of the rushing wind, the sound of that gun going off was deafening. I could not think. My impulse was to get away. I was terror personified as I dove without a parachute out the open window frame to my certain death on the rocky hillsides below.

I was falling as helpless as a dodo bird or a Thanksgiving turkey and we were not that high up, with the hard surface of a tree-studded slope of granite rushing up at me and the wind was ripping the scream from my open mouth, and it was in those terrifying last seconds I found out that *riding the broom* had nothing to do with traveling from Chicago to Los Angeles on the hardwood stick handle of a dust mop.

CHAPTER 8

In that weightless moment of pure terror my reality shifted sideways. Well, not really *sideways*, but I do not have any words to express the otherworldly experience of what happened next. How do you explain the rationally inexplicable? Well, for one thing, I wet my pants.

I figured I was dead. I was sure of it. I said to myself, *So this is what death is like for an ordinary B-grade daredevil stunt girl like me.* But if I was dead, it was the oddest sort of ending, something I could never have imagined. I always thought death was the great blankout, the finish, the last stop, the final resting place…but here I was dead and things were still going on. Simple yet marvelous things.

While I was still aware of a sense of falling, I was no longer falling through ordinary air on my way to disaster. Gravity became irrelevant as I moved through flashes of light and dark that speeded up until they were a stuttering blur. And then, nothing.

Okay, so maybe *now* I could be dead. But no. I felt muddy dirt on my hands and knees. I heard a warning cry of crows calling from somewhere in the distance. There was a wind rustling through leaves.

I opened my eyes. A giant full moon stared down at me. The breeze was stirring the leaves of full-grown cornstalks. I was on my knees in a muddy cornfield. I was somewhere, I had no idea where. I was still wearing the old leather jacket, and Grandma Jenny's woven bag was still around my shoulder. Aside from that, I was totally stark naked.

I do not know what you would do, but I panicked. I jumped to my feet and bumped into somebody behind me. I screamed like a little girl. I turned, ready to make one of my martial arts moves, only to find myself looking into the crude grinning face of a scarecrow.

"Jeez, you gave me a fright!" I said.

Yeah, that was me, Juniper Rose Warner, ex-Hollywood stunt girl, now finding herself newly dead and reduced to talking to stuffed straw people. However, recently deceased or not, I had no qualms about raiding the poor guy for his beat-up old farmer's overalls. Hey, you would too if you were caught in a cornfield somewhere without your panties!

As I was pulling the overalls on, I saw my knee and ankle braces were both missing…but I apparently had no need for them anymore. There was no more of that ugly black bruise on my ankle, and my knee felt perfect. So from this odd business I started wondering if dead people somehow got their wounds all healed in their new way of being.

That sort of aimless wondering did me no good at all, so I also stole the checkered shirt from the poor scarecrow and pulled it on. It was about ten sizes too big, but I was not about to complain. I rolled up the sleeves and buttoned the single remaining button to partially cover my ladyness as best I could. Then I put the old leather jacket on over that. After all, as dear devious Auntie Regina had so often reminded me, I was a debutante from Winnetka with high standards to live up to. Err, maybe that should be *die* up to.

It was, in brief, an entirely confusing moment. There I was, barefoot and no underwear, standing in a cornfield in itchy borrowed overalls, in the middle of nowhere, reaching into my farm-boy overalls to get rid of some irritating sticker things that were bothering my behind. This could not be heaven, and it did not feel like hell, either.

Then I heard a clatter nearby and saw a small aircraft lifting up into the night sky. And hangars. I saw the dark mounds of several hangars about a hundred feet away. Dead or alive, I was near an airport! I thought the plane might have been a Curtiss Robin, or maybe that was just my imagination. It *could* have been; it was a monoplane with an overhead wing.

I had to keep moving. I decided to creep as quietly as I could in the direction of the nearest hangar, if only to see what it was like being a dead person around live people, but right then I heard shouting and the noise of young people crashing through the cornfield. They were heading in my direction. I heard enthusiastic voices, yelling and laughing, and the gang sounded like they had been drinking.

"I am sure I heard a girl scream. Come on, Al! Somewhere near here!"

"Ah, Rudy, you're a nutcake! Come on, we gotta get out of here."

"Vell, chust a little further."

Wait a minute! Al and Rudy? The brothers Schotenheimer in the full spring of their youth? They were five or six rows away as they ran past me, but it had to be them! I waited about ten

126

seconds and then jogged in the opposite direction, heading for the hangars.

The nearest structure was lit in a far corner with a single hanging lightbulb. I walked in and saw a bald man with a white mustache so thick it covered his mouth. He was scratching numbers on a chalk board. The sign over the wide open door said, "Warner Aviation"!

I tried to speak in a calm voice.

"I am sorry to interrupt your work, but is John Warner anywhere around here?"

He looked at me, not seeming to be very surprised to see a barefoot young woman asking for John Warner. Maybe it was the old aviator's jacket. Maybe I belonged.

I was surprised to hear a girl's voice. "He ain't here, you dirty tramp! What you want with him, anyway?"

I would know that whiny voice anywhere. It was Regina as a snarly teenager!

The bald man gave Regina a weary sigh, and then turned to me.

"You just missed him. That was him that just took off."

"When will he be back?"

"Not for two months!" said bad bopper Regina.

"Shut your mouth, Regina," the mustachioed man said.

He stuck his rough-skinned hand in my direction and we shook hands. "I'm Otto Warner, John's brother."

"Foster brother," Regina said. "Otto, you know you was adopted."

The bald man ignored her.

127

"He'll be back in maybe six weeks. He's on his regular route west."

"Is that his schedule?"

I pointed at the chalk board. It read Pittsburg, Indianapolis, Springfield, Ames, Kansas City, Denver, and Alamo.

"Easier to see on the map." He pointed out a map with red push pins that ended at Denver.

"Does not seem right," I said. "What's this?"

I traced the fairly straight line east from Trenton to Springfield, Illinois, and then pointed to the jump north to Iowa.

"Iowa? He has a special pickup. US government," Otto said.

"That's none of her business," Regina said.

It was my turn to ignore her.

"Okay, I see it ends in Denver. You said 'Alamo.'"

Otto grinned and shook his head.

"Not *the* Alamo. Short for Alamogordo. One extra stop in godawful rural New Mexico."

"That government shipment?"

Otto shrugged. "I guess."

"You get out of here, bitch!" Regina said. I had the urge to slap her.

That was when she moved in on me. She must have been expecting to start the usual girly catfight. I stepped back and as her momentum carried her past me, I helped her along a little with one of my patented moves, a good push to the small of her back. She lost her balance and slid on her face across the not very clean floor of the hangar. That seemed to take the fight out of her. She staggered to

128

her feet and let out a dramatic sob, followed by the wailing exit I knew so well.

"Family," I said. "Where is Jenny?"

"Never around," he said.

"Because...?"

Otto caught the nuance in my question. Apparently that was something I was already supposed to know.

"You *are* family, right?"

"Yep. Cousin Juniper."

He nodded, accepting me at my word. For a family of liars, we sure could be gullible.

"Don't get me wrong," he said. "Nothing upset between her and John. She's just got her own life. Shows up for Christmas and Easter, mostly. They live independent lives and John seems happy. God bless 'em both."

"So how would I catch up with John?"

"He'll be back in a few weeks, like I said."

"I absolutely cannot wait for that."

"Well, aim for Iowa, maybe. He'll lay over in Indiana or Illinois, so if you take the train, you might be able to catch up."

"I thought air mail was faster than this."

"Maybe someday," he said, giving me a wry grin and scratching the top of his head where his hair used to be.

It was my bad luck to leave the Warner hangar the same time Alfie, Rudy, and their gang were coming back from looking for me in the cornfield. Sure, it was just my teenage uncle Alfie and his goof-off pals, but still, not knowing exactly what was going on, I was not about to jump out there, particularly not in my scarecrow outfit. I ran toward

129

the next hangar but it was locked tight. I saw an old pickup truck parked nearby. There was nothing else I could think of, so I dove under a pile of rotten old canvas tarps in back. Wow, did it smell bad under there!

I once did a stunt for a farmer's daughter comedy, my bit being a fall through the roof of a chicken coop, with feathers flying and chickens flapping around. The art director insisted we use a real chicken coop, and these tarps smelled at least as bad as that. *Chicken crap is the worst smell in the world!* But beggars cannot be choosers. And with that, I was sure I probably was not dead, after all; dead people may smell bad, but they do not have a sense of smell, do they?

But then, as if to prove my run of bad luck was still holding, the returning teens came right over to where I was hiding. They popped open the caps on some longneck beer bottles. Rudy and Alfie piled into the truck and another boy went around to the front and cranked the engine. After three tries, the motor started up. Alfie put the engine in gear right away and the pickup with me in it lurched forward, speeded up, and chugged away. The kid who had cranked it up had to run and dive into the back end with me and the two others in the cab were laughing like they had done something really funny. The guy who had managed to dive on board was panting and shuffling around right next to me, and he actually propped his feet on my butt as the truck bumped its way down a rough rut road.

"Hey," I complained without thinking.

Not too smart, right? But how would you feel, falling out of the sky and getting all naked and dirty

130

and you are wearing scratchy overalls and no undies and you just missed meeting your long-lost grandpa and then after all that nonsense and abuse, some creep uses your bum for a footstool!

I poked my head out from under the canvas. The kid went all wide-eyed and I used his confusion to swivel my legs around and give him a big shove that sent him off the end of the pickup. I figured he would probably be all right as we were not going too fast. I was right, because I watched as he got to his feet and gawked at the truck.

The last I saw of him, he was still standing there, picking his nose in the moonlight as the pickup truck with me in the back swung onto a paved road and began to gain a little speed. I pulled a corner of the tarp back over me and sat looking backward as we drove ahead into my uncertain future.

CHAPTER 9

The pickup truck continued on and on. I had no idea where we were going. It rattled and chugged along at a steady pace for several hours while I bumped around in back. The last dark edges of late night were losing their daily struggle with the faint gray edges of dawn, and we seemed to be driving directly into the new day, so I figured we were heading east, but whether it was light or dark would make no difference to me. I was wide awake, and feeling more and more disoriented. In my wildest nightmares I could not imagine being trapped in 1939 and heading to an unknown destination in a primitive pickup truck driven by the teenage versions of my uncle and his brother.

Think, Juniper, *think!* I kept telling myself. *Don't do anything rash or stupid.* But it was hard. Whenever we came to a stop sign, I was tempted to jump off the back of the pickup and run. What stopped me was the notion that this truck might be the thread that connected me to my past—that is, to my real life in the future. If that were the case, it had to be a mighty thin thread. However I had transported myself here, there had to be some way to get back to my old life. Or was that foolish? Could I go back? Did I really have to go back?

Maybe I would have to go back before a certain time or I would be stuck here. Or maybe I would wither up and die. Or maybe if I went back I would die. I might get back for a split second, only to take up where I left off, ending my dive out of the Curtiss Robin by smashing into the rocks below! What a terrible end to my autobiography! Time travel poets could sum it up in two lines. *Look at that! She ends with a splat!*

And so mulling and fretting and not deciding one way or the other, I stayed huddled under the musty old tarps as we passed through town after town...and my amazement grew and grew as I recognized the full implication of what I had done. From the shape of the cars and the look of the buildings, there could be no question I truly had transported myself back in time by means I did not understand, and I was now trapped somewhere in the past. *Juniper Rose Warner was lost in time beyond recall.*

Well, we would see about that. There had to be a way to get back to my own place in the universe. Had to be! Hell, I had actually seen Regina when she was a pouty, pimply adolescent! If Reggie could learn to *ride the broom,* it had to be something *I* could do.

So, okay—something I could do. But what? What was this weird science fiction all about? Did I actually *ride the broom*? And if so, how? What was the broomer's secret? Maybe weightlessness? I had been falling, I was about to splat myself into nothing on a rocky hillside, and I had been transported...no, I had somehow *transported myself* to another time and place. But how?

It could not be easy as free fall, or every time I had hopped a bike across a stream or fallen out of a building I would have ended up somewhere and sometime else. So what was different about this time? All I could remember was I had been scared out of my wits and falling to my certain death, but if that was the answer, people would never die falling off cliffs and there would be no broken bodies from jumping suicides. No, it had to be something different in *me*. Maybe other people would die in the same circumstances, but I wouldn't because...because I had powers. Special powers. A gift of some sort.

And that started my thoughts skittering back to Grandma Jenny's old Irish tale of Aidana, the fiery one, and her special blessings given to her by the strange ebony-skinned man who had fallen from the sky. Those powers were supposed to be passed on to Aidana's female descendants, through the generations, for all time.

It came clear as a bell in my mind. That *meant me too!* Me, Juniper Warner. In spite of everything my mother and father had told me to banish such thoughts from my mind, I had powers!

That realization washed through me like a wave of some sort of mind-bending radiation, fast moving but soon fading into the distance. I was getting that familiar sick feeling in the pit of my stomach. I was feeling dumb and dangerous, like a monkey with an AR-15 assault rifle. What exactly had I inherited? If brooming was so simple, I would have used it that time Regina pushed me down the stairs when I was a little kid! And what if I *hadn't* turned on my strange ability at that last second after Alfred's brother Rudy forced me out of my grandfather's airplane without a parachute? I would have been smashed to a pulp! How could I be sure to turn on my magic the next time I needed it when I was not even sure what I had done? I had used it because I had to, but that did not mean I could do it again. Think, Juniper. Think, think, *think!*

134

I found myself looking at the square-cut diamond ring on my finger. I decided that could not be it. Regina could ride the broom and she did not have a ring like mine. She had tried to take the ring from my hand. That ring was important, it did *something,* but whatever it was, the power of the ring had to be something else. I started thinking maybe Jenny had somehow activated some potential in me at Cedars-Sinai before she died. That might be it. But being activated in this case was dangerous. It was like being fired off to somewhere on a rocket ship without knowing the destination or how to steer the damn thing. How could I learn about my powers without killing myself?

Wait, wait, wait, I whispered to myself. I had to think this through. Actually, in one way I probably was not going to have much choice in the matter. I would get the chance to test my newfound abilities a lot sooner than I wanted. If I did not—well, I would not survive whatever lay in store for me, and I would never get back to my own time.

I took a deep breath and tried a yoga move, raising my hands high over my head for a moment, which was about the stupidest thing I could possibly have done. Thankfully, nobody had been looking out the rearview mirror right then. Jeez, I had to settle down or I was going to be out of the game before I had any idea what it was about!

I blew out the air I had been holding in my lungs and tried to think of something, anything constructive. How the heck was I going to learn to hone my skills, if indeed I had any? What had I been thinking about as I fell from the airplane over the Grapevine north of LA? I was screaming, totally freaked out of my mind. About all I could come up with was the notion that the last thing I saw was the plane as I tumbled down, that last moment before I hit the ground. The Curtiss Robin!

And I had seen it again flying overhead after I'd appeared in the dark in that muddy field! There was my link. Different time, different place, same airplane! Well, maybe not…there was Rudy…old Rudy had been there, and then young Rudy… Oh God, it was confusing!

So maybe. Maybe while I was falling I had to think hard and very specifically of something or maybe even some place or some person and some moment in time and in some fantastic way I could transport myself to the place and time where that person or thing was. And maybe that first time when I took my first shot at brooming, since I was not thinking of a specific time and place, maybe I had ended up close but not precisely where or when I might have landed—that is, if I had known exactly where I wanted to go.

It seemed to me that was a lot of maybes, even for a stunt girl used to throwing her body around Hollywood movie sets. Still, for the moment it was all I had to go on. *Better than nothing*, I whispered, trying to calm myself down.

Under other circumstances—if I would have been sitting in my hillside apartment living room in North Hollywood munching popcorn and watching a movie about Al Capone or Charles Lindbergh or Howard Hughes—it would have been fun to watch the brand-new and slightly used automobiles putter by, cars that in my own age would be valued antiques or at least rare curiosities. But things being

136

what they were in the raw here and now, I found everything that should have been fresh and new to me a bewildering distraction.

I leaned back against the cold corner of the truck cab and that was when I spotted a familiar V-shaped pattern in the sky overhead. It was Regina's harpies, and if I was ever certain of anything, it was that they were scanning the ground beneath them for me. Regina must know I had broomed back in time and she knew where to look for me!

I tried to make myself as inconspicuous as possible under the foul-smelling tarp. If her harpy bitches spotted me, it would be five to one, and it would be all over for me. But they passed by quickly and disappeared into the dark horizon, leaving me to my disconnected thoughts and my mounting worries.

How could it be that these flying troopers could even fly in the first place? When I had asked Benjamin, he raised one eyebrow.

"You like to know how things work," he had observed.

"There was no way that flying bike should be able to fly. It is just too heavy, and the wings are too small."

"Powers and enchantments always seem like magic, but they are not magic," he had said.

"That is not really an answer."

"From what Jenny told me, people like her can change the weight of objects."

"You mean…make them lighter?"

"Yes. Or heavier. But not forever. It is like a charge on a battery."

137

"So when the three ladies took aim at the harpies diving at us?"

"It was probably Tillie's score. Tillie is the best shot. Margotha is too old and shaky, and Blu just likes to blast away for the fun of it."

So my evil aunt somehow had the ability to change the density of matter. She could charm heavy motorbikes into flight and probably sink battleships, too. That seemed like an awful lot of power to place in the hands of a greedy and unstable person. My mind flitted back to the legend of Aidana. Did her alien lover have any idea of the trouble he was unleashing when he gave her supernatural abilities that would be passed on to future generations?

As the old pickup chugged us steadily in an easterly direction, I became more and more aware of the smell of sea salt in the air. And then we were motoring in a seaside resort community. I recognized it as Atlantic City, mostly from a show I had watched on cable television. By now the sky overhead was looking like lumps of wet clay and it started misting, just the beginning of a sodden, miserable early morning.

Young Alfie and Rudy seemed to know where they were going. Alfie steered the pickup without hesitation to one of a half-dozen seaside piers that ran perpendicular from the sandy shore out into the choppy water. The truck came to a halt. The engine gave a sputtering last couple of knocks as he turned it off, and as I watched stealthily, the two teens slammed doors and trotted away to join two older men who were standing on the boardwalk near one of the piers. The men were bundled up for the cold damp, huddled in their greatcoats, and they had woolen scarves wrapped around their necks and short-brimmed hats pulled low over their eyes.

Their attention was toward the sea. For the few short moments I stared at them I could not figure what would be so important that they would stand there with an icy sea breeze in their faces. It was hardly the place for a smoke and a friendly chat. I squinted but there was nothing to see. I got out to get a better look.

The teenage kids went right up to them, which apparently was not the brightest move they could have made because one of the older men turned angrily to the closer of the two and struck him a savage blow to the head.

"Rudy! You idiot boy! My son, you are dumber than ze Polish bricklayer! I did command you, yes. I said to you and your brother, you must stay back at ze airport!"

The man was shouting so loud I could make out the words through his heavy German accent. Young Rudy was waving his hands like he was trying to explain himself, and he was pointing at the truck, where by this time I was foolishly standing in plain sight, looking like a full-size Raggedy Ann doll, dressed as I was in the clothes I had swiped from the scarecrow.

And at that same moment I caught a glimpse of what the men with the binoculars were looking for. About a hundred yards from the end of the pier I could just make out the outlines of a dark, cigar-shaped tube rising from the choppy seas! I was not prepared for what I saw, and I am quite sure my mouth dropped open in a way that was entirely unbecoming for a deb from Winnetka. I had spotted a submarine, and what was more, it had the unmistakable mark of a Nazi insignia on it!

I could make out the little tower on top and the floating upper one third of the vessel that bobbed above the water line. And I watched as several men jumped from the sub into the water and begin to swim toward a small open frame outboard motorboat. The boat seemed to be in some peril as it dipped up and down in the rough waters. It looked too small to be carrying as many men as were swimming toward it. But any concern I might have had for the boaters was interrupted by a distant voice.

"Hey, you! Vas is goink wrong mit du?"

Bad news—the man who had struck Rudy was shaking his fist in my direction and shouting at me.

I was going to get a great chance to try out my powers because I did not see anywhere I could run or hide. There was no time for me to crank up the engine on the old pickup, and even if there was, from what little I knew about it, cranking up was a two-person deal—while one person cranked, you needed somebody in the driver's seat to enrich the gas with some sort of a pull knob.

What a rude man Rudy's father was! He did not have to keep shouting at me! I already knew that I was not welcome because I saw a flash and heard the bang of a pistol. The man who had punched young Rudy now had one of those nasty German-looking pistols in a two-handed grip and was firing in my direction. I knew about pistols from all the scripts I'd read, plus the courses I took so I could add *proficient in firearms* to my stunt girl brag sheet. Not much chance they could hit me at this range, but then something whizzed right past my ear and I decided I had better test my legs with a little running.

There was a second pier next to the first, and as this seemed like my only avenue of escape, I made a run for it. I know, you're thinking, *How dumb is that?* because, of course, piers run out and then you come to the end and there is nowhere else to go. But with the sound of Rudy's farmer's boots slapping the worn wooden planks behind me, I certainly was not in one of those analytical frames of mind.

Young Rudy could run nearly as fast as me, and I could hear his panting behind me. *Time to do the unexpected.* I spun around and pulled to a stop. I held up one hand, and he unthinkingly stopped. Not giving him a chance to consider what was going on, I flashed open the old leather jacket I was wearing, and with only one button on my shirt he could see the smooth melon part of my full and lovely girls that were not covered by the overall straps, which was actually most of them. Hey, this girl is in show biz. I know sex sells.

Rudy stared at my tits like he had been hit with the flat side of an ax. In that moment of stunned ogling, the poor boy was unprepared for the spinning karate kick that caught him full in the face. And I am inclined to believe that is how Rudy Schotenheimer got the broken nose that led him around through the rest of his mortal life.

The older men were running toward us now, and both were shooting as they came. So with no further pause to take a bow—stunt girls do not get to do that, anyway—I took a few running steps,

141

leaped off the end of the pier, and wished with all my might that I was back in my favorite place in the world.

CHAPTER 10

Yes, I had been visualizing myself materializing back in the present where I would be sitting in my dear Horny Hudson in the driveway of Grandma Jenny's bungalow, but I was new to this damn brooming business and maybe it was my fault since I did not close my eyes like you are apparently supposed to, *When you wish upon a star and wake up where the clouds are far behind you.* So as I was plummeting off the end of the pier hugging my traveler's bag with one hand and holding on to my nose with the other, the last thing I saw before I closed my eyes was the black Nazi emblem on the white tower of that submarine and in the next few seconds when I opened my eyes after that light-and-dark shuttering thing I actually was *in a submarine!*

Only, praise the lord of carefree gypsy movie stunt girls, it was not *that* submarine off the coast of Atlantic City. It was a German sub called the U-505, and I was in the Chicago Museum of Science and Industry. Dizzily, I looked around at the familiar inner chambers where, as a kid, my fourth-grade school companions and I had played hide-and-seek, much to the outraged protestations of the outraged museum guard staff.

The sub's insides were deserted, but I peered out and saw a line of tourists, parents, and school kids waiting to get in. One of the kids saw me and pointed.

"Hey, how come she gets to go in early?"

I had the presence of mind to yell to the puffy-faced museum guard standing nearby.

"Just about finished in here!"

143

Lucky thing it was somebody other than old grouchy-face, the surly fellow who used to yell at us kids and send us to our teachers in sniffling disgrace.

As I made my way out of the side entrance that the museum had engineered into the sub, the same little brat spoke up again. "Hey, how come you don't got no shoes?"

"'Cause I work better barefoot," I said.

"How come?"

"That way I can tell when the floor is still wet."

"Can't you just see it's wet?"

"Huh. I never thought of that. Thanks, kiddo."

I reached out with one hand and tussled his hair, and hurried away to disappear into the early-morning tourist and school kid crowd. Part of me wanted to head over to the Field Museum to have a look at Sue, the frightening T-Rex skeleton, but I figured if my new talents could take me anywhere I wanted, maybe I could go way back and see her in real life.

I got out of there as fast as my now-tiring legs would carry me. I bought a Chicago hot dog with catsup, mustard, and that special green relish from a vendor who had set up his umbrella at the base of the museum steps. Yes, I was gratefully back in the present, but now I was facing a new set of problems, the most pressing being, *How was I going to get out of these itchy hayseed pants and into a decent set of underwear?*

It was mid-morning, and the weather was pleasant enough, a rare warm early spring day. I hitched a ride over to Clark Street and pawned Grandma Jenny's Indian head gold piece for far more than enough money to buy a bra and some nice cotton underwear, a sweats outfit, cushy socks, and a pair of good running shoes at the Macy's that used to be Marshall Fields. I remembered a shopworn travel agency on nearby Michigan Avenue that had always seemed a little desperate. The way I saw it, keeping up with the high rent had to be a bitch. I walked over there and purchased a plane ticket back to Los Angeles. It was a little dicey because I did not have my ID, but I was in their system so I lied and said I had left my wallet in the car. That was more or less true, but I did not bother to tell them the car was in Los Angeles. That was what the priests in the confessional used to call a *sin of omission.* Read that as *It is okay unless they catch you.*

Now you know that today you will never get on a plane without your ID, but this was indication that my present day was altered from how it should have been. The girl behind the counter chewed her gum and handed me my ticket, proving she could do both at the same time. The little things, the big things, everything was slightly *wrong.* I could feel it. Was it already too late to save the world from Regina?

My plane did not leave until that evening, so I sat on a street bench in Rudy's old leather jacket and my comfortable new clothes, pondering what sort of trouble I might get into if I caught a train out to Winnetka to see if I could get a better fix on what mischief Regina was stirring up. No, I was not crazy enough to want to see her, but I figured I just might be able to get into the carriage house, and from there I could make out if the main house was empty.

If it was, maybe I could get in there and do a little righteous snooping.

That sounded like a plan, so I walked over to the Randolph Street station and caught the commuter train heading north. As my seat in the passenger compartment gently jostled me along, I was overtaken by a stronger uneasiness. Since finding myself in the museum U-boat, I had twice been bothered by that push-pulling quake sensation I had experienced in Los Angeles right after my grandmother's funeral. And somehow, the present—my present—increasingly did not seem exactly as I had remembered it.

It was a lot of little things. One of the ads on the train said something about *Mach Schnell!* and another advertised a river boat cruise through Greater Europe, and a third was promoting a *Nutsy Nazi* television game show! And when I had bought my hot dog earlier that day, the vendor had simply responded, *Danka*. This had to be Regina's doing. Was there such a word in the language as *Germanization*? Or, as my agent, good old word-mashing Sumner Blinker, would have said, *Gerblized Germanization-ism?*

I found myself missing my real life. That one, the day-to-day existence of an ordinary Hollywood stunt girl, was feeling very remote and far away. Whatever my evil aunt's ultimate goal was, it looked like she had already set her grand scheme in motion. Maybe she was doing it as fast as she could. Maybe this was all the universe could take, restructuring things bit by bit until there was a total new reality. *The world according to Regina.* Great

God of Stunt Girls, there had to be a way to stop her!

I splurged on a taxi from the Winnetka train station. The driver was a grouchy old guy with a flat cap squashed on his bald head. He had a big yellow union driver's sign clipped on one side of his cap.

"Were you in the war?" I said. He looked old enough to have been in World War I, I guess, and that would make him about a hundred.

"What war you talking?" he said.

"You know, the big one. The best generation. World War II. We take Hitler out."

"Cheezus H. Christ! You best not talk like that, young lady."

"Why not?"

"*Vas is los mit du?* Germany kicked our ass in World War II. Where you been, on Mars?"

Not much I could say to that. I did not want to anyway, because after that outburst I was in a state of shock. We drove on in silence until he let me out on Sheridan Road, two blocks from my aunt and uncle's house.

"I'm tryin' to be nice to you, young lady. You keep your mouth shut, you hear, dummkopf?"

I said I would be quiet as a mouse and walked away with my head down, doing my best to look like I was sorry. I took the path down to the beach and slipped across the back lawn. As it turned out, the carriage house was deserted, the key was under the mat, and they had not changed the locks on the door! I guess when you set out to take over the world, you cannot think of every little detail.

I knew I might be walking into some sort of crazy Regina trap, but I was too tired and

147

bewildered to care. I turned the key and slipped in the door. Joy of joys, all those years since I jilted Georgie-Porgie and they had not cleaned out my clothes or thrown away any of my things! There you have it—my aunt was too busy warping history, and my uncle, as usual, was out making money.

I waited until the sprinklers went on in the backyard and then I ran a tub full of hot water. What a luxurious feeling, cozy and warm in my old tub with bubbles all around me! I was nearly drifting off to sleep when I noticed the light on the phone next to the tub. The button for the line connected to the main house was lit. So somebody was home after all! This could spell the worst sort of trouble.

Hoping I still possessed my stealth skills from my wild teen years, I carefully picked up the receiver, and heard my Uncle Alfie's voice bellowing on about something. He sounded upset and maybe worried.

"No, of course she is not moving too fast! This is Regina we are talking about. She knows how to do these things!"

A man's heavily German accented voice cut in on Alfred, and this second person did not sound happy. I recognized that voice. Rudy Schotenheimer, renamed John Warner, Alfie's brother.

"How could Regina know such thing? Zis haf not been tried before. Never!"

"Well, you have to leave it to us. You see everything moving in the right direction, don't you?"

148

"Ve vill certainly not be leaving it to the discretion of you! Regina vill meet us at the Plaza Hotel in New York City for ze charity event. Early in May. You hafen ze date. Ve make everything firm from zere."

"But Rudy, that is not necessary. It's all set and everything is moving in the right direction. We will handle everything from here!"

"No. No, no, no. You see nothing stable yet. Things yet to do. A plan begun is not a plan in final. Regina vill be at Plaza greet-fest. She must be zere. No exception!"

I carefully set down the phone and hauled my wet butt out of the tub. So Alfred was in on this madness! Timid Alfie, so intent on keeping the household peace that he nightly drowned himself in his whiskey tumbler. Fierce Alfie, taking out his frustrations on the gardeners. Clever Alfie…yes, that was the one. The never-quit business tycoon racing all over the world to keep Regina in silks and furs. Safe to say I had underestimated him. Score one for functioning alcoholics everywhere. Good old Uncle Alfred was not just keeping the peace in the Warner house—he was *the peacekeeper*.

I scrubbed myself dry and got into some of my favorite things, a great pair of jeans and a Waylon Jennings T-shirt that had seen better days. I shrugged into the old aviator's jacket and slung Jenny's travel bag over my shoulder. Then I slipped out the door, leaving everything just as I had found it, except for the drying soap ring around the tub. In another half hour I had caught a taxi and made my way to the railroad station. Lucky me, I was just in

149

the nick of time to catch the hourly commuter train heading back downtown.

They offered good wi-fi at O'Hare, so I had a bright idea while I waited for my flight. I used another chunk of my gold money to buy a small tablet at an outrageous price. It was probably worth it, because with a little googling I found out a lot was going on in the month Grandpa, the real John Warner, disappeared. On May 7 in 1939, Germany and Italy announced to the not-nearly-wary-enough world their ambitious new alliance, *the Rome-Berlin Axis*. And there was a huge German-American Friendship Ball held at the Plaza Hotel on the first Friday in May of 1939. Celebrities in attendance included Regina and Alfred Warner, and a Rudy Schotenheimer and his wife Donna. The old newspaper clipping said a Teutonic Youth Award was given to some lucky blond kid (there was an old black & white photo), and a substantial donation was presented to the Friendly Hands Across The Atlantic Charity.

This gala event looked like something I probably should attend if I was going to save the unsuspecting world from dear deadly Aunt Regina.

Meanwhile, back at O'Hare, a middle-aged, slim, and balding fellow wearing a dark turtleneck sweater, matching dark pants, and shiny black shoes had been giving me a suspicious look while I banged away at my keyboard. He found a seat at the other edge of the seating area and opened his own laptop. I managed to click over to the stunt website just about the time he got going on his machine and that earned me a big frown from his direction. I guess he was just a little late in uncovering my

Internet query. Screw him. I watch movies, I can spot the bad guy when I see one. I clicked over to upcoming stunt assignments. A new movie titled *The Foolish Failed Escape Attempt* was looking for stunt doubles who could jump motorbikes. I logged on to my email and shot Sumner Blinker the usual nag.

Hey Sumner, I am perfect for this gig. Get me on it.

The reply came like lightning. It had to be Joanie manning the keyboard, since Sumner was still learning how to use his Olivetti portable typewriter.

Hey, yourself. How's the leg?

All healed. Ready for action.

Okay, will try.

The flight to Los Angeles was uneventful, except I found the male flight attendants guilty of a disgustingly superior attitude. After my request for an actually functioning set of headphones was ignored for over an hour, a fellow named Reinhold dumped an unwrapped mess of wires on my lap. *Fly the unfriendly skies.*

"Reinhold, these ear buds look used."

"Yeah. So what?"

"Well, I do not want to catch ear rot."

"You get what we got."

He started to walk on, but I held up one hand.

"I like your toothbrush mustache," I said. *Hey, why not butter up the hired help? Could not hurt.*

My strategy of harmonious surrender had rewards, of a sort. He unbent a little, passing me a forgiving, if slight, smile, somewhat like an elephant trying to hide a fart. He smoothed out the

151

fresh little spriglets sprouting under his nose with the finger of one hand.

"It is all the fashion. Like Charlie Chaplin and Oliver Hardy."

"And Adolf, himself."

"Yah, of course!"

He grinned and did a sort of informal heil salute.

"And that haircut? Reminds me of *der Führer*, too."

"Very popular right now. We call it 'ze Untercut.'"

"By the way, when did the great man die?"

He laughed and looked at me like I might be crazy.

"His retirement life at Mount Vernon is very good, you know, the Mount V, it was Silly George's place?"

I said I had heard of it. That was the surface social side of me. The inner other side that occasionally had a serious notion or two recognized that Regina's overwhelming remake of history was spreading like poison gas. The changes were everywhere. America had lost the big war and the exploits of George Washington, one of the greatest of our founding fathers, had been reduced to foolishness.

The airline steward had a notion of his own.

"I think Adolf lives to be 125 if he lays off the schnapps."

"Happy wife, happy life," I said.

"Oh, Eva, she is long gone. Adolf have more woman than ancient *Playboy* man Hefner."

"Good to know," I said.

I could not wait for that plane to land. But I did have to wait. We all did, as all the passenger planes had to go into a holding pattern, delayed by a priority military flight in from German Nicaragua.

CHAPTER 11

When I deplaned, the fellow in the dark outfit who had been trying to break into my notepad action was nowhere in sight. The only luggage I had brought with me was Grandma Jenny's travel bag, so there would be no stop in baggage. And that was a good thing, because as I made my way out of the terminal there was a rifle shot and a chunk of wall splintered behind me. I was being fired on from the roof of the parking garage across the street! I was frantically looking for cover when I heard the lovely sound of Horny Hudson's mellow beep.

"Over here!" Benjamin yelled from behind the steering wheel.

I raced out into the street and did a rolling stunt dive into the back seat and my gray-skinned friend took a sharp left, actually driving in and through the parking garage along a narrow lane between parked cars, then finding a way out the other side. We crashed through a wooden barrier, careened a half block against traffic that scattered in front of us, turned onto Century Boulevard and were on the freeway north headed for Hollywood Hills before I had the chance to ask how he had happened to show up at just the right time.

"Margotha alerted me you might be in need of my services," he said.

"You would make a great stunt driver!"

"Thank you, but I do not think I have the complexion for it."

"We could fix it in makeup!"

I crawled over the seat back into the front and snapped on my seat belt. Benjamin gave me an approving nod.

"Safety first. Once we get to your bungalow we should be safe for a while…at least until Regina tries her next trick."

"What will that be?"

"I do not like to think about it."

Even barreling along at high speed, I could see changes everywhere. Detroit and Japan had stopped making cars. Every newer car, truck, or bus on the road was a Volkswagen, a Mercedes, or an Audi. And the big American flag flying from the Veterans Administration building in Westwood still sported red and white stripes, but there was one white swastika on a field of black where the stars should have been. So now we had the good old *red, white, and black* for a flag.

"Sumner Blinker has been arrested," Benjamin said.

"Sumner? But I talked to his office earlier today!"

"But not to Sumner."

"Well, there was no way to tell. Email, you know."

"It was not Sumner, we can be sure of that."

"What did they get him for? Bad taste in his Mister Hollywood outfits?"

"Seditious acts against the government. He has been sent to a camp in the desert to the north."

"The world is upside-down crazy. We've got to stop this!"

"Blu, Tillie, and Margotha have a plan. But it is dangerous, and it involves you."

155

"I am the girl for the job," I said. "At least, I think I am."

As if on cue, I heard the familiar Groucho Marx snicker of my cell phone. Benjamin lifted one hand from the steering wheel and pointed to the glove compartment. I fetched it and hunkered down out of the wind.

"Hello," I said.

"This is the Sumner Blinker Agency," a polite voice intoned in a crisp English accent. "This is James, his assistant."

"Where's Joanie?"

"Err...vell, Joan has been, ah, retired. Sumner requests to know if you are fully recovered and prepared to accept employment."

"Put him on the phone."

"Err, he ist out of the office for ze moment."

"What sort of employment?"

"A temporary assignment. I believe you are to attempt a motorcycle leap across a barrier of some sort. Ah, vait, here are some specifics: A barbed-wire fence, twelve feet high, with sharp barbed wire on the top."

Benjamin was nodding *yes*, that I was to take the assignment. James, the fellow on the phone, took my hesitation to mean the opposite, that I might not take it.

"Err, *Sumner* said to tell you that you might be able to direct two days. Second unit, of course...vatever zat means."

What it meant was that I was being offered the golden plum that producers in rare moments of soft-headed generosity occasionally held out to people like me. It was not really all that much, but it was

156

something, a little bitty next step in the business. Directing stunts was fifty percent camera placement and the rest was luck, in the hands of the demigods of fate, the wind, the direction of the sun, and a hundred other things. But directing second unit was the next step up if I was ever to move past my present low position on the totem pole of filmmaking.

And yet any fool could see it was a trap. It was highly unlikely this phony replacement for Sumner would on his own initiative offer such a prize to me.

"Let me think about it for a minute," I said.

As we headed north over the pass that led to the San Fernando Valley, on my right I saw a line of red, white, and black Nazi flags where Hebrew University used to be, and that gave me an idea.

"James, you still on the line?"

"*Ja*," he said.

Not so English after all. Since he wanted something out of me, I thought I might be able to pump him for a bit of information.

"James, I am doing a survey for, ah, *Popular Aryanism* magazine. Can you tell me, in your personal opinion, just exactly how did Germany win the war? Just what in your opinion was the most deciding moment?"

"Oh, that is a schoolboy question. It was when Hitler buzzed London with an atomic bomb. Just that one A-bomb. A is for Adolf. After that, the vor iss over. There vas a German ship in the Atlantic off Washington, DC, and that one vas set also mit a V-2 rocket, but Chicken-heart Roosevelt, he vants none of that tough love from der dear Führer."

"I see."

I *did* see. Regina had done something to ensure the Nazis got the atom bomb before we did. Now all I had to do was get my brain trust of three old ladies and a gray-skinned man to figure out exactly what she had done, and then go back to the exact point in space and time, the historical juncture, and foil her evil plot. *Comic book stuff, but how to do it in real life?* A voice from the cell phone intruded on my pondering.

"So you vill do the motorcycle stunt?"

I thought I would play hard to get.

"I want double scale for the directing gig, plus my normal stunt wages."

"Yes, off course."

"Okay, I am all in."

"You start tomorrow, call at six, front gate, Volden Und Disney Studios," the crisp voice said. "Buena Vista Boulevard, you know it?"

I told him I knew it and that I would be there. Why not? Hell, they were paying double scale. That and the fate of the world hanging in the balance. You would have done the same thing, especially if you had *powers*, even if you did not exactly know what they were or how to use them.

CHAPTER 12

My three witchy lady pals, Benjamin, and I were sitting in Grandma Jenny's living room, gathered around the remains of an extra-large Straw Hat double-cheese stuffed-crust pepperoni pizza with dill pickles and sauerkraut on the side.

"You are not really that old," I said to Margotha.

It was a rhetorical question. She looked ancient as an old sea turtle, and before she spoke there was a pause as if she were swimming up from the depths of the ocean.

"Aye, but I am. I was of an age before Chaucer thought to scribble about Canterbury. In point of fact, he blathered about me in there. Men, braggarts and boasters all. They kiss, they tell."

"You were the—"

"Aye. The Wife of Bath. Poor Geoffrey claimed I had five husbands. If he only knew! Ten times five, maybe. I don't know. I lost count."

We were passing the time while we waited for something to happen. I had no idea what it was, but Tilly had assured me it would be *both entertaining and enlightening*. Her ring tone chimed in *Ist das nicht ein Schnitzelbank?* She grinned like a little schoolgirl.

"Not long now!"

"What the heck is a *schnitzelbank*?" I said.

Her grin broadened.

"It's a sawhorse. You know, half a bench. Carpenters have two of them and they lay boards on them for sawing and hammering."

"That makes no sense at all. What is that song about, then?"

"It's for beer drinking. It doesn't have to make sense."

My head was swimming, trying to catch up.

"So you are German?"

"Fifth-generation American. But it's good to pay homage to the old ways. Bratwurst on dark rye and a cold mug of Tucher."

"Zum Gluck gibts Tucher!" Blu said, raising one fist as if she were clutching a mug.

"You speak German, too?"

"Naw, honey, but you hang out long enough with Tillie, you learn stuff. That there is a beer slogan. It means, 'Lucky thing we got Tucher!'"

Tillie's face lit up with happy memories. "It's a Hefeweizen-style beer brewed in Nuremberg. The greatest of all the wheat beers, the standard by which all others are judged."

"About common expressions," Blu said, leaving the three words dangling in the air like unfinished skywriting.

"What about them?" Tillie said.

"Well, a person don't have to be 'incredibly stupid' to be stupid."

"True," Tillie said. "So what?"

"So why the dumb fools use 'incredibly' if just plain 'stupid' suffice?"

"You're talking about Regina, are you not?" I said.

Blu admitted she was.

"Any fool in the present can change the future. Every living creature do it all the time. But when

160

you take the path back and try to change history, why, there are *reasons* why dat be forbidden."

As her words trailed off, she quickly drew an odd and complicated sign in the air, indicating expanding dimensions, and then she pursed her lips and crossed her hands with two diagonal slashing motions, a clear gesture meant to ward off a great evil, then brought her hands together in an agitated dance meant to illustrate an exploding object.

I raised my eyebrows.

"Earth blows up?"

"Worse than that, honey chile."

"The solar system?"

"Think galactic," Tillie said. *"Scheista gevault und Kerfluoi!* A super-nova, it takes out a big chunk of the Milky Way!"

"That could happen?"

Blu sighed.

"Has happened before, and it will happen here, unless we can stop her," Tillie said.

"And you know this *how*?"

She gave a little nod in Margotha's direction. The ancient witch seemed to waken with a little start, then shrugged and nodded as if to confirm Tillie's fatalistic conclusion. When she spoke, it was in a way that confirmed she knew a lot more than her usual quaintly archaic speech patterns let on.

"Aye and verily, young Juniper Rose. Gravitational disruptions caused by Regina bending our timeline have already begun to destabilize our sun. If we cannot stop her foolish and senseless course, we are all going solar ge-splat."

161

"Nothin' new under the sun," Blu said. "Civilizations fry demselves before they bloom to…well, nobody knows to what exactly…let's just say to whatever something dat der destiny might have been."

Jenny's bungalow was built in the Craftsman style made popular over a hundred years ago, and the warm and inviting atmosphere in the room suddenly felt claustrophobic to me. I found myself longing for some of that modern *bring the outside in* feeling. I was having a panic attack.

I was surprised. We were inside a comfortable and lovely human habitat. Benjamin had assured me the place was now mine, but I still could not believe it. It was too wonderful. I had been thinking that, with my luck, sooner or later someone would show up and try to take it away from me. As luck would have it, I was right, and worse, it looked like it was going to be sooner rather than later. Regina was going to kill us all!

So far, the ladies had done a bit of business with Benjamin looking on with an approving smile. The business had involved the dark-green front door and some sort of *scoot-hoot-out-lout!* charm intended to ban evil presences.

As Blu reached for the last slice of pizza, there was a knock on the door.

"Right on time," she said.

I had no idea who it could be.

"Maybe we failed to tip the pizza delivery man enough?"

Blu grinned and took a huge bite out of her pizza slice.

"No. This would be your meddling auntie."

162

"You have to invite her, my dear. Otherwise, she can't come in."

"Are you sure that is a good idea?"

"Part of the plan," Tillie said.

I peered through the eyehole in the massive door, and it was Regina, all right. She was dressed in one of her trim pastel pantsuits with a starched white collar and she wore an expensive beige pearl necklace and a matching pearl ring. I could see she was controlling her anger, but just barely. With her arms folded and chin raised, she was looking east across the Los Angeles basin to the ridge of mountains, pretending she did not have a care in the world.

I opened the door a crack. She took that as an invitation and she shoved the door open and pushed past me to confront the three old ladies.

"Hey, I didn't invite you," I said.

I returned to stand next to the trio, facing the woman who had killed her own mother and had repeatedly tried to kill me.

"You opened the door."

"All right. I did not know that counted. What do you want, Regina?" I said.

"You know very well."

Her response was cold as ice. It was her classic approach to anything that displeased her—freeze it to death.

"Too late for you, nasty evil bitty bitch," Margotha said in her dry old voice. "The orb is closed."

"You be outside de circle," Blu said. "You be the outsider in dis game."

163

"Not in my own house! This house belongs to me!"

The three ladies looked at me, but they said nothing. I did not know exactly what the play was, but clearly it was my move.

"Get out," I said.

"I will not leave my own house! I raised you from a timid little mouse! You are still a mouse! That's your name. Mousy Jousie, little Ju-Ju Bird!"

I have to admit, it was hard standing up to the ridicule I had suffered since I was a little girl, but the memories of my dear Grandma Jenny overwhelmed me and anger toward Regina rose up in my throat like bile. Jenny had believed in me with all her heart and I knew I had to do my best for her. I tried to keep my voice calm and level, like the heroine in a Disney animation when she faces off against the wicked dragon lady.

"It is not your house. I must ask you to leave."

"I will not! Never!"

"Then I command it."

I raised one hand, pointing at her the way I had seen her do hundreds of times when challenged by some social rival—and Regina hesitated and took a half step backward! But she was not quick enough, and I felt the tip of my finger lightly touch the back of her hand.

She recoiled in furious agony, and I saw her skin instantly become wounded and bloody as if it had been gashed by a clawed hand.

"Oh, dat there's gonna leave a scar," Blu said.

"You'd better put something on it, dearie," Tillie said.

"Balm of aspic, mayhap," Margotha muttered.

164

It had been my impression that Regina, flesh and blood, was in the room with us. But now her image began to fuzz and sputter like a bad blue-screen video image.

"I'll get you for this!" she hissed.

And then she was gone.

"Not really her," Tillie said.

"Naw. Dat jist be her avatar," Blu agreed.

"Still, Juniper gave her a good one! Reggie felt that one right through the ether," Tillie said.

We took our seats in our wooden ladderback chairs around the empty pizza box. It looked to me like I had renewed the fury of my mortal enemy.

"I am not seeing anything good coming from this."

"No, no, no, our plan be mighty good," Blu said.

"Well, somebody better explain it to me, because I am not sure what good it does to send Reggie off in a flaming rage. She's going to come back for me."

"You shall see, my dear," Margotha assured me, and the three ladies clapped their hands and laughed. They stood and reached for their travel bags that were sitting in a bunch nearby on the dark-stained oak floor.

"Well, we must be on our way. Benjamin, if you will apologize for our haste and perhaps explain things?"

And with that, they did their fading trick and in another moment were gone.

Benjamin nodded and turned to me.

"Remember how you wanted to return to the Hudson-Named-Horny, but you ended up in a submarine?"

"Yes?"

"You have to be very clear about exactly where you want to go. Time and place. Precisely where and when."

"Yes, but…"

"The moment you touched Regina's image, she automatically and inadvertently passed the information—her time and place—on to you."

"I do not think so."

"Think about it. Feel the moment. Where was the wicked Regina, the person, not the avatar?"

What happened next was oddly normal. The answer came to me like something I had known all along.

"She was at the Plaza Hotel across from Central Park in New York City."

"Exactly where?"

"In her usual suite."

"What time of day was it?"

"Evening. Maybe six at night."

"And what day and year?"

I knew the answers. It was May 5, 1939. The day of the German-American Friendship Ball.

"Well, then," Benjamin said, "You had better get going."

"No, I have to do the motorcycle jump."

"The fate of the world is in your hands and you want to do a stunt over a fence?"

"My first director's credit," I said, "but it is more than that. I think I am somehow fated to make

166

that jump. Anyway, I do not think we have a choice. Take a look out the window."

A squad of army soldiers was lounging around an olive-green troop carrier that was parked on the road in front of the bungalow, and I thought I caught a glimpse of the harpies squad flying overhead. There was no way they were going to let me make a mad hundred-yard dash across that road to the flier's cliff so I could broom my way back into history.

CHAPTER 13

Trapped as we were, Benjamin and I sat in the living room of my bungalow. I tossed a worn script of the movie on the coffee table between us. It looked like everybody but the producer's girlfriend had seen it before it got to me, plus there were a lot of stamped approvals on it.

"It is a spoofy Nazi remake of *The Great Escape*."

"I never watch movies, but I do know the winners get to rewrite history."

"Why do you never watch movies?"

"The flickering screen annoys me. I think it has something to do with my reconstituted eyes, and video is not much better."

I gave him an inquiring look. There was a lot I did not understand about Benjamin.

"Well, video has 30 frames per second instead of 24. That would help a little bit."

"Tell me about the story of the escape. Why was it great?"

I tried to explain. "*The Great Escape*, the original movie, was produced less than 20 years after V-E Day—short for 'victory in Europe.' America was still in full pride, so Hollywood did an action flick about a bunch of Allied prisoners who escape a POW camp. Looking for big box office, you know. Lots of money."

"I believe I have heard of it. This is the one where the actor Steve McQueen does a motorbike stunt where he jumps over a fence."

"Right. Steve plays a character called the 'Cooler King,' and some film buffs claim that is what started fans calling him the 'king of cool.'"

"And you are going to replicate his famous leap to freedom?"

"Well, that was not exactly Steve's jump, though his PR guys worked hard to impress a generation of moviegoers he was the man with brass balls. Stars like that all think the same way: Screw the stuntman. What is one more little lie in the land of make-believe?"

"And this bothers you?"

"Well, sure! It takes money out of a stunt person's pocket when the star claims he or she did the gig."

"But is not the real point of concern for you that, in a remake of *The Great Escape*, would not the Germans be the heroes?"

"I am not sure I follow."

"I think that would mean that in this new movie there is no way the Cooler King gets to jump with success."

"Yes, it is a trap set for me. There is no way they want me to survive."

"And if you are going to try what I am thinking you might, you will be cutting things very close."

"Well, my friend, I do not see any other way if I am going to save the world as we know it."

He stood and stretched.

"In that case, you had better get some rest, Queen of Cool."

"Do you have to go?"

"Well, it would only be polite."

"Maybe do not leave me. I…I feel something I am not used to. Lonely, I guess. Scared, too."

"We can lie down in bed together."

"What?"

He smiled, amused at my reaction. "It is just a friendly offer. Actually, I am sexually inoperative. I think you call it cuddling."

"How about if we sit together out here?"

"That would be acceptable."

I found a fuzzy yellow blanket and we put up our legs on the recliner sofa.

"I will regulate my temperature to something toasty-warm," he said.

I thought it would be like hanging out with a plastic man, but when he put his arm around me, he was human-like to the touch. He had no hair, but a lot of men were shaving these days.

He sighed and frowned, looking across the room at a portrait on the wall that had to have been painted in the early 1800s.

"Who is that?" I said.

"One of Jenny's lovers. Charles-Joseph-Laurent Cordier. Jenny met him in Rome."

"What year was that?"

"1811, I am pretty sure. She hired Jean Auguste Dominique Ingres to paint his picture. Mr. Cordier was in Rome as a representative of the French emperor and Ingres had left the Villa Medici to make a living painting portraits in Rome."

"I thought the men hired the artists to paint their mistresses."

"Sometimes it works the other way."

"I guess it does. That is an actual Ingres? It has to be worth a fortune."

"Well, no. Jenny donated the original to the Louvre. That's just a copy."

"Did my grandmother have many lovers?"

"Before, sure. But not after she met John Warner."

"My grandfather must have been special."

"Yes. He was bright, funny, and inventive. I knew him well."

"So they had a special love."

"He could make her laugh, and that is a rare thing, when you…when you have powers it can be hard to find humor in the world."

"I think I would have liked him."

"I am sure he would like you. You remind me of him. You are your own person, making your own way. He was like that with his pioneering air pilot ways. Always finding a better solution to the problems of the day."

After that, the silence lengthened between us.

"What exactly are you, Benjamin?"

He paused, thinking over my question.

"I am still myself. I am still human, sort of."

"An advanced species," I said, giving him a joking tap on the arm.

"Subspecies, maybe. If humans have a soul, then it feels like I still have whatever that is. In other words, I am still me, except that I am totally not the original biological me any more than a rock fossil tree trunk is the original tree it once was."

"How did you become this…what you are?"

"Well, I wanted to live, and Jenny said she only knew this one way."

"No, I mean, how is it possible such a process exists? It is not…natural."

171

"No, not to this planet."

We nodded to each other as if we had discovered something important. Maybe he did, but I was off the deep end and he must have seen it.

"We do not know any way sentient biological beings can get to another solar system to start life on a new planet, not even one of the closest stars in our galaxy. When you think of such an enterprise, even traveling at close to the speed of light, such planets would be years and years away. Human lives flutter past like May flies. But the dark ones found a way."

"Dark ones?"

"You know. Like in Jenny's story. Your ancestor saved one."

"You are saying Aidana met an alien."

"That is my interpretation of the story. I talked about this with your grandmother. As nearly as we can tell, they are not really our friends."

"Then what are they?"

"More like distant allies, some few who owe us a debt of honor. But some, not even that."

"So they cannot be trusted?"

"Jenny did not think so."

"Good to know," I said. "Could you turn the temperature down a degree or two? Getting a little warm here."

"Yes, of course. This is a very rare joy," he murmured. "To rest with a human friend."

"You do not actually fall asleep, do you?"

"Actually, I do. My brain patterns function the same as ever. You could say I run in sleep mode. Be sure to say your prayers."

172

"I do not know any that I think will do any good."

"I will say one for you."

He started the Lord's Prayer, and I must have been tired because I was asleep before he got to *Thy will be done on earth as it is in heaven.*

CHAPTER 14

The next morning I showered and got into one of my skin-colored neoprene underlayer suits and a pair of faded jeans the girl at Aardvark Antique Clothing swore were from the Great Depression. I donned a tight sports bra to protect the girls and shrugged into a stiff old World War I khaki shirt I picked up some years ago at a military collectibles store. It was always something of a surprise to rifle through the wide and varied wardrobe I had picked up in over a decade in the trade, everything from medieval armor to an auto racing suit with an STP oval patches sewn on, an outfit that was supposedly once worn by the famous Richard Petty.

With a few of Jenny's old gold coins in my pockets, I slipped her travel bag over my shoulder and made for the door. I kissed Benjamin on the cheek and gave him a confident good-bye smile that I did not really feel. I was playing right into Regina's hand. I had to be on my best game or I was going to end up one dead stunt girl.

It was no big surprise to see a squad of smartly uniformed soldiers waiting outside my front door. I was briskly taken in hand and we piled into a VW Heil! SUV and caravanned through morning traffic north on the 101 to the Malibu Canyon cutoff. We left the freeway and headed south on a two-lane blacktop road to a brushy area near Malibu Flats.

We were only about a mile from the ocean, but we were surrounded by low hills and the air was still and stifling hot. The movie people were putting the finishing touches on a high fence with razor wire on the top. That did not seem right to me, and I went looking for somebody to complain about it.

I wondered who I could irritate the most. The film director looked like he might do for starters. He was a joyless little fellow with a pimply face and the scowling features of a discontented high school economics teacher. His name was Hector Jenkins, and to me he did not seem headed for the stellar heights of the biz. I decided I would try not to make his life any easier. Two directors on the set, you know, is the much the same as two roosters in the cockfight ring.

"Hector. In the interest of historical accuracy, in World War II they used barbed wire. Razor wire was not invented until maybe Korea or Vietnam."

"Vell, I do not know," he said.

"Exactly," I said. "But I *do* know. That means your guys fix it or I do not jump. *Mach schnell!*"

He rolled his eyes. His prissy little assistant director sniffed in my direction.

"She is such a bitch!" the girl said.

"I heard that," I said. But I had the advantage, so I kept on walking. By this time I was on to their game. I was certain they needed me to jump that fence so they could kill me in glorious 3-D and surround sound.

So I stalked away like some miffed prima donna and Hector went into a huddle with his sniffy AD, the producer, and the script girl, and the upshot was we had to sit around for a few hours while they sent away for the right kind of wire. Toward the end of our little hiatus I got restless and went over to take a closer look at my bike. They were stringing the last few strands of the historically accurate wire

175

and most of the cast and crew were lollygagging around, taking a break. I had already checked the bike out, but you can never be too careful, and sure enough, at the last minute some fool art director must have convinced props to strap a set of leather pouches over the rear wheels.

"What the hell are you people doing?" I said.

"It looks so much more authentic," the art director said. She had short straight hair shaped over one eye in the feminine version of the Hitler cut, and she gave me a *haut* look that said, *Who the hell are you to ask?*

"I am the stunt double, and I am also second unit directing today. You knew that, right?"

The art director cast a dubious look in Hector's direction, but he gave her a curt nod. Hector raised one eyebrow to me.

"Ve tink mit the leather bags it haf more of the authenticity, no?"

"Okay, but I am going to have to give it a few runs to see if the extra weight makes any difference."

"How should zat insignificance make such a difference?"

"Balance. It is all about balance, me bucko, in both life and art. So I need a couple test runs."

But he was not going to let me go without an argument.

"You are now wearing zat clutch bag vitch ve never see before."

I was wearing Grandma Jenny's woven travel bag over one shoulder.

"You are making my case here, Hector-Protector. Balance is everything."

I looked from the art director to Hector, who suddenly seemed distracted, as if the real world was way too much for the pure *artiste* in him. He shot a quick glance at a nebbish-looking fellow who was fooling with a radio transmitter. When the fellow saw he had caught my attention, he held the transmitter to his face and started talking, at the same time pointing off in the distance. I followed his gesture. There was another crew member standing on a small hillock near the fence jump, but he did not seem to be holding any sort of device up to his ear. Something was cooking, all right.

Franz, one of the four cameramen, came over to check on what the delay might mean. He looked right at me, but he did not recognize me.

"Hey, what's up, *Fraulein*?"

This was a little weird because this Franz had been on a few shoots with me back when the world was a simple, sane place. Back then his name had been Frank and we had actually tossed around in the hay a little bit. Nothing of Georgie-Porgie's slick-stick professionalism, but Frankie was not a bad shooter in sort of a fresh and enthusiastic schoolboy way. Now he did not seem to recognize me. I grinned at him.

"Hey, Frankie, you ready to go, hot stuff?"

"Always up," he responded automatically, as I knew he would.

"That is the word around town. Stay sharp, my good man."

He gave me a dubious wave and headed for his camera position. I was hoping old habits never died. Frankie had a trigger finger. With my vague

177

warning, I knew he would be ready to roll film even on a test run.

The art director looked like she wanted to protest, but I gave her a rude stunt girl shove.

"Out of my way, Nazi bitch," I said as I headed for the bike. I slung my leg over the chassis and grabbed the bars. The motor was still warm from my earlier runs, and the wheels spun a little on the dirt road as I headed away from the milling pack of crew members.

In thirty seconds I had rounded a bend and found myself alone in a small patch of bushy live oak. The thick patch of low-lying oaks made a screen, sufficient for my needs. I slammed on the brakes. The bike skidded to a halt and I was able to take a look in the saddlebags.

As I had suspected, they were packed with gray, putty-like stuff. I was no expert, but I had been on a Mafia gang picture where I had to leap in the direction of the camera while a car exploded behind me. Spectacular shot, the craggy mountains of Sicily in the background, but that is not the point. I knew an explosive rig when I saw it. I carefully pulled wires from the putty and then buckled the straps back up. No need to risk my life on a crewmember with a premature trigger finger.

I was going to take the run. This probably sounds crazy to you, but you have to remember that, while in this alternate universe things could get confusing, in my old life back before Regina's Nazi Time, I was already living in two worlds. In my old life, I was a stunt girl who would do anything to get that directing credit. In my new one, here I am, out to save the universe as we know it from being warped into Regina's vision of herself as some sort of evil queen—but I still wanted that damn film credit on my résumé, no matter which world we ended up in. And according to the rules of both the stunt union and the director's guild, all I had to do was to make this jump and I got my double paycheck deposited directly into my bank account—and two days after that, the regulations say they have to record my very first Directors Guild credit, one for a prep day and the second for a shoot day.

No time like the present, I told myself. I kick-started my ugly little beast-bike and skidded my way back around the bend and into the open, accelerating as I headed for the jump. You would have thought some giant shoe was stepping on a bunch of ants, the way the crew scurried out of my way. I was too busy adjusting my angle to notice if the guy with the transmitter was jabbing his little buttons. I hit the ramp just right and flew up and over the barbed wire with inches to spare. Below on the ground in front of me I could see a row of large packets of gray putty! Boy, they were not leaving anything to chance! *My ending was going to be a cinema spectacular!*

I reached the apex of my jump and in that split second, as gravity took hold and started to pull me down, I closed my eyes and visualized Regina's suite at the Plaza. But then my old habits came back and I foolishly had to take a last look and out of the corner of my eye I saw another crewmember with binoculars. From where he was, he could have seen me behind the screen of live oaks while I was defusing the explosives in the saddlebags. *Damn lousy live oaks!*

Distracted as I was, the word "oak" hung in my overloaded brain, and so instead of materializing in Regina's suite, I popped up in the Plaza's Oak Room Bar with Grandma Jenny's travel bag around my shoulder, wearing nothing but that frayed khaki World War I shirt. That damn Aardvark Ancient Garb place had sold me fake jeans!

CHAPTER 15

It was early evening, and the all-male crowd was enjoying pre-dinner drinks while their ladies were off somewhere primping for a fine evening of dining and dance. The Oak Room Bar in the late 1930s strictly prohibited unescorted ladies, much less girls who were presenting their lower half *au naturel*. As I was actually standing barefoot on top of the bar above the milling throng, it was easy for me to spot the two dark-suited bouncers who were moving in to grab me and throw me out on my bare behind, or worse, into a paddy wagon for a one-way trip to the local jail. Too bad for them they were having a hard time making their way through the crowd of whistling, hooting males who thought they were being treated to some sort of Special Gentlemen's Event.

Hooray! I was on stage, and in my Hollywood life I never had been one to miss an opportunity for fun or that devil thing called career advancement. After a coy moment where I used Granny's travel bag in an attempt at bashfulness, I offered a shy smile and broke into the hesitant beginnings of a bump and grind. Shades of Gypsy Rose Lee! In a moment of happy recognition, the grateful crowd of males raised their glasses and broke into a cheerful chant, *More, more, more, more!*

I hip-and-rolled my way to the far end of the bar, where I went into a fast stunt dive through the crowd, followed by a mad dash out the door. And before the pair of bouncers could make their way through the push-and-shove, I disappeared into the nearest ladies' room.

181

Just my luck, there was a female attendant. I pressed a small gold coin in her hand and whispered, "You did not see anybody come in here." She winked and nodded. I made my way into one of the stalls and stood on the toilet seat. Not ten seconds later, the two bouncers came clumping into the room.

"Get outta here!" my new friend shouted. "This is women only, you stupid dumb schmucks!"

"Some naked broad come in here?"

"Like we got naked broads running around the Plaza! You caught a case of the stupids? Ain't nobody in here but me, you frickin' creeps!"

I was sure they were scuttling along, hunched over and peeping under the stalls. But to their eye, the place was deserted, and my friendly attendant helped by going into histrionic high gear.

"Get out of here right now, you pervert creeps! I'm calling the cops!" Her voice rose into a shrill scream. *"Help! Police! Rapists!"*

"Okay, okay, lady. Don't get your balls in an uproar."

"Women don't got balls, you dumb shits!" she shrieked.

And with that, they left in a hurry.

Once I was sure they were gone, I hopped down. It took me no more than a minute or two, but when I opened the door and walked from my little dressing room, I was magnificently dressed in one of Jenny's slinky black gowns. Tightly fitted on top, with pleats falling from the waist to just above the knees. Classic black, never goes out of style. Full skirt, excellent for beating a hasty retreat. Black shoes, simple, sensible, fitting the outfit. Even

Jenny's knit bag, slung over one shoulder, took on a look of elegance. The attendant gave me an approving look over.

"Jesus H. Christ, sweetie, you sure got in your getup fast!"

"That's show biz," I said.

"Let me touch up your hair, hon."

"It's a wig."

"Hon, you went in that stall a strawberry blonde, and not a minute later came out with black hair. Let me touch it up a bit."

I allowed that might be a good thing, and when she was done she would not take another gold coin.

"You're probably going to need it where you're going," she said.

I was afraid she was correct on that one.

CHAPTER 16

A half-dozen stiff-faced men in uniforms were guarding the elevators, so it did not look like I was going to be able to get up to Regina's rooms. Instead, I demurely window-shopped my way along a crowded hallway lined with establishments offering services and elegant items for ladies and gentlemen of substance.

But no sooner did I round a corner to the next row of shops when I saw the two energetic bouncers coming toward me. I could not be sure whether they had spotted me or not, so I slipped into the closest doorway. The place turned out to be a hair-and-nails salon called Top to Toes. It was only half occupied so I settled into an empty chair and spun it in a half circle so I was facing away from the door and the large window looking out on the passing crowd.

"You are having a reservation?" a trim, silver-haired woman asked.

"No, I am trying my best to hide from two brutes who think they own me."

"You need a haircut."

"It is a wig."

"I know that. Everybody in the world knows that. Your hair underneath is too much."

"Oh. What should I do?"

"Put this dryer over your head. After the brute-men go, I will fix."

With her help, my head was under a huge dryer in less time than it takes to tell it, and just in time as one of the bouncers yelled from the doorway.

"Hey, ladies, anybody see a naked broad running around here?"

184

The woman with the silver hair pursed her lips, shook her head, and made an annoyed gesture with one hand as if she were shooing off a pair of mangy stray dogs.

Once they had gone she gently took off my wig.

"You have beautiful hair. Like fire, it is so. Why do you hide it?"

"I am hiding from some very rude and bad people who do not like me."

"Pity. Who would not like you? Well, we will make everything better under the wig."

And over the next half hour, she did. Thinning and shortening my unruly curls allowed a more snug fit for my close-fitting false head of hair, and by the time I left I was feeling that no one could possibly recognize me as the randy daredevil who had suddenly appeared in the Oak Room Bar without any panties and put on a show. Being up there in front of a herd of males had given me a rush. If stunting failed, maybe I would have a second career in a different kind of limelight. I guess it was not exactly the right time for humor, but come on, if the world is taking a dive and me with it, there has to be room for a last laugh.

As I left Top to Toes, the early evening browsers were crowding the arcade. Well-dressed couples moved along the gallery chatting as they looked over the bounty of jewelry, health and beauty, and specialized foods. I took a sudden interest in the display of expensive French perfumes in the windows of Kringler Parfumer as a small squad of New York's finest jogged by. Probably looking for that audacious and naked female bounder, but the men in blue looked right past me and hurried on their way.

As I reentered the hotel proper, all the action seemed to be coming from the Palm Court, a huge, high glass-ceiling gathering room featuring a small chamber orchestra that was playing Strauss waltzes. I headed in that direction. It was quite an impressive place. A large variety of leafy green potted plants and four tall palm trees flourished under a glittery Tiffany glass ceiling, and there in the center of the room my aunt Regina was the focus of adoring male attention. She was wearing an elegant navy blue silk gown as she waltzed with a portly gentleman who sported manly sideburns. *I had found her! Victory at last!* And it had to be my good luck to catch up with her in a public place where her choices in ways to kill me might be limited.

I spotted her travel bag at a deserted table and sidled over to take a seat next to it. More luck. Nobody seemed to notice me, so I started to go through her bag—you know, looking for a clue or something.

That is, I thought nobody noticed until I heard a low male voice behind me.

"Going through Regina Warner's things, are we?"

He was a handsome young fellow, I figured maybe in his mid-thirties. He was a few inches taller than I was. I looked him over with some interest. After all, I may have powers but I do have my extraordinary human side, too. He had a penetrating look with dark brown eyes, curly black hair, and a quizzical smile on his lips. I reddened and managed to stammer my excuses.

"My Aunt Regina," I said. "I need to make a few entries in her diary."

"Well, you better do it. The waltz is ending, and she'll be here in a jiffy."

I groped around in that damn endless pit of her purse and just managed to snag her diary and slip it into Grandma Jenny's woven bag, which by this time I was pretty much coming to think of as my own. I turned toward the fellow who had now seated himself next to me.

"I am Juniper Rose Warner. And who are you?"

His smile broadened.

"Haliburton Hamilton, at your service. I am pleased to meet you, Juniper Rose. You may call me Hal. Just so long as you do call me."

"Oh, not that old line."

"Tried and true beats fresh and unreliable."

Things were looking up. I might actually get one last roll in the hay before Auntie Dearest blew up the galaxy.

"And what do you do, Haliburton Hamilton?"

He looked like he was about to conjure up some sophisticated lie, but raised his eyebrows and looked over my shoulder. That was my cue that Regina had arrived. Not that I needed a clue—it was easy to follow the annoying yip of her voice over the sound of the orchestra. The band was striking up the lively Druck zua Polka. My luck was turning sour. Regina disdained the polka. She thought it was for peasants and drunken fools.

"You are sitting in our chairs," she said in that haughty tone of voice I knew so well.

Hal stood and moved between me and Regina.

"I'm sorry, Miss Warner, but we were tired from too much dancing. We were just leaving."

She gave me a second look and her eyes narrowed.

"You!" she said in that icy whisper. Regina could freeze a hot potato at a hundred yards. She knew voice control like the ladies with powers of mind control in Frank Herbert's *Dune* novels. No, they were amateurs compared to my lovely aunt.

"Sit!" she commanded.

I ignored her, of course. If I were a poodle or a German shepherd I would have flunked obedience school.

"Nice dress, Reggie. A little tight around the hips, maybe. Been getting into the strudel? Midnight runs to the old German deli?"

"I should have killed you when I had the chance."

"You mean that time with me as the Easter Sunday morning target practice? Or the shove down the stairs? Or the push off the cliff?"

"Jenny can no longer protect you."

"Are you sure about that? How did my bike stunt turn out for you?"

A look of uncertainty flashed across her face. Regina was not that hard to read, once you realized she was fifty percent fear, fifty percent greed, and fifty percent rage. Yes, one hundred and fifty percent, that was the right number, and it was all bad.

I nodded in the direction of the portly German fellow standing at her side.

"Are you not going to introduce me to your…err, date?"

Her cheeks puffed and I was afraid her head would explode, but she was a lady of manners and etiquette, if not principle. Her moral compass had been broken a long time ago, assuming she ever had one.

"Baron von Kurtzmark, this is my niece, Juniper Warner."

The fellow was about six inches shorter than my five foot ten, and his belly puffed out his vest like one of those Bismarck-mustachioed corporate bosses who hang out in the playing cards of a Monopoly game. He even had one of those monocles on a black silk string attached to the buttonhole in his black jacket, the same place that held a white carnation.

"Enchanted," he said, in a voice that burbled from deep in his chest. "Vould you care to dance, my child?"

My aunt's expression changed from rage to one of alarm, but before she could get a word in, I sprang to my feet and took the old fellow's hand.

"*Merci beaucoup*," I said.

"Ahh, the French… Do you do the polka?"

"Not so much," I confessed.

The baron made a grand gesture to the band, an arch wave with his left arm that ended with an imperious finger snap. I was relieved to see it was just a signal to change the music; his move looked too much like a salute to *mein Führer*. The band, however, was in tune with his gesture and dumped the folk dance for a light waltz. This dance I knew well from my cotillion days, the practice lessons where nice young men and women of promise had

189

their first brush with the carefully orchestrated contact sport of high-society romance.

"Sooo, vere are you from?" my new dance partner asked.

"Oh, Chicago," I said.

"You verk mit our Regina, then?"

"Yah," I said, getting into the dialect thing. "I do so. Lived mit her, actually, for many, many years."

"Great projects in the work."

"I know. It is so vonderful!"

Of course, I did not know much of anything. But how would it hurt for him to think I was solid on the team? Maybe I could dupe him with a bit of rapturous babble. I pulled him in a little closer, cursing that I had decided not to have the girls enhanced.

"Everyzing for Adolf! I was there when the submarine boys came on shore. So glorious! So dangerous! So thrilling!"

The baron might have had too many sips of the schnapps, but he was nobody's fool. Maybe I had gone overboard with my gushing. For a second there I thought he was looking at me like I had to be a spy. And then he raised his eyebrows in astonishment. I saw he was looking over my shoulder. A delighted smile graced his blubbery cheeks.

"Ma-TIL-da!" he said.

And then Tillie Noonschnapper joined us. The minute she touched my shoulder I knew how to dance the polka after all, and the three of us formed a little dancing trio. Tillie joined the conversation as if she knew all about it. Actually, the way she talked

190

it was as if she was one of the ringleaders. She nodded enthusiastically.

"Operation Ziggity Zag is going well. Our troopers are prepared to pick up zis Spedding fellow und his magic rabbit pellets."

"Oh! Matilda! I should haf known you would be in on it!"

I gave a furtive look around the room and caught Regina's angry glare.

"Yes, but should we be talking about Spedding here?" I said quickly.

He smiled and whispered in my ear.

"Chust some few more days, unt ve haffen ze Frank Spedding and his pellets on ze sub!"

"For ze vadderland," I whispered back, giving him a light kiss on his ear.

Tillie gave me a little wink.

"One more dance with my lover-boy."

The baron reddened as Tillie gave me a little wave good-bye. I took my cue and made my way back to Regina's table, where she wasted no time trying to lasso me into her corral. The very second I arrived, she stood and slung her travel bag over one shoulder.

"Well, we're late, dear niece. Come along, now."

She reached out to grab my arm, but I slid to the far side of Haliburton Hamilton, my new protector.

"Where are you going, auntie? Can you not fetch Frankie by yourself?"

Regina took on a look of thunderous rage.

"Frankie?"

"Spedding," I added, just to make things clear.

That brought the thunder.

"We must go back to my room! At once, child! My assistant will escort you!"

It was the first I had seen of the big, tough fellow with the crewcut blond hair and the scar on his chin. He shouldered Hal aside and moved in on me. He placed his big meat hooks on my shoulders. Too bad for him I had this simple but neat trick I had learned in the chop-socky movies. As his grip tightened on my shoulders, I managed to squirm around and elbow him in his stomach. He bent over like a wet pretzel.

"Too much of that good Cherman food is *nicht ser gut* for you, *nein*?" I said in German that I was sure was just as chop-socky as my karate move.

Hal was quickly back at my side, brushing his coat and bristling with indignation. It was good to see he had attitude. I was going to need reinforcements to get out of this one.

"We have not eaten yet, auntie-sweets," I said. "I shall certainly see you later, alligator. I promise. After a while, crocodile. Just like at Georgie-Porgie's wedding."

I held up my crossed fingers to make the point. *Cross my heart and hope to die/I have better fish to fry!*

Hal took my arm and hustled me in the direction of the lobby. Whatever this sweet guy did for a living, he was a smooth operator. I liked the way he was helping maneuver us out of my sticky business with Auntie Dearest. And the way he carried himself in his tailored suit and tie. And I particularly liked the way he looked at me. Interesting possibilities.

But then reality set in. *Do not get carried away, babes,* I told myself. *The fate of the entire free world is resting on your...err...shoulders.* I almost said *boobs,* which might have been a more appropriate way of looking at things. I was thinking more and more that maybe Sumner Blinker was right. Maybe I should have that operation, you know, move up a half cup size or so. Nothing drastic, just a little something to help me get ahead in the game.

So, with me thinking semi-unladylike thoughts, we gingerly skirted around a dancing floor that was now annoyingly cluttered with couples. The polka had been replaced by the jitterbug. I love the jitterbug and was tempted to break into one of my moves, but then I took a quick look back over my shoulder. Regina was frantically pawing through her travel bag, no doubt looking for her missing diary.

"Oh-oh. Regina is on to us! Time to get us out of here!"

"I've been trying! Come on, my car should be outside."

We rushed across the lobby and a valet was conveniently standing there, or maybe my new savior had something to do with that. Hal gave him some money and said something to him in German that I did not catch, and then he hustled me out through one of the revolving glass doors.

Unlucky for me, it seemed like I just could not catch a break. The bouncers I had run into earlier in the Oak Room Bar were right there behind us. I was thinking those guys should really give it a rest as they came barreling into the revolving door slot directly behind us. I jammed the heavy plate glass backward with my foot and they crashed full force into it. It was a trick I had learned when I stunted for a dumb comedy about some idiots who try to reverse-steal goods into department stores. The revolving door stunt had probably been the best gag in the whole stupid flick. All I can say is, it worked just as well in real life. I was pretty sure one of the goons broke his nose on the glass. And in the next moment Hal had my hand and we were running for a line of parked cars.

"Here it is," he said.

An attendant standing next to a steel-blue Buick convertible held out his gloved hand for the gratuity. Hal flipped him a heavy coin that he caught smartly in one hand, waving us on with the other.

I knew that car.

"You own a Buick Special!"

"Yes. Dynaflash straight eight. Fastest car on the road."

"Second fastest. The Hudson is faster."

"No, it isn't."

"Yes, it is!"

We were trying to get away from the most dangerous woman in the known universe and I was about to have an argument over my beloved Horny Hudson! But then I heard the gunshots and that snapped me back to the moment.

"Ah, heck, they are shooting from too far away! They can't hit us with pistols at this distance," Hal said.

A bad premonition made me shiver and I instinctively reached out and gave him a shove as he was opening the passenger-side door for me. In the

194

next second, he grunted and grabbed his right arm. I glanced over and got a shock.

A long, feather-tipped arrow was sticking through his arm! If I had not shoved him right then, it would have gone through his chest!

I looked back and there was Regina in her ballroom gown busily nocking another arrow into a giant long bow! *Where the hell did she come up with that thing?* You would think that a fancy place like the Plaza would make you check your weapons with your hat and coat, but I guess this was the result of Regina's forceful nature, or maybe she just summoned her bow up out of thin air like magic. That woman was an endless source of surprises, and most of them seemed to be designed to kill me!

It was panic time. At least, it was for my new pal Hal. This James Bond 007 guy could be human after all. I put my hand on his head and yelled "Down!" forcing him to duck and probably saving his life as another arrow whistled past, this one missing both of us.

Regina must have lost her Zen center of calmness, or whatever people like her called it. I snapped off the front end of the arrow that was sticking through Hal's upper arm, the same way Alfred had done to the one sticking through my prayer book that was not a prayer book that long-ago Easter Sunday morning.

No time to be gentle or nice, I muttered to myself. I unceremoniously yanked out the end with the feathers and shoved Hal into the car. A third arrow whizzed by me as I scurried around the rumble seat and jumped in on the driver's side. Our lucky day, the valet had left the engine running.

I heard Hal's weak voice trying to instruct me on the ways of his automobile, which I already figured had to be one of his most treasured possessions.

"Three-speed manual transmission…"

"Yeah, three on the floor."

"You are a good gal, but are you sure you can drive a stick shift?"

"Oh, yeah. I got this one," I said.

CHAPTER 17

The tires squealed on the concrete as I laid rubber down tree-lined Fifth Avenue, getting us the hell out of there. I was hoping for a fast getaway, but traffic was too heavy. We barely made it a block before we had to stop at a busy intersection. A mustachioed traffic cop held up one hand and coaxed a line of cars and trucks to cross in front of us.

"How do you feel?" I said to Hal. He was still gripping his arm, and I could see blood around his fingers. He had looked better.

"Sleepy...I feel loopy."

"Regina puts knockout drops on her arrowheads. Or sometimes poison. My uncle Alfred told me."

The look on Hal's face was one of pure fright.

"P-poison?"

"Do not worry about it, Hal. I think you got lucky. If it was poison, you would be dead already."

"Uncle Albert?"

"Regina's husband."

"You're not really related to her?"

"Yes, I am. Not my fault. Bad luck for me."

"S-so I'm supposed to trust you?"

"Get real, Hal. I heard you speaking German back there. The *real* question is, am I supposed to trust *you*? How do I know you are not the king of the bad guys?"

"My stepdad was ambassador to Berlin. After he and Mom were divorced, I spent half my time in Germany and the other half in New York City."

"What about your biological dad?"

197

"Oh, he's still around. But that's another story."

There was something vague and suspicious about that reply, but I had no time for more questions as I caught a glimpse of my crazy aunt in the rearview mirror.

"Hang on for your life!" I said. "Here comes the Bat Out of Hell!"

I had to admit she was creative. Regina had commandeered a horse from one of New York City's finest and was charging after us with her steed at full gallop. She was quite a sight, with her skirt riding high above her hips as she kicked the wild-eyed brown stallion, a large horse that looked like he was having the race of his life. I should have known my aunt would be an accomplished horsewoman, though I had never seen her ride. She was managing a full gallop without holding the reins, and she held her bow sideways, string taut and arrow ready. And it was an unusual arrow with what looked like a small egg-shaped gray object, probably a grenade, at the tip.

No way I could wait for the traffic to change. I practically ran over the startled cop to get through the intersection. I pulled right, bumped the curb, and zoomed along on the sidewalk, scattering a flock of angry pedestrians, and then I wove good old Dynaflash through the intersection. The astounded traffic cop tooted his shrill whistle and waved an angry fist, but by that time I was through the last of the cross-traffic and hitting the gas. Lucky thing, too, as the grenade arrow exploded, destroying a red, white, and black United Germanic Empire mailbox on the curb behind us.

"Pox on her! Pox, pox, pox!" I shouted into the night air.

I did not really know any curses, but I hoped maybe my words could drudge up something on the spur of the moment, and maybe I was right—in the next moment, Regina's horse was brought up short by a fruit cart drawn by a donkey and she went flying over her own mount! I found myself hoping she would break her neck, but she was too clever to be finished off like that. She disappeared in mid-air to the astonished disappointment of the traffic cop, who went off balance as he swung his baton through the space where she had been flying not more than a few seconds before.

Traffic now definitely was thinning. I picked up speed and left the mess behind us. That gave me a little space to reflect on where I was going with Haliburton Hamilton—that is, if he was still interested in a bit of hot sexual fun and games after we patched up his arrow wound. He was some attractive hunk o' manhood, but on the other hand, he was awfully glib. He seemed to have an answer for everything, and the stories flowed easily out of his devastatingly handsome demeanor. Something had to be wrong. He was just too good to be real.

Still, on the other-other hand (say, if I had three hands), maybe I could use the moment of confusion to my advantage. I had told him Regina dipped the tips of her arrowheads in sleeping potions. That was not quite the full story. More accurately, I might have told him *truth serum*. Evil Auntie was the complete bag of tricks. Maybe it was time to see if Regina's chemical approach really worked.

I shoved Hal on his punctured arm. That seemed to do the trick; he groaned and gave me a sleepy, heavy-lidded glance.

"Hal. Haliburton. Haliburton Hamilton. How do I know you are not a spy?"

"I'm not getting blood on the seats, am I?" he asked drowsily.

"I've seen all the really good spy movies. That avoidance technique is not going to work with me."

"Spy movies?"

"You know: 'Bond. James Bond. Shaken, not stirred.'"

"Are you crazy or something?" His speech was slurred, but at least I knew he was not going back to sleep with me poking at him. He was a tricky guy, but I could not help myself. I was attracted to him. He reminded me of a young Robert Downey Jr., or maybe Rock Hudson.

"Come on, Hal. You are just avoiding the question. I am suggesting you might be a traitor and you are worried about messing up the seats?"

"Not avoiding. 'Evading,' as in 'evading one's taxes.' It's not illegal. And it's my sister's car. And the seats are leather."

He reached in back with his good arm and awkwardly bundled a classy woman's scarf under his bloody jacket. It was clumsy and I nearly ran a stoplight trying to help.

"Is that your girlfriend's scarf?"

"No, it is really my sister's. And I am not a spy. Are you crazy? You're the one who is most probably the real spy, hanging around with the likes of Regina Warner!"

"She is my aunt!"

"You said that! But you were sneaking things out of her purse!"

"You could have stopped me. You wanted to see what was in there, too."

"Liar, liar, bloomers on fire."

I was working up to yell at him, but in the next second he yawned and, still using his good arm, took out a wallet. He flipped it open and when I saw what was in there I ran a stoplight and nearly hit a Schlitz beer truck. There was a card with a picture of him a few years younger and the big black letters "FBI."

I started to apologize, but he was sleeping or unconscious. I had no idea where the nearest hospital might be, so I drove him to the address on his identification card. It took less than five minutes to get there, but it was very much unlike any FBI headquarters I could have imagined, unless FBI stood for "Foreign Booze Importers." America in the late 1930s was full of surprises!

CHAPTER 18

Hal was stirring and mumbling when I brought his shiny steel-blue Dynaflash to a screeching halt in front of an ordinary-looking brownstone. Practically before the whitewall tires stopped smoking, two men in dark suits rushed out of the building and took over, dragging his limp body toward the front door. They were going to leave me with the car, but Hal put up a mumbling fuss and they allowed me to tag along as they half-carried him up the concrete steps. We crowded into an elevator and were whisked up.

The doors slid open and I saw that, across a hallway, a black-tie party was in full swing. The apartment looked like it took up at least the entire floor of the building. There must have been fifty couples milling about in a crowded ballroom. A jazz pianist was hammering away under a glittering chandelier, and champagne was flowing from a corner bar setup that was handled by two maroon silk–vested waiters who were having trouble keeping up with the demand. The men hustled Hal through this happy madness to a side corridor and we all jammed into a bathroom with confusing reflections of mirrors on every wall, not to mention the ceiling and the floor.

Quickly, they stripped Hal to his waist and examined his wound. I watched and was satisfied to see he did not have any other scars on his well-muscled chest.

"Twenty-two caliber," the first man said with a little sniff, rubbing bar soap on the wound, which predictably made Hal scream a few choice profanities.

"No. Thirty-two," the second said.

"Ash wood arrow," I said. "Steel tipped, dipped in something bad, probably morphine."

They looked at me like I was nuts, so I pulled the two ends of the broken arrow out of my travel bag and handed them over. "He was shot by Regina Warner. Can you arrest her?"

"*The* Regina Warner? I don't think so," Unfriendly One said.

"How do you know it was Regina Warner?" Unfriendly Two asked.

"For one thing, she is my aunt. And then, at least a dozen witnesses saw her do it in front of the Plaza Hotel."

They looked at Hal, who nodded wearily. With no further discussion they swabbed some dark brown liquid on his wound and crudely taped up his arm, and then we took a smaller private elevator with glass doors up two floors to the rooftop balcony, where a meeting of sorts was taking place. We passed a level where a small swimming pool, also with glass walls, was populated with naked young men and women who seemed entirely preoccupied with each other.

"That has to be hard to do underwater," I said.

The two men gave me a sad look and shook their heads.

"We wouldn't know," Unfriendly Two said. "Pool play's off limits to the hired help."

"The pool or the play?"

"Who wants to know?" Unfriendly One said.

"Sorry. I did not mean to hit a sore spot."

And then the elevator arrived at the rooftop balcony. The doors slid open and we were ushered over to a poker table with a canvas awning over it, where three cigar-smoking old guys sat around with roughly equal piles of money in front of them. They were being watched over by two sullen young men who looked to be of Italian extraction. The group had been there for a while, judging from the empty beer cans and half-empty bottles of whiskey on the table.

"This isn't the FBI," I said.

"A lot of places can say that," one of the older men said. He was beefy and tired looking, and had not shaved in a day or two. He was wearing a wife-beater undershirt and striped shorts.

"Nice dress. Sensible shoes," he said.

"You, too."

"Yeah. Well, we dress for comfort. I'm Charley. Charley Magnolia. Pleased to meet you. Do you think you could recapacitate Louie here, so to speak, before he kills you with the revolver in his waistband?"

"'Recapacitate' is not a real word," I said, "but let me give it my best shot."

Hal shouted, "No, Dad!" but the scene was already in play.

Charley gave one of the sullen young men an almost imperceptible nod and heavy-lidded Louie made a sloppy grab for the heavy revolver he had stuffed in his pants. It was a long-barreled .45, which seemed a bad choice, as the tip got caught in one of his belt loop holes. But my whirling-spin kick was already in motion, and I showed a lot of granny underpants as my practical shoe caught

204

Louie in his unsuspecting middle. Air went from him with a big whoosh and he stumbled backward before he landed on his big butt in a crumpled mess.

Charley gave me the once-over. "Where you learn to do that, Missy Fancy-pants?"

"Hollywood. That is show business. But you are going to catch a cold, dressed light like that."

"Nah. I got internal combustion. Hey, I like this broad. Louie, put away the peacemaker."

Charley frowned at Hal.

"Rocco, I told you that fake ID was going to cause trouble."

"It got me into the Kraut shindig."

Rocco, indeed. I noticed Hal's foreign accent was dropping into the Bronx. And with it, my James Bond fantasies were dissolving into the Hudson River. I waved my hand in Charley's face for a little attention.

"Look, I have a real problem! I think my aunt is out to sabotage the entire United States of America, and time is running out here. In fact, we may be in overtime."

Charley raised his eyebrows at Hal.

"Overtime? We can't afford that."

"She says Regina Warner is her aunt," Hal said.

"What do I have to do, take out a billboard? She is my aunt!"

Charley grunted and snapped one of his suspenders. It made a slapping sound on his sweaty chest.

"We think your aunty-poo is bootlegging liquor from Europe. That right there is our interest. We don't know nothing from nowhere about no frickin' sabotage, pardon my French. We sent young

205

Haliburton Magnolia here to keep an eye on her. By the way, Haliburton was his mother's idea. I wanted Rocco."

"Rocco is a nice name."

"Yeah, but that didn't happen. Well, tell us about the sabotage thing."

"There is a plan to hijack mysterious bunny rabbit pellets from the US government. I don't know what they are. Men snuck into New Jersey off a German submarine. My aunt is involved. I don't know how."

Charley screwed up his face like he did not believe me. Who could blame him? It was a very tall story, standing there alone with no props. Somewhat like me, I might add.

"Lots of stuff you don't know," Charley said. "Bunny rabbit pellets?"

"It's probably code for something," I said.

"How many men got off the Kraut sub?"

"I saw maybe six or ten. But there may be more."

"Was there any cases of booze? What are they going to hijack? Maybe gold bars or something?"

"No booze. And I do not know exactly what they are up to. They are supposed to do it in Iowa, but they have a big head start. They might have already done it."

"Wait, slow down, young lady. Where in Iowa?"

"Ames, Iowa. But we are wasting time talking about it."

"We got a plane doin' nothing, parked handy at the municipal airport. We use it for shipments and stuff."

"That's a great idea," Hal said.

"Yeah, it is," Charley the underpants man said. "And since you got us into this thing, you get to be pilot."

"I suggest Hal take a few hitters," one of the other men at the table said. "And some pea shooters."

"Good idea," Charley said, laying down three queens and two jacks. "They might find something to shoot."

"Why would you do this for me?" I said.

"Right. I don't do nothin' for nothin'. You say you are in motion pictures. You think you could get Rocco here into the flickers?"

"Well…sure. Maybe. He is a pretty good actor."

"No maybes. Here's the deal: Haliburton Hamilton. I wanna see it in the bright lights. You got three years. Shake on it?"

He pointed to his cards and raked in the pot. Then he stuck a meaty paw in my direction. It was like shaking hands with a grizzly bear.

"You gotta deal," I said, showing that I knew the language.

We took a taxi to the municipal airport, also known as LaGuardia Field. On the way, Hal tried to explain, but I shrugged it off.

"Look, Rocco, like I said, you are a good actor. You help me, you get to try Hollywood. I am serious. I will hook you up with my agent."

Actually, I was thinking about Old Man Blinker, my agent Sumner's father, but Hal did not have to know that. And then I had another idea.

By now, you know I am something of a schemer. In my spare time I had been translating around the edges of the arrow hole in my white prayer book, and that was not easy, the combination of Old Irish and Latin being a bit of a mind-twisting wonder. But I had learned some interesting tricks, and a few notions were starting to fall into place. There might be a way to broom Haliburton Hamilton along with me back to my real world—if he was brave or foolish enough to take a shot at it.

CHAPTER 19

We winged up into the late-night sky from LaGuardia in a stout DC-3 painted all black except for a big American flag on the tail structure. I did a double take on the flag. It had 48 stars with eight rows across and six high. A little thing, you might think, but jarring as a reminder I was back in the 1930s, way out of my own time.

Durable Hal was in the pilot's seat with me insisting on sitting next to him, my excuse being I wanted to make sure he did not fall asleep and crash the plane. We were less than five minutes out, still clawing for altitude, when I started bugging him to teach me to fly. Flying the DC-3 would be ten times more complex than flying the Curtiss Robin, what with the two engines and all the knobs and gauges, but I was getting the fundamentals, and once we leveled out at eleven thousand feet he let me take over the controls, so long as I *didn't do nothin' stupid.*

"So, Rocco, how did you acquire your European accent?"

I expected him to revert to his Haliburton Hamilton persona, but there was no reply from the pilot's seat. In fact, Charley's son was out like a light. I gave him a shove.

"Hey, Hal, you are supposed to be flying this goddamn airplane!"

Still no response. He did not look like he was breathing. And if anything could frighten me more, it was the ugly green glow coming from the arrow puncture on his arm. *Regina, up to her evil ways!*

And then she was in the cockpit, standing right behind us. I guess it was her, or maybe more like some ghastly projection because she looked a little fuzzy around the edges.

"Ask him if they have deposited the gold in my account," she said.

"Regina, how can I? He is out like a broken lightbulb!"

"He'll answer you," she said, reaching past me to give him a little push. Hal groaned like he had been stabbed.

But this was the aunt who had lied to me and tried to kill me on more than one occasion. I saw no reason to help her with anything.

"I have no reason to trust you!"

"Juniper, don't be foolish. We're on the same side! This is our only chance! Ask him if the payment has been made!"

"No way," I said.

But Regina's truth serum apparently did not need me, because in the next moment Hal answered in a low voice.

"*Der Führer* sends regards. Payment is complete. Zurich Federated Bank."

He began to rattle off a series of numbers. She tried to cut him off, but he just kept speaking in his spooky monotone. A sequence of twelve numbers. I have always been good with numbers, so I committed them to memory.

Regina looked uncertainly from Hal to me, wondering, I was sure, if I could have done the impossible and caught those numbers. She made up her mind—she was not going to leave anything to chance. Before I realized what was happening, she had slammed one hand on the control yoke and sent the plane into a steep dive. Hal, who apparently treated seat belts like they were optional, paid for his bad choice by floating up and smashing into the ceiling.

I tried to push Regina away from the controls. It was probably too late. We were in a full dive, the engines screaming, the ground approaching as we went into a free fall. I know, I could have wished myself anywhere, but things were not so simple. What about Hal and his mob hitters? They would be heading for certain death. Luckily, there was another way.

The moment I touched Regina's upper arm, her muscles jerked as if she'd been hit by white-hot lightning, and deep gashes appeared as if I had dragon claws. The two of us were close, falling together inside the cockpit of the DC-3. She hissed in my face like a wounded bobcat. But even as she flailed with her good arm to claw at me, she began to fade from my sight.

"Hal," I yelled. "Rocco, old buddy!"

There was no answer. I grabbed Hal's arm with one hand and tried to remember the old Irish phrase for throwing out evil spirits, but I was also trying to fly a plane with only the barest grasp of how to do it, and I yelled the only thing that came to mind.

"Out, out! Damned spot!"

I know it was plagiarism. Still, Shakespeare had been dead for hundreds of years and he was not going to mind, and after all, rumor was Grandma Jenny slept with him, so what is wrong with a bit of phrase-borrowing between friends of friends...of friends? But it did not seem to matter—my evil aunt let loose her grip on both Hal and the plane. There was a burning, sizzling smell in the air and Hal woke with a start.

"What? What's up? What's happening?"

He shook his head as if he was swimming out of a deep sleep.

"Fly the goddamn plane, Rocco!"

It was a close call, but Hal managed to pull us out of the dive, with the bottom of the plane scraping through the tops of some willow trees at the edge of a small lake.

We were not that far off-course, and he righted us, took us back up to about eight thousand feet and got us heading in a westerly direction.

The evil green glow was gone from his upper arm. Hal's flesh did not look any worse for the wear, and I was fondly wishing that somewhere in creation my aunt was furiously running cold water on her gashed arm.

"And do not even think to come back!" I yelled to the thin air in the cockpit, sure that somewhere, somehow she could hear me.

"You're acting rather strangely," Rocco said, once again assuming the cool demeanor of a young English gentleman.

"Yes, well, Auntie Dearest just took over your soul and tried to crash your daddy's airplane!"

"Hard to believe," he said, shaking his head.

"Look at your arm."

Where the arrow had pierced one side of his bicep and come out the other side, the skin was now smooth as if he had never been shot.

He stared at it for a moment. "Impossible," he said.

"Nothing is impossible, Rocco. And you better start coming clean with me. You are in bed with the Krauts and you know more about Auntie Dearest than you are letting on."

"No, I do not."

"You speak fluent German."

"And Italian. You going to hold my education against me?"

"And you knew the Germans paid Regina a lot of money for something. You even knew her bank account number."

"I do not."

"You said it out loud when you were under her spell."

"Well, I may have seen it once, but I never—"

"Where did you see it?"

"Look, we figured she's trying to get into the booze biz! Of course I know some things about her!"

"How did you find that out?" I said.

He was impatient and angry with me. This Haliburton "Rocco" Hamilton had more tricks up his sleeve than Harry Houdini.

"We have friends in banking. We own a bank or two. Hell, this is getting us nowhere!"

He clammed up and would not say another word as he flew us toward Iowa. For me, that was a good thing, as I had plenty to think about. First, I was increasingly puzzled by Regina's unexpected appearances. It was true that I had thrust myself into the situation by brooming back to the place and time I felt had to be the key starting point for her berserk plans. And although I still did not know exactly what she was up to, I had to be worrying her, or

213

why would she not simply ignore me? I had to pose some threat to her. There was no other motivation for her to continue her frantic attempts to put me six feet under. Well, about that last one, she had always wanted to *snuff me out,* to use Hollywood gangster talk, so maybe it was just that black-spider witch thing. But still—why? There should be room enough in the world for two…witches?

The word stole into my mind like forbidden fruit. Was that what I was? What we were? And why could there not be two witches, or a half dozen, for that matter? After all, there was Blu and Tillie and Margotha. There was so much of this business that was unknown to me, and the way things were going, if I did not get a lot smarter—and fast—I would be a dead little witch-apprentice before I knew the half of it.

Another thing: What about the suave and handsome fellow sitting next to me? What about *Mister Rocco Magnolia,* or whatever his name really was? Whose side was he on, really? In the Plaza Hotel he had helped me get away from Regina. And she had taken a shot at him, unless that arrow had been meant for me. Hal spoke British English when he was not talking like a gangster, but he spoke German and Italian, too, and his mobster father clearly was Italian-American.

"I went to school in Switzerland," he volunteered.

"I do not really care," I said. "Shut up and let me think."

"We're already past Lake Michigan. We'll be landing in a few minutes."

"Well, then mind your own business, which would include getting us safely down on the ground."

He did his best, but the airfield landing strip turned out to be little more than a rectangle of grassy meadow, and the DC-3 ended up stuck in a muddy cornfield at the far end. We had barely come to a mucking stop in the mud before Rocco's mobsters jumped out the side door and ran toward a hangar to one side of the airstrip. To make matters worse, as I hopped out, I heard a now-familiar sound of a radial engine, and I looked up just in time to see my grandfather's plane once again lifting into the sky and disappearing to the west.

Damn it, I had missed him again!

CHAPTER 20

And now there was gunfire in the distance. Maybe somebody was shooting at us and maybe not, but I could hear the deadly whispering *thwickit! thwickit! thwickit!* noise of bullets slapping through the cornstalks around us. Maybe they were stray shots, and maybe not. Too close for comfort, that is what I was thinking.

I was already kissing dirt, as we stunt ladies say, when Hal yelled, "Get down!"

"You're a little late with that one, Rocco!"

In the next second, he ended up on top of me while bullets continued to clip through the corn leaves.

"Some guys will try anything for an easy lay," I said.

"Hey, I'm saving your life here!"

His face was inches from mine. I kissed his nose.

"Come on, Romeo, get off me. We've got a world to save."

It might have been fun, but the timing was awful. I squirmed out from under him and scrambled to my feet.

"That was John Warner's plane! My grandfather! We are too late again!"

"That could be a good thing. It means he got away from the Krauts!"

The gunfire had died down except for a random stray shot or two.

"Gotta find out who won, Rocco," I said.

We shrugged in agreement and then put our hands up like we were surrendering and walked

216

through the muddy field until we came to a damp grassy meadow and then a big barn halfway down the airstrip. There we found Aunt Regina standing with regal disdain in the center of a half-dozen men dressed in black pants, turtleneck shirts, and skullcaps—and they in turn were surrounded by two dozen of Herbert Hoover's finest, men wearing suits, shirts, and ties and carrying tommy guns. The US government necktie bunch had won and now they had to sort out the good guys from the bad guys.

"Okay, I see the Germans and the feds. Where are *your* guys?" I whispered to Rocco.

He gave me a grin and a shrug.

"Why waste your resources if you don't need to?"

"FBI," one of the feds said, waving us to step toward them. "Who are you and what are you doing here?"

"We're American citizens. We're with you," Hal said. "May we lower our hands?"

"Any firearms?"

Hal gingerly took a small revolver from a pocket of his jacket with a thumb and one finger and dropped it to the ground. It looked to me like he had experience with this sort of thing. With a father like his, that was not at all surprising.

"This is John Warner's granddaughter," Hal said, talking briskly like a man who did not want to get shot by accident. "We are just a couple of ordinary citizens, but we heard these German creeps were going to intercept a special delivery shipment of the US mail."

"You heard right."

217

"And the mail plane took off okay?" I said.

I looked at Regina, who was standing tall and rigid with an aloof expression on her face. I followed her gaze. She was looking in the direction her father's Robin had disappeared. She was holding the arm where I had clawed her, but to me she did not look angry or even mildly disappointed. In fact, if I could read anything there, I would say there was a look of faint triumph on her face.

"What is going to happen to them?" I said, referring to Regina's men.

"Treason," one of the FBI men said.

"And her?" I nodded in my aunt's direction.

"The same. I'm no judge, lady, but I'm guessing *Hanged by her neck until dead.*"

Regina gave a scornful little *pah!* which was one of her standard imperious gestures, as if to say, that will never happen.

"Don't laugh, lady," the man started, but he was interrupted by a sudden painful bee sting on the back of his neck. "What the—?"

I pulled Hal aside and whispered in his ear. "Something is very wrong."

"What? No. We got the bad guys."

"Just a couple of them. And Regina does not look like she has been defeated. Just look at that smug and superior expression on her face."

"Isn't that her natural expression?"

"Well, yes." I had to admit he had a point. On the surface, everything seemed okay. The plot had been foiled, John Warner had taken off with his precious cargo, the German saboteurs were captured, and they all were going to be hanged for treason. But my deceitful aunt was not fooling me.

218

She had gotten away with something, and I was starting to think we were all in worse trouble than we knew.

Meanwhile, the feds handcuffed the disheartened Germans and began loading them into an olive-colored school bus that had thick bars on the windows. Five presumably dead bodies were unceremoniously dumped into a box-like delivery truck with a Frau Gertie's Fresh Eggs sign painted on the side.

I was fully expecting *something* to happen, and in the next moment it did. There was a muffled shout from the single hangar at the far end of the runway, and a man who was tied hand and foot appeared and began hopping awkwardly down the runway toward us. I ran to him and untied the dirty rag that was gagging him. He was a sturdy, broad-shouldered man who looked to be in his late thirties. He was dressed in a tweed suit and was trying to appear as professorial as possible, considering he had taken a brutal beating. His face was bleeding and he had bruises on his forearms and shoulders.

"Let me help untie you," I said. "Are you Frank Spedding?"

He nodded. "Where is John Warner?" he managed to gasp. "Where is he?"

By this time, the FBI man was standing over us, and you know how they always try to take control of everything.

"John Warner took off a few minutes ago," the FBI man said. "You are going to have to come with us now, sir."

That was rushing things, considering that I was only starting to untie the ropes around Frank Spedding's wrists.

"Hey, back off, man," I said.

"Bitch," he muttered.

"That attitude will earn you a kick in the balls."

"You silly bitch, I'm warning you—"

"Does your mother know you have a potty mouth?"

All this chatter was doing nothing to calm Frank Spedding.

"The postal pilot took off with the package?" he said.

"I guess so. I do not think he would have left without it. You do not see it anywhere around here, do you?"

Frank craned his neck and strained at the remaining ropes around his knees.

"No, no, no! Not good!"

"Frank, you are going to bust a gut!" I said. "Let me finish untying you!"

The FBI fellow tried to push me aside, but he found I was more solid than he had figured. A good female figure like mine, grounded with a healthy butt, is not that easy to shove around. He had to talk around me while I worked at untying the last of the thick ropes around Frank's legs.

"Look, fellow, who are you, and just exactly *what* is not good?"

"He's Frank Spedding!" I said. "My grandfather John Warner, who is a regular US Postal Service air mail flyer, was supposed to pick up a government shipment from him!"

Frank nodded, looking at me rather than the buttinski federal fellow.

"Well, did he manage to get away or not?"

The FBI man gave him a suspicious look.

"What do you think, fellow? The only thing we have is that empty box over there."

There was a heavy-looking box about the size of an infant's coffin lying out in the open on the asphalt apron about halfway to the hangar.

Apparently that was not a good sign, and the worried look deepened on Frank's battered features.

"That *empty box*, as you put it, is a lead-lined container!"

"Well, so what?" the FBI man said. He idly preened his dapper mustache with the index finger of his right hand as he pointed the same finger on his left at the innocent-looking container. But the self-pleased look fell from his face like a used napkin when he heard the reply.

"In a few days our pilot John Warner will be dead from radiation poisoning."

And just when I thought there could not possibly be any more bad news, angry cries went up from the men guarding Regina's van. In spite of the fact that she had been secured with handcuffs locked to her wrists and those had been snapped securely to metal bars that were welded to the inside frame of the heavy vehicle, my aunt had disappeared into thin air.

Hal looked at me.

"What do we do now? My DC-3 is stuck in the mud at the end of the runway."

"If the radiation doesn't kill my grandfather, Regina will. We have to get to him!"

"It may be too late," Frank Spedding said.

"*Maybe*. We have to try!"

Frank gave me a doubtful look.

"Well, you can borrow my motorbike, if that will help."

222

CHAPTER 21

Frank and his wife turned out to be serious cycle enthusiasts. Once she was brought up to speed on our problem, the wife insisted on outfitting Hal and me with oil slicker jackets, pantaloons, flat leather cyclist hats, and goggles. The plan was to lend us their sidecar Harley Davidson.

"If you don't run into any trouble, you might catch up to the Curtiss Robin in a day or two at most," Frank said.

As a final touch, Frank's wife suggested that Hal and I goop our hair with a product from England that she said would prevent *hirsute tangling and premature male balding.*

"Well, male baldness does not really run in our family," I said. "And me not being male, I think I will decline."

Hal was looking like he wanted to avoid male baldness, so she happily scrubbed some in his scalp while the three of them sang:

Brylcreem, a little dab'll do ya
Brylcreem, you look so debonair
Brylcreem, the gals will pursue ya
Simply rub a little in your hair

And that is how, as a starry night descended on the Midwest of 1939, I found myself on a 1938 Harley Davidson with a wide-eyed Haliburton Hamilton more or less cowering in the sidecar as we went thundering along, making our way south from Ames, Iowa, to Kansas City. There is no sound quite like the deep throaty growl of a 1930s Harley knucklehead, and I resolved that if I ever got back

223

to my own time and place, I was going to buy me one.

I glanced over at Hal from time to time, and I have to say, there was not a single hair out of place on the dapper fellow's head. There was something to be said for British hair maintenance products, though I am sure Hal's cyclist's flat hat helped as well.

We topped off the knucklehead's tank in Des Moines and went roaring on south. I figured we would probably miss my grandpa in Kansas City, but Professor Spedding said he was supposed to make a fuel stop in St. Joseph on the western edge of Missouri, so we decided to cut west, bypassing KC entirely in the desperate hope to catch up with him at his next fuel stop in central Kansas.

It was dawn when we arrived at a bridge over the Missouri River. It was a little dicey because, although a local grease monkey told us bikers used it all the time, it turned out to be a Union Pacific railroad bridge with thumpy railroad ties under us instead of asphalt.

No problem. We went chattering down the tracks and it looked like clear sailing until the last minute, when the bridge itself began to pivot in the middle and swing away from both ends! It was a swing bridge, so-called because it swung sideways to allow riverboat traffic to pass through. Great for barges and casino paddle-wheelers, but not so good for us. We were clattering along toward the widening space where the railroad tracks had been only moments before. I tried to squeeze the brakes with all the strength in my hand, but that was when I found out we no longer had any brakes. We were rushing along at nearly fifty miles an hour to the brink of disaster.

And then, naturally, who should be standing gracefully next to the precipice other than good old reliable Regina.

I reached for Hal.

"Rocco! Grab my hand!"

But Hal's hands were frozen to the rail on the sidecar.

Regina could not have been more delighted. She pumped both fists high in the air, claiming her wonderful victory over me. And yet even then she was not quite finished.

"Watch out for Sue!" she yelled as we zoomed past the end of the railroad tracks and into thin air.

Sue. That one-syllable word struck fear in my heart. I only knew one Sue, and her bones were featured at a prime spot in the Field Museum in Chicago. Sue, the Tyrannosaurus Rex skeleton that had haunted my girlish nightmares, thanks in large part to my aunt's endless cruel teasing. Now, as Hal and I went off the edge of the railroad tracks, I suffered a horrible mental image of that prehistoric monster actually alive and of her giant dinosaur teeth snapping in my face. And then I was alone and tumbling down, down, down through the shuttered event horizon of endless eons of flickering nights and days.

CHAPTER 22

I guessed it was daytime, though the sunlight was muted with a misty fog so dense it was improbable that it should exist at all as anything less than a liquid. The air was enormously dense and heavy. My lungs tugged at it, but it felt so thick it was barely breathable. The sun was somehow *different*. It looked more red-orange and maybe bigger, though I found myself thinking that had to be impossible. There were some weird bugs hopping near my face and mosquitos big as crickets tried to land on me and take a sip from the wiggly hollow straws sticking out from their faces.

I was lying on my back in a few inches of swampy muck. Naked, of course. I realized I had better get up before the local wildlife ate me alive or sucked me dry. I lurched to my feet, lost my balance, and tumbled right back into the stinking muck. Maybe it was better to stay down for a bit, half covered in slimy water. Maybe hugging the swamp floor made me a smaller target. Nothing in sight was in the least bit familiar. I crawled behind the thick root of a bushy fern tree and tried to collect my scattered thoughts.

I was starting to get a small idea of how *brooming through time* worked, if not the big picture. One sure thing—it was dangerous. Then too, the items in a travel bag were only good if I was traveling back to the time when they actually had existed. Try to go before they had existed and they would not come with you. Maybe other witches somewhere knew why, but I certainly had no clue. I could only hope, if I could ever find a way back to my own time, that my travel bag would be waiting for me.

I could see nothing farther than a few yards away. I was closely surrounded by odd tree trunks with thorny scales, and brushy dense patches of giant ferns. None of the plants looked like anything I had ever seen in my life. How comforting it would have been to spot a maple tree or one of those live oak bushes I had been cursing just before I did my jump at Malibu Flats.

Bubbles were popping on the surface of the scummy water next to my ears and the rank smell of methane was in the air. I knew I could not stay here. *Come on, Juniper Rose, time to make your move!*

With one quick motion I did a one eighty and pushed off the spongy ground. And just in time! I dove sideways as a giant head crashed out of the thick ferns and a huge set of jaws snapped at the place where I had been lying not seconds before. Sue was here! The actual, live Sue from my childhood nightmares, and this was her place, her territory, her time! Sue, no more an ancient fossil! Sue in the flesh, a hundred times more terrifying than when she was an old wired-together pile of bones! Things were looking hopeless, but you know my ways by now—the stunt girl's code is *Never shy, never lie (we don't always stick to that one), and never say die!*

I took off running down the fetid trickle of a stream with the giant beast thudding behind me. I knew I had only seconds and after that I was going to be one dead stunt girl. Oh, where was Steven Spielberg with one of his dramatic rescue scenes? I needed a jet pack, a stun gun, or maybe Arnold

227

Schwarzenegger all charged up from fighting alien predators.

And then he was right there. Well, not Steven or Arnie, but somebody even better. It was this tall, dark, and handsome guy with flashes rippling like personal lightning under his translucent ebony skin! He appeared out of nowhere, standing tall and heroic between me and the vicious Sue. In the next moment he did something I did not fully see and there was a flash of brilliant blue light and a *zap!* noise and big old Sue the unbeatable T-Rex turned around and ran off making sounds that were more like whimpers than roars!

The man was staring at me.

"Stop looking at my private parts," I said. I would have looked at his, but he was wearing what looked like a toga.

"You have no parts that are private."

"True enough, though indelicately put! For mercy's sake, give me a fig leaf or something!"

He did a showy finger-snap and I ended up with a shoulder-to-toe sack dress. I wondered what I would have to do to get some underwear.

"Is that thing going to die from what you did?" I said.

He looked uncertainly in the direction she had disappeared, and then put on a brave face. It was my guess that he did not know. I guess alien males are just as easy to read as earth men.

"Don't be foolish, mortal girl. The rule is minimum disruption. Always. Follow me. There is shelter this way."

He started to jog away, and I guess that meant our conversation was over, unless I wanted to talk at his back.

Hey, another guy who spoke in *British* English, as in *Bond is the name. James Bond.* Where did these guys get the idea they had to talk like Brit royalty to be cool? First there was my pal Hal coming across like he just stepped out of *Goldfinger*, and now I travel back to Jurassic times and find a second wannabe hero who talks with his nose stuck in the air. I must admit, it was catching and I found myself looking for precise language to take him down a notch or two.

"He gets it from you," a girlish voice with a bit of a lisp said in my ear. "You think your studly male heroes should all talk like that. And he is the master of your emotions. At least he thinks he is."

I swiveled my head and found myself staring at a translucent violet-shaded pixie fluttering about six inches in front of my eyes. She gave me a nod to show she was trying to be helpful, but she was way too close and I was seriously beyond my normally at least slightly calmer state of being, so I backhanded her with one irritated swipe of my left hand. Oh, did I tell you I am "left-wristed"? That means I write and play table tennis with my left hand. On the other hand (no pun intended), I am right shouldered—that is, I throw with my right hand, and I throw pretty well. I can fire a fastball better than most men. But I digress.

I ping-ponged this oddly fluttering pest with my left and it was like shooing a May fly, since the creature had very little substance, if any at all. Just a light brushing sensation and she went flying a few

229

meters to bump into a tree trunk with big rhomboid designs on its bark.

"Who the hell are you?" I said.

"My name is Zandor," the Dark Man muttered without breaking his pace or turning around. The pixie was not hurt, but she looked quite startled. She shook her head in wild desperation and held a finger to her lips.

"He can't know I'm here!" the little thing said. "Don't say anything out loud. Just think it and I can hear you." Well, she did not actually say it out loud, but I heard it in my head.

"Who are you?"

"My name is Mipsi. Aidana thought of me as an air sprite." She indicated Dark Man. "He doesn't know for sure if I can communicate with humans."

"We will go to my cave where we can find shelter," the ebony-skinned man who claimed his name was Zandor said.

He made another of his grand gestures and I saw some semblance of a distant cave fashioned out of a hillside covered with lush green vegetation. Any dummy could see it was a hastily fashioned disguise for a flattish flying saucer sort of a vehicle, a set that was something low-budget filmmaker Roger Corman might have had his guys slap together for one of his cheap but highly profitable cheeseball flicks. But for once in my life I kept my mouth shut, and I tried my best to shield my thoughts from my new pale purple sprite friend. Actually, I was gratified to see that that worked, because in the next moment I felt a mental nattering.

"What are you thinking, Juniper?"

230

"Nothing. Nothing at all."

"You have to let me in. You have to."

"I do not have to do anything I do not want to, pal."

I felt a zapping electronic sensation as we made our way inside the phony cave entrance. Zandor took a seat on something that looked like a rock, located a bit higher than a ledge. He pointed to a somewhat lower slab of rock.

"You can sit there. Do not go outside. Any small action in this time can have disastrous consequences."

"Yes, your majesty. Where's the bed o' love?"

"What are you talking about? I came here to rescue you."

I wasn't buying it. I took a deep breath and did the old yoga trick to force my heartbeat to slow a little.

"That is bull. Look, I have my own take on the Aidana legend."

"Please enlighten me."

"You lonely male demigods are all alike. You pull the same old gag every time. You are wounded and a long way from home and only the affection of a mere mortal can heal you."

It was an interesting moment. While we were talking, he was surreptitiously fidgeting with a few sticks and sharpened stones on a small table to one side of his rocky seat. Since I had the feeling we were in the formative stages of our demigod-and-mortal relationship (if you could even call it that), I fell back on my naturally skeptical (call it wary) nature. I tried concentrating on the small things, like his fingers dancing through the rubble on the table.

231

What I saw was that the veil of his illusions dissolved like fog and showed me he was rapidly—nearly desperately—working a series of levers and controls on a switchboard that was now only thinly shielded by a fake rock wall.

Don't let on that you can see right through this bozo's tricks, I told myself.

"What are you thinking, Juniper?" a voice said in my head.

"Nothing, Mipsi. Nothing."

"You must let me in! You must!"

"No, thanks."

Zandor let out an exasperated burst of air. I had a feeling it was all for show. He probably had a direct solar link like the gray men and did not need any oxygen.

"You are being very foolish!" he shouted. "I loved Aidana! She was my first true Earth soulmate!"

"I do not think so. And stop yelling at me. For one thing, this is our planet. Maybe you can screw us, but you do not get to make the rules."

"Well, not for very long."

"What do you mean?"

"You're setting about for your own speedy extinction."

"Am not," I said.

"Are too. Why do you think I am here?"

"Your insatiable desire for a little Earth-nookie would be my guess."

"Do not be absurd. Let me explain it in terms you can understand."

"Do not talk down to me."

"Time is a river."

"Oh, *bla-bla-blah*. I know the shtick. If we continue to disrupt the space-time continuum by trying to warp the present to something different we will blow ourselves up. But I have a problem with you."

He gave me a calculating look.

"What is it?"

"Where have you been since you knocked up poor Aidana?"

"I did not 'knock her up,'" he said. "I just gave her certain powers as per our agreement."

"Sex for powers. Nice."

"There is nothing wrong with that."

"Do not get pissy with me. I do not believe you are telling the entire complete absolute truth. Men are such terrible liars. You should send girl aliens to do your intergalactic dirty work. And you did not answer my question."

"You annoy me so badly I can't even remember what your question was."

He turned and gave me the once-over. I think he was seeing me for the first time as something slightly more than a dimwitted but alluring island maiden he could buy with plinks on a ukulele and a few shiny baubles.

"You answer me one question, and then I'll answer one of yours. Tell me: what do you think I am?"

"I think you are a nasty-tempered little space-boy who has lost his way."

Mipsi fluttered into view behind him and gestured a huge thumbs-up, *Yes!*

The fellow I was thinking of as Dark Man frowned. "Okay, what is *your* question?"

233

"I am saving it for later."

I stood and walked across the length of the so-called cave and saw it distracted him to the extent that he was no longer really thinking about our conversation. That led me to believe he may have different abilities than my own, but like ordinary humans he had difficulty doing two things at once. Maintaining the illusion of a cave to cloak his transport vessel was costing him big time in the concentration area, and maybe it was sapping his solar reserves as well.

I pushed aside a beaded doorway, revealing an ornate room of carved flower vases and plump pillows surrounding a heavily draped bed.

"Ah, here it is, the legendary bed o' love. Nicely done, I must say. I like the Pompeiian mural on the wall. You know the whole damn city was cindered by a volcano, right?"

I could see it was news to him, though he looked more annoyed than interested.

"Well? What sort of a deal did you have in mind?" I said.

"I don't know what you mean."

"It is simple, kind of like the rest of you. If you play your little drama true to form, first you are going to show me some huge wound where Sue nearly killed you."

I walked up to him and before he could stop me I pulled aside his loosely drawn toga, revealing a huge, open wound with dark fluid spilling from it.

"And there it is."

My gesture also revealed he was well hung as any mortal, and the tip of his stiffening ebony rod was glowing like an LED light.

234

"And there *it* is!"

I was tempted to backhand his manhood with a quick left like I had done Mipsi, and he seemed to get my mood because he backed away and the glowing end of his lust dimmed and sagged a little.

"If I have the story right, at least according to you, I have to come across with a hug or two and then you give me powers. Being blunt about it, this humble Earth savage screws you cross-eyed and you give me beads and trinkets."

I do not think he liked hearing my take on interplanetary relationships. I pulled the edges of his robe together.

"Here, let me make you a little more decent. I bet you are not so superior to me. I bet you do not even know if there is a God or not. Not really know."

He gave me a bleak look.

"You Earth creatures have come something of a ways since Aidana."

"What did you expect? It's been over a thousand years."

"Would you stop jabbering? I don't have the energy for this."

"Then how did you figure you were going to keep up with me in the sack?"

I figured he was pulling something of a con job, but he chose that moment to fall on the floor of the cave, and with that motion the rock shifted to metal.

"Hey, come on, I never said for sure that I would not go down with you," I said. "If your life really depended on it, I could make you forget every eight-eyed sentient being you have ever convinced that you are a demigod. I will make your testicles howl for mercy, if you have any. Just do not ask me to bow or genuflect. I am not good at that."

But he did not move as I rattled on in my chatty way, not even when I touched him, and then gave him a little shove. And when I turned him over I saw that the huge wound in his chest and abdomen had not changed. It still looked like he had been ripped open by Sue's terrible claws. That chilled out my attitude something considerable.

"Ah, shit. Just another Earth babe sucker for love," I said, gathering him in my arms.

I hugged him to me, hoping the old legends were true that he could be revived by an act of affection. Nothing. Not a flicker of an eyelid or the twitch of an arm. He was not nearly half as heavy as I had calculated, and so I stood and easily walked over to the bed o' love with him in my arms.

CHAPTER 23

I had to say it looked like Zandor went all out for seduction. Inside his vehicle/place/whatever it was he had constructed a sort of Romanesque love bed, a plump and luxurious curtained-off mattress like you see in those awful French films spoofing a Renaissance play where Zeus rides down from heaven on a chariot or a thunderbolt to make love to some mere mortal girl who will become a legendary demigoddess of the hearth, of the dining room table, and maybe the herb garden. Things like that. There was a scented fountain with rose petals floating in a quiet pool. There was a mural with fluffy fat infants with fluttery white wings were playing lyres and shooting off golden arrows into nowhere. It was the whole up-to-date deal, maybe right for an alien sex god who maybe had been off planet for two hundred years or so. And to think he had fired up his 3-D printer and had it working overtime to churn out that stuff just for little old *moi*, as Miss Piggy might have put it.

But the bare-assed fact was that Zandor the alien, the myth, the legend himself was not coming around, so I set his limp frame on the Roman mattress as gently as I could and put a fluffy sort of a leaf-blanket on him. Then I wandered around a bit, trying to absorb what I could of technological wonders that were probably at least a couple hundred times more advanced than anything Steven Jobs or Bill Gates could have imagined, even after a wild lost weekend smoking dope and staring at a crystalline moon over Silicon Valley.

237

I was snooping around, trying to find the control room, if there was such a place, when I ran into my little violet firefly light bug pal. Mipsi buzzed me a few times and then hovered in front of my face. She spoke in a chirpy voice, looking sort of like Disney's Tinker Bell though she lacked Tink's womanly hips in favor of a lithe Asiatic appeal.

"Hello again, Earth Creature. Are you civilized?"

Huh. *Civilized.* I wondered—if I said no— if she would be inclined to fry me like the creature from Mars did in Orson Welles' *The War of the Worlds*. For once, I decided on prudence rather than smart-ass.

"Mipsi, I think I am civilized. I am Juniper Rose Warner, flung back millions of years in time by my evil aunt who is about to destroy half the galaxy, if Dark Man has it right."

"Well, Zandor— 'Dark Man,' as you call him—does tend to exaggerate for his own advantage."

"I have suspected that myself. What are you doing here?"

"I'm a point-of-light sprite. The last survivor of a lost, exploited, and then exploded race. We blew ourselves up on the way to glory, no thanks to Zandor."

"And Dark Man was trying to help?"

"I wish he would have tried harder. He might have been the exploiter. I thought we did have a chance, but he got distracted by my beauty."

"Oh," I said, trying for polite.

238

"No, here, look. Here's me, in translation in your spectrum."

The light purple dot expanded and became a full-blown human-like goddess, beautiful and gorgeous, but translucent so that all her inner body parts showed.

"Nice," I said. "But maybe go a little more solid."

"No, too hard. Can I turn it off now? It takes a lot of energy."

"Right. With a set of bazoomies like that you could name your own price."

"He has kept me with him. I have nowhere else to go."

"Why would he do that?"

"His job is 99.9% traveling in a semi-comatose state from assignment to assignment. Even with wormholes and faster than light technology, he spends most of his life bussing around."

"Huh. Who knew?"

"He's bored and lonely, and I am his captive. His love slave. I can adapt to any form he can imagine, and it keeps him from going crazy...more crazy than he already is."

She did a ripple, something like shuffling a deck of cards where the players were lifeforms of every variety from squids and spiders through cloud bursts of light and blasts of dark energy.

"Amazing, you are."

"You, I thank."

"Are you sure your civilization is lost and exploded?"

"Well...no. But I have no way to figure that one out. Zandor says it is."

I figured I was lost in time at least fifteen million years beyond recall, and I needed all the help I could get. I was starting to think my situation might not be entirely hopeless.

"Look, Mipsi, you help me and I will take you with me when I get out of here."

"You promise?"

"Yes. Cross my heart and hope to die."

"Okay, yes, and I cross my heart, too. But I do not think it will be easy for us to get away from him. I've been trying for…well, a very long time."

"But now there are two of us."

I reached out one finger and I thought she would touch it with her own, but she somehow reverted to her point-of-light presence and then zipped inside me.

"Is this okay?" I heard a voice inside my head say.

"A little distracting, but yes, okay."

I did not have to say the words, just think the idea.

"I'll be quiet unless I can help," she said.

"But Dark Man will know where you are?"

"He will think I am lost in the swamp. I like to go exploring and he is always rescuing me. Now that he has you, he will not look too hard. Perhaps this time you can distract him with your incredible seductive powers."

"I do not have powers like that."

"You must have. He's only attracted to the best of the best. Look out. Here he comes all pumped up in his male boastfulness."

Indeed, there he was, all healed and striding toward me. He looked a male fluster of proud

240

nakedness with his flag flying at full mast. I ducked behind his bed o' love.

"Whoa there, big stick! Where you going with that thing?"

"Well, you said you know the drill."

"Nice choice of words. Look, dark boy, we are trying to fight our way out of a Jurassic quagmire and all you can think about is poking me with that nasty thing?"

"Nasty?" He wilted like a petunia in a hot house. "That is not proper appreciation for the gifts I offer."

"This the same deal you offered Aidana?"

"Well, yes."

"Well, no! Here is the way I see it. We do the big *hup two three four* and then you give me superpowers and after that I spend the rest of my short life burned at the stake or nailed to a cross. I do not want your deal. The truth is I probably already have those powers, inherited from Aidana. So, no thanks."

"But you have to—"

"Forget it, limp dick. I do not have to do anything except get back to my own time and save the world from my crazy aunt."

"Well, you need me to do that. Now come on, be reasonable and let's make wild passion fly and then we'll get back to that world-saving thing later."

I did not know what angry words were about to fly from my mouth, but before I could say anything, Zandor's place shook violently and big claw marks appeared in the ceiling.

"Uh-oh," I said. "Time for plan B."

He was staring at the rip marks in open-mouthed terror.

"You *do* have a plan B, do you not?"

Apparently he had nothing of the sort. I grabbed his hand and dove headfirst out of the entrance of his combination travel and house of love van.

"But my transport carrier?" he said.

He looked terrified, but I did not know what else to do. I only had one power that I knew how to use, and there never was a better time to get it working. I grabbed his hand.

I was thinking *There is no place like home, there is no place like home, there is no place like home*. That was what I remembered Dorothy had done to get back to Kansas. And there was some tricky business about having to click the heels of her red shoes, but of course I had no shoes at all and so I skipped that part. Nonetheless, the magical transport system I had nicknamed *brooming* seemed to operate with its usual efficiency and Zandor the Dark Man and I (and, hopefully without his knowledge, Mipsi) were *transponderized* back home.

Yes, but *home* was apparently not where the heart was, because we showed up in the present day, right in the middle of a festive cocktails-and-Teutonic-tidbits gathering in Regina's spacious living room in Winnetka. And, you've guessed it— it was with my usual splendidly naked appearance. I may have been flunking Brooming 101, but I was going to get an "A" for streaking.

CHAPTER 24

What can I say about the new order of things? Upon our return from the Jurassic Period, I was jerked back to a harsh reality in the modern age. I saw Regina's plan to change history was well on track—the men at her little party were almost entirely military officers decked out in Nazi uniforms. If history was this easy to fudge around, why could people not do it all the time?

But then there was a brief elemental shudder to remind me all was not right with her new world order. A crack appeared in the high ceiling overhead and a little dust filtered down. It was my impression that the ceilings always seemed to go first. Might be a new order of things business opportunity there, Juniper Rose Plaster Repair. Nobody else seemed to notice the ceiling. They were all looking at me, and who would blame them?

It was early summer and the French windows were open to catch the lake breeze. The women were floating about in elaborate gowns and the men wore dark olive-and-black military uniforms proudly sprinkled with medals and bars and stars indicating rank and (one supposes) valor. And then there was me. Remember, I was returning from what was perhaps the longest broom ride ever achieved (I should get a medal for that), and so I had managed to show up in the usual unprepared-for-brooming travel garb—that is, totally stark naked. I gave Zandor a frantic look.

"Zandor, a little wardrobe, please!"

He gave me a vengeful grin and manufactured me up a cartoonish super-hero costume, with golden

243

stars on my nipples, tight red girdle-like panties, bullet-stopping bracelets (at least I guessed they would stop bullets), flowing cape, and all. I guess you can call that Dark Man humor.

"Oh, Christ Almighty!"

I shot him my dirtiest look. If a glare could kill, he would be a dead alien.

On the other hand—and it was a good thing— her majesty Regina was not in attendance. Probably off in her boudoir, entertaining Germanic royalty with her witchy charms. Thank whatever God there was in this alternate reality for small favors. We were already in enough trouble without my evil aunt shooting spells and poisoned arrows at me. Still, we were in quite a pickle even without her.

Two guards in SS uniforms drew their lugers and pointed them at Dark Man and me. They were a problem I had not anticipated.

"Schwartzen!" they said in one voice as if they were twin dolls from some creepy WWII stage drama. They fired together, but one bullet seemed to go right through Dark Man without any effect, except that it struck a stately old lady behind him in the middle of her bountiful bosom. She tumbled to the floor while making bubbly gurgling sounds and a pool of red blood spread on the otherwise spotless white carpet beneath her. The cleaning bill on that one was going to be enough to give Regina the jabbering fits.

The second bullet bounced off my stomach and caromed back into the man who had dared shoot at a super-heroine. I had to give Dark Man credit; his outfits held up under fire. But more SS troopers

244

were moving in and I could see we were running out of options.

I did a barefooted dropkick on the closest Nazi's chin and Dark Man cindered another with a finger-point zap. The poor German fellow turned into a carved charcoal brick replica of himself for the barest of seconds before he lost resolution and collapsed into a pile of soot on the floor.

"Wow," Mipsi commented in my head. "That's *really* schwartzen."

And then the place seemed full of troopers. I had no idea where Regina was getting her reserves, but angry men came pouring in through the front door, the back door, and the side doors.

I grabbed Zandor's hand and we dove out the window into the French garden just in time as I heard a familiar shrill voice behind me screeching, "Where is she? *Where is she!*"

CHAPTER 25

Was I never, ever, ever going to get this brooming thing right? I had the thought that maybe it was not my fault. Maybe it was not an exact science, but then that notion gave way to the realization that Regina was able to pop up when and wherever she wanted. If she could do it, why not me? I just had to admit I was a novice at a complicated discipline. I had been more or less flung (out of an airplane) into this strange universe where I had powers I barely understood, much less was able to control. Where could I go from here without committing total disaster?

Following along with my mishaps, you recognize that brooming could take a *broomer* to a different place and time…or to a different place in the same approximate time. Somebody really expert like Regina could probably go nearly exactly where she wanted, as she had when she showed up for Jenny's funeral…well, maybe not exactly *when* she wanted, since she showed up a bit later than she had hoped. Good to know, but time was passing and I was getting nowhere fast.

I had to concentrate. I had the capability to broom, at least some beginner's abilities. I just had to figure out the process. Maybe practice would make perfect, like when I had to do fifty-two tumbles off a third-floor roof for a stupid sick comedy that never made it into theaters before I was able to make my deadly fall look *comic* enough for the director. *Death as a joke. Where do these guys come up with these ideas?* That guy had fumed he was going to take film footage overages out of my

246

paycheck, but I guess maybe there is such a thing as an evil eye because I fixed him with a full glare and that bill never came in the mail.

Anyway, this time, as Dark Man and I were diving out the window in Winnetka, I was thinking *My California home* and that worked out a little better although not much, as we popped up at my apartment on Fredonia Street instead of Jenny's bungalow and Zandor had to cinderize two snide blond art directors who had taken over my place and seemed to think they were going to be the next Deutschlandic wave in Tinseltown. Anyway, that black soot was the very devil to clean up and thank the Almighty for Hoover vacuum cleaners and for the calming thought that none of this was really real, or at least would not be real if we could just save John Warner and get time back on its track where it was supposed to be running before Regina got the idea she could warp everything and become the mistress of the universe.

Okay, my mad aunt aside for the moment. An observation or two about my own brooming here and there like a mad lightning bug. I tried to calm my nerves by telling myself we were simply taking the local train with a lot of stops along the way. Frustrating, but maybe I was getting somewhere. It was not as if I was becoming a total *mistress of the broom*, but maybe I was progressing a little better than Mickey in *The Sorcerer's Apprentice*. After all, I had brought us back from the Jurassic jaws of Sue to *right here, right now* time. Maybe for my future broom stunting, all I had to do was get the exact time and place right in my mind before some angry lunatic shot me or threw me out of another airplane.

But that said, I saw one other major, serious problem. With all this fumbling and zooming around, we were getting further and further from saving my grandfather. Somehow, some way, I had to untangle this mess in which I had trapped myself. And that meant I had to buckle up my courage and once again *broom away!*

"One more for the road, Schwartzen-volk," I said. I tackled Zandor at a moment when we were out on my patio. He was gazing longingly in through a window at my bedroom and so he was not expecting me to take him down. Anyway, my impulsive dive took us together over my somewhat shaky redwood patio rail and past where Duke the Ducati and Putt-Putt were still parked, until at the very last moment before smacking into the crumbled asphalt on Fredonia Drive we finally did broom away to arrive a few blinks later at dear Jenny's bungalow.

CHAPTER 26

Benjamin must have had some way of anticipating our arrival because he was standing in the living room with a robe ready for me. He was delighted to see I was actually wearing clothing, a sweat suit I had picked up at my apartment.

He was less enthusiastic about the appearance of Dark Man. It seemed they knew each other from Jenny's time.

"Zandor," Benjamin said. The chill was evident even in his nearly emotionless voice.

"Ah ha, Gray Skin! Still sucking solar, I see."

Benjamin turned to me.

"You are carrying a parasite. You must eject the intruder immediately."

"Oh, Mipsi. She says she is an innocent point-of-light sprite," I said.

"What, Mipsi is here?" Zandor asked.

Benjamin ignored him, talking directly to me with more passion than I had ever seen in him.

"She is a sweet but deadly innocent who will take over your body and then your soul!"

"How do I get rid of her?"

"Command her to go…if you still can."

I felt a soothing bath of warm emotion all over my body and heard a soft, pleasant voice inside my skull.

"Oh, don't listen to old Benji. You and I are just getting to know one another."

That soft, cajoling voice alarmed me more than you can imagine. It reminded me of some of my aunt's clever ways. *First comes the pleasure, and then comes the pain,* as the old country western song goes.

"Out! Out! *Out!*"

"You can't make me go!"

"I think I can!"

I ignored the flaming pain that swarmed me. If it was mind games she wanted, it was mind games she would get! I visualized crushing Mipsi in a very, very dark place.

"No. Don't do that!"

My own pain mounted but I ignored it. *Hell,* I told myself, *we stunt girls live for pain!* I pushed even harder and after a moment she let out a furious scream and popped out of my fingertip, the same place she had slipped in.

"And stay out!" I said.

"Well, all right! You don't have to be nasty!"

Benjamin nodded.

"Remember, point-of-light creatures cannot get in without an invitation."

"She told me she was the member of a lost race. She said Dark Man here rescued her and since she had nowhere else to go she became his love slave."

"Probably partially true," Benjamin said.

Mipsi nodded and as if to prove her abilities, rippled through a catalogue of portraits of famous seductresses from Helen of Troy to Napoleon's Josephine, Marlena Dietrich, and Marilyn Monroe.

I backhanded her simpering Marilyn caricature. It proved to be another lightweight creation, solid in outward appearance but feather light, and she flew across the room, bounced into a wall and slid to the floor, her skirt riding up to show the spread of her

250

famous legs. The Marilyn portrait giggled and looked up at me.

"Stop it," I said. "You're making me dizzy. And Marilyn had more integrity than that, both on and off the screen."

"Not what I heard," Dark Man said with a chuckle.

I was really beginning to dislike him.

"You do not know nearly half what you think. Marilyn just ran into the wrong man. Men, if you count Bobby."

Benjamin coughed discreetly. *Time to get serious*. He took me aside and spoke in a low voice.

"Since I am still seeing all things Germanic on the news, am I to assume Regina continues to run unchecked as she revises the pages of history?"

"Yes, but now we know what she is up to. Her plan is to steal America's first shipment of enriched uranium ever. Hitler gets the bomb first, drops one on London, the war is over."

"Useless," Dark Man said. "Just give it up. Once an emotional race like yours gets atomic weaponry they wipe themselves out."

"You do not know that!" I said.

"Come on, you're only one step up from the monkeys!"

"Not a hundred percent of the time!"

"Ninety-nine percent!" he shot back.

"You jilted aliens are really nasty."

"Am not!"

"You turned Daphne into a tree!" I assumed, since those were myths, after all. But my assumption was correct, since he shot back with,

"She got off lucky!"

251

Benjamin, as ever the voice of reason, placed a hand on my shoulder.

"Tell me what happened."

"We were in Missouri, chasing after my grandfather. He had a head start but we figured he would be stopping to refuel his airplane and we might catch up."

And that was when Haliburton Hamilton made an appearance from the bedroom. I do not think I was ever so happy to see anyone in my life.

"Rocco!" I said. And I fairly flew across the room into his arms.

Dark Man frowned as I rushed over to Hal. Good old Rocco gave me a warm hug and then held me at arm's length and smiled the smile that had probably lowered a thousand ladies' slips if not sunk them entirely, and even though I told myself I did not care about his too-smooth ways, he was here and I knew there was hope yet for the world.

"Hal, how did you get here?"

"Ben picked me up panhandling in the street."

"But I left you about a hundred feet in the air, falling into a muddy river in 1939!"

"True enough. But it seems my dad had a brief but torrid affair with a lady named Blu Baxter, who showed up with some sort of giant butterfly net to catch me before I hit the big muddy water. Ancient history, she said, talking about my dad. No hard feelings there. All's well that ends well. And oh, yes. She sends you her regards."

"Huh. Your dad and Blu?"

"Don't judge a goober, a gumbo, or a goombah by their wife-beater T-shirts. Old Charley's always had some good moves with the ladies."

"Where is he now?"

A shadow crossed Hal's classic movie-hero features.

"From what I understand, he died in the war. Battle of the Bulge. He was a hero. That's just another reason why we cannot allow this Regina abomination to happen. Life sacrifices should not—must not—be made in vain."

"But you—we could go back and save him!"

I know I was talking about Rocco's dad, but I was thinking about my grandfather, John Warner. I had not fully thought it through, but I am pretty sure that had been my plan all along: get on the bike and go barreling across the Midwestern plains to save my grandpa. Hey, I am a simple stunt girl turned apprentice witch. I was going to go back and save him. And then I was going back just a little bit further to take part in a fight over this very bungalow where I would make the difference by helping my grandmother crush wicked Regina.

Hal shook his head.

"No, Juniper, we cannot."

"But…I could take you. People like us…we have the power!"

"No. Blu explained it to me. Please. Listen to me. My dad died in the war. Your grandfather John Warner died earlier, in 1939. Regina killed your grandmother Jenny a few weeks ago."

"But we could bring them back! All of them! They do not have to die! We can do this!"

They were all looking at me, even Dark Man, with resigned expressions on their faces. It was enough to make me cry, and in fact that is what I did. My spirit crumbled into a thousand pieces and I wept as I realized the foolishness of what I was saying. I did not need anybody to tell me the simple facts that I had been ignoring or hiding from myself since I had seen Jenny on her death bed at Cedars-Sinai. Yes, we had the power to undo the past. But how would that be any different from what Regina was trying to do? Our abilities were also our dark and relentless curse. The second we let down our guard and thought only of ourselves, our power became deadly dangerous, more liable to doom humanity and take out the entire solar system than all the atomic weaponry in the world!

I had been rushing across the country to save my grandfather, but the truth was, nothing and nobody could save him without changing the past, and that would be just one more rip in the fabric of a universe barely managing to hold itself together.

The words burst unbidden from my mouth. "Then…what are we doing? Why go on? Why do I have to go on?"

"Well, you don't have to," Benjamin said softly. "But we have a plan."

"But if somebody doesn't stop Regina…" Hal said.

"Of course, it is ultimately hopeless, but I am here to serve. The plan is the same as before," Dark Man said. "We set aside our personal problems, at least for the moment, and make sure Hitler does not get that bomb."

"Denver," Hal said. "We ought to be able to meet up with John Warner in Denver. Plenty of time to take over the plane and fly it on to Alamogordo."

There was a rumble as a major quake hit the bungalow.

"I take that back," Hal said. "We better get going now. I think we're running out of time."

I nodded, wiping the tears from my eyes with one swipe of the back of my hand. I was too dumbstruck by my own emotions to say anything, but I knew in my heart that my allies in this room were right. And if I could not bring back Jenny or John, maybe at least I could do something for the people I cared for. I might be able to finish John Warner's mission, and that would be something.

"Okay, time to go."

"That's my girl," Rocco said, putting his arm around my shoulders. I looked up at him and managed a faint smile, but he was not looking at me. His attention was across the room in the direction of Dark Man, and the expression on his face was as dark as that of a wronged Mafioso prince.

CHAPTER 27

I took poor, nervous Rocco by the hand and we jumped off the sheer face of the cliff in front of Jenny's bungalow. Back again in 1939, it was early evening when we finally caught up with my grandfather. We had boarded a United Air Lines DC-3 passenger flight from LA by way of Phoenix, Gallup, Albuquerque, and Taos, hoping to backtrack from Alamogordo until we crossed paths with him. And it looked like we finally figured something right.

We ended up east of Colorado Springs, at a small ranch with a tiny airstrip runway that my grandfather owned. He had bypassed Denver entirely, only stopping to refuel where he could before continuing in his mission to get to Alamogordo. Benjamin filled me in when outlining our plan. This was the place John Warner had called home, a small ranch in the hilly southeastern corner of Colorado with the Rocky Mountains looming in the distant west. Benjamin had heard Jenny mention it, but he had never been there, and we only found it with the help of a small hand-drawn map he had once seen in one of Jenny's notebooks.

I took a chance and went ahead of the others and broomed myself there, and lucky thing it turned out okay, my clothes were old enough to make the journey with me, and after a few flashes of night and day I was standing next to the Curtiss Robin, not two hundred feet from a house and an old barn.

Even though the ranch was showing some signs of neglect, it looked like it had once been a sweet little farm. There were about fifty acres of pasture

256

with a stream meandering through it, and some additional land that had been planted in corn, except that had dried in the field without being harvested. And there was a small wooden-frame homestead with one light burning in a front window.

The house faced west with a view that sloped down into a shallow scoop of a valley and then back up to the towering presence of the Rockies nearly a hundred miles away. Close by and to one side of the house was a straight length of unpaved roadway, and when I saw my grandfather's Robin parked there I knew that had to be his private runway and I had finally caught up to him. I was relieved to see the plane looking sprightly and ready to lift off into the evening sky.

When I ran up to the house I finally found my grandfather, John Warner himself, slumped in a rocking chair on the front porch. He looked like he might have been sleeping, but he straightened up and then stood with some effort and limped toward me. I found words tumbling from me as I ran into his outstretched arms. I had always wanted to meet him, and I finally was.

"Grandpa Jack!"

"Little Juniper Rose, all grown up and come back to the past to help out!"

"You knew I would be coming?"

"Jenny said so."

He was pale and worn and gasping for breath. He was losing his hair in big tufts and there were bad spots on his skin. But his eyes lit and he smiled a weak smile when he saw me.

"Grandpa, I've been missing you by seconds all across the country from New Jersey!"

257

"That's nobody's fault at all, Juniper. That's the way she's meant to play out."

"But—"

He put his finger to his lips.

"Shush, now. Somebody's about to show up."

There was the distant mutter of motor vehicles and a string of trucks approached down the two-lane blacktop that fronted his ranch. They stopped at the tall pole frame with the wooden "JW" carved in a timber slab and then turned into the gravel drive that led to the house.

In the next few seconds, about ten squat, square black vans and armored trucks roared up and surrounded us.

Regina stepped from the leading van and all but ignored us while she directed her men to my grandfather's airplane. Everybody, even Regina, was appropriately dressed in black T-shirts and pants. It was like the movies, when the lady in charge of proper garments hands out the right clothing.

"Get over there, you fools! I want the bag from the passenger seat! It's behind the pilot's seat, you idiots!"

She yelled at the top of her lungs and rudely shoved a pair of the thugs closest to her toward the Robin. They found and easily lifted a big bag from John Warner's plane. Two of the largest men shouldered it and trotted off to one of the armored trucks, where they carefully laid it down inside.

Regina snorted her old familiar chuckle as she saw the big sack they carried was a dog food bag.

"Magic dog food! A touch of the old Papa John Warner humor! How clever!"

She turned her attention to us, giving me a look of amused disgust.

"Little Jousie. I should have killed you years ago."

"Remember, you did try," I said. "Repeatedly. Like to try again?"

I moved toward her, remembering my touch had once scalded her skin, and I guess she was remembering, too, because she backed away and stood behind two of her tough-guy henchmen.

I was remembering something else about Regina from the old days. We used to play this deadly game where we would quietly position ourselves, with her aiming to have a good shot at pushing me over a balcony railing or out of an open window, and me quietly sliding to one side or the other, using people around us to block or parry her moves. But now it seemed to me she had another object for her deadly little game.

"You want to kill Grandpa," I said.

"You think I came out here to godawful nowhere to pick sagebrush?"

"But he's your own father."

She shrugged.

"Once John Warner is dead, he can hardly be expected to deliver his shipment to Alamogordo, can he. History changes once and for all. Your side loses, I win."

She looked around me at the figure hunched in the rocking chair.

"Hello, Dad," she said. "Did you hear I killed Mom?"

"You'll go to witch hell for that one."

259

"Oh sure, witch hell, I can't wait…but your Jenny is gone forever."

"Maybe. But maybe dead isn't dead forever. You ever hear that one?"

An uncertain expression clouded Regina's timelessly smooth features for a few brief seconds, but she recovered nicely.

"Rubbish," she said. "You don't know anything."

"Better get going," John Warner said. "Juniper's friend Rocco and his government pals are on their way over here just about now."

Regina sneered like she did not have a care in the world, but my grandfather pointed and from where we were we could actually see Rocco's small army of vehicles speeding along the road from the north, and if she wanted to make her getaway she was going to have to do it now.

"I guess we'll have to be content with the rabbit pellets. You still don't win."

She gave me a last appraising look, trying to calculate her chances of getting around me for one last shot at taking down her father. She shifted her weight from one leg to the other, and I did the same. And then she gave out an exasperated curse and ran for her van.

CHAPTER 28

I thought I should go after her, but when I started to make a move, Grandpa held me back.

"Let her go. She's going to make a run for the border," he said.

"But we could stop her!"

"She'll cross over at El Paso and her little troop will shoot their way across Mexico to the East Coast. A lot of trouble for her, but I'm guessing in the end she'll probably make it."

"But—"

"And when she does finally get to Cancun or Manzanillo or wherever, a Nazi sub will meet her. She doesn't have Frank Spedding, but she doesn't think she needs him. The Krauts will carefully store that priceless bag for a trip back to I'm guessing Hamburg."

"But—"

"Back in Hamburg, they will find that her eighty-pound bag of premium dog food actually contains forty pounds of premium dog food and forty pounds of lead weights."

"Oh…"

A faint smile lit John Warner's face.

"I'd like to be there when that happens. My daughter Regina always was a mean, spoiled little brat. But she never was all that smart."

He studied me for a moment.

"Think you can fly the Robin? Upslope most of the way, just follow the two-lane blacktop. One stop to refuel. Benjamin Greyfellow will light a fire by the side of the road; you land on a flat stretch there. Take off again. A few hops and you complete my mission for me, close the loop, history intact, the world saved."

"I think I can do that," I said. "But we have to get you to a hospital."

"No, not me, Juniper. Me, I'm done this time around."

"But—"

"Juniper, what little I know about it, Jenny taught me. Time is like a river. What our stupid daughter is trying to do is divert the whole damn stream. In the *real* river, my river in my time, you know I disappeared. Well, what you *don't* know is that I was the one who delivered the pellets to Alamogordo and I didn't know enough to protect myself from that devil radiation. Now somebody has to do it to get things back on track. Doesn't matter who. But it must be done."

"Oh, Grandpa…"

"Don't worry, Juni-Rose. You will be safe. We have the pellets packed in a lead casing again. Interesting how this thing we call time works out. Events seem to almost want to move back the way they flowed originally."

The expression on his face turned sad.

"Of course, they can't bring back the dead."

"What about you now?"

"When we lived through this the first time, I *did* die. I don't see any way to change that. Wouldn't want to, actually. Well, maybe a part of me would, but for the most part, no."

And then he brightened a little.

"There's so much stuff we don't know. I believe I'll be meeting up with my Jenny a bit farther down the stream. Don't you doubt that one for a minute. I think we will. I'm pretty sure about it."

I saw him cross the fingers on one of his gnarled hands, *Cross my heart and hope to die.* Or, more accurately, *There has to be something more than this. Come on, Lord, what is a life down here without a heaven up there?*

It was easy to see why I loved my grandpa.

CHAPTER 29

Grandpa Jack gave me his old leather aviator's cap and a white silk scarf and a pair of Grandma Jenny's snappy tan horse riding pants. I was quite the romantic historical figure as I pulled the cap on, wrapped the scarf around my neck, and climbed in his Robin. The radial engine roared in my ears and the chill evening air whistled through the open windows as I bumped the Robin along his pasture runway. The sturdy little plane gathered speed and I found myself hoping I would know the precise moment when there would be enough speed to launch us into the night sky.

Just another stunt gig, I told myself. *Come on, Juniper Rose, lift this baby off the ground!*

Frank Spedding's lead coffin with its heavy load of enriched uranium pellets was holding us down, but there was one last bounce on the dusty dirt runway and we staggered up into the sky. I cautiously pushed us into a slow but steady climb and we leveled out at about six hundred feet over the roadway, heading south for the first of several fuel stops on my way to Alamogordo.

It was icy cold and I was glad to have Grandpa's maroon woolen sweater on under my old leather jacket, and twice grateful for my flying lessons. When Uncle Alfred's brother Rudy taught me the rudiments of flying the Robin, I do not believe he had in mind that I would actually live long enough to use his instructions, but here I was, gliding along under a full moon with a silvery ribbon of two-lane asphalt below me. I was thinking how flying the plane was easy, like riding a flying bicycle, and that this was going to be one easy ride for an experienced stunt lady like me.

But then a voice started up right next to my left ear and then my right ear and then back again, and things turned very bad. It was Mipsi the parasite sprite, demanding to be let back in.

We yelled at each other and she wheedled, whined, and pestered me without a moment's rest for the better part of an hour while the road wound only too slowly beneath us. I was trapped with her in the narrow confines of the Robin and there was no way I could get away from her. She battered and hammered away at me, making little runs to bounce off my forehead or my ears.

"Let me in! Let me in! You've got to let me in! You've got to!"

Finally I shouted in exasperation, "Show yourself, you little twerp!"

"Oh, was that all you wanted?" She blinked into my line of sight, a purple apparition sitting on the control panel in front of me. "Now will you let me in?"

"No, I will not! I do not see one good reason why I should!"

"I can tell you Dark Man's secrets. That's a very good reason."

"I already know about him. He is a lonely creep who likes to sex Earth girls like they are animals. He calls it making love with a god, like he is showering us with his glory. I call it bestiality."

"Well, face it, you *are* animals."

"Don't push me, Mipsi!"

265

"Dark Man has a plan to destroy you all. I'll tell you about it, but you have to let me in. I have to be in, I have to be in!"

"No, Mipsi. That is not going to happen."

She fluttered close in front of my face. It was way too close for my comfort, and I had to swat her away.

"Ow!" she said. She sat in the farthest corner of the cockpit, which was not nearly far enough for my comfort, and pretended to be hurt.

"Stop looking like you have been injured. You are not getting in."

"Oh, very well then. Hey, look, there's our first fuel stop down below!"

I saw a tiny fire by the roadside in the near distance. But then there was another spot of flame, and a third, and then dozens all along the way. In fact, there were dozens of intertwining roads below, each one looking as real as the next.

Mipsi gave me a smug look.

"You're going to need my help to sort out which is the right one. Now will you let me in?"

I was so angry my hands were shaking on the controls, but out of nowhere I heard Grandma Jenny's calm voice. *I'll bet she responds to mind control, dear girlie.*

Mind control. I reached out with such a naked fury that I nearly crushed the poor sprite to death. Once I realized I was firing a howitzer rather than a pea shooter, I backed off and heard her gasp in relief.

"Oh, for Jupiter's sake! You nearly crushed me to death!"

"You deserve it. What an annoying pest you are!"

"I won't do it anymore."

"That is right, you certainly will not."

Without knowing what I was doing, more out of angry frustration than anything, I imagined her in a fruit jar with holes poked in the lid for air, and in the next second, there leaning in a corner of the Robin's simple wood veneer control panel in front of my wide-eyed astonishment was a furious little Mipsi-in-a-bottle, battering and ramming frantically in a vain attempt to get out. My wish had actually become reality!

"Make the fake fires down there go away and I will let you out after we land."

"Now, now, now!" she insisted. "You let me out now!"

I picked up the bottle and held it near the open window.

"No, not now. And if you do not do as I say, it is *Sprite overboard!*"

That settled her down, and the bonfires below began to wink out. When there was only one left, I circled at about two hundred feet and came in for a landing. As it was, I was a little too hesitant getting the Robin to touch wheels on the ground and we came right up on a curve and practically ran off the road into a ravine before the plane came rolling to a stop.

My first flight piloting an airplane! I could hardly wait to add this one to my stunt girl résumé! Proficient at piloting ancient aircraft!

Benjamin and one of his gray pals refueled the plane from ten-gallon cans.

267

Dark Man handed me a bottle of Coke. I took a sip and that opened my eyes.

"It's the real thing," Benjamin said with a smile.

I felt the jolt that had made Coke so popular until the 1950s.

"Wow."

Dark Man frowned at me.

"By the way, where's Mipsi?"

I pointed to the Ball jar resting on the floor of the cockpit.

"I had to bottle her up. She wanted back in."

"You should have let her in. Otherwise she'll die."

"There is no way that is going to happen."

"When did you get so headstrong?" he said.

"*You* can let her out of the bottle, dark boy. And you can let her in your head all you want. After all, she's *your* sex toy."

"She looks a little…tattered."

"Not my problem, Zandor."

Looking up from his duties pouring gasoline into the fuel tank, Benjamin gave me a nearly imperceptive nod. I reached for the jar and tossed it to Dark Man. He took great care in catching it.

"She has to live in a biological presence or she will die."

"Then she can live in you."

"I am not exactly a bio-form. It works, but it is not the perfect solution."

"What are you, then?"

"Silicate, actually." His frown deepened, and I got the idea he was angry with himself for having

268

said too much. "We will have to talk about this later."

"I do not think so," I said. "Have her take refuge in a goat or a moose."

Actually, there was a lot more I wanted to discuss with Dark Man, but I was thinking that a sour attitude on my part might knock a little of the smug out of him.

He sighed and beckoned with one finger and Mipsi zipped inside him.

"You no longer trust me," Zandor said, sending a *poor me* look in my direction.

"When did I ever trust you? You know the old saying, *Trust but verify*."

"I don't even know what that means."

"How about *Good fences make good neighbors*?"

"I don't get that one either."

"I did not think for a moment that you would. You only think of yourself."

I climbed up onto the side strut of the Robin and pulled myself back in the cockpit.

"Am I good to go, Benji?"

Benjamin actually smiled. I think he liked his new nickname. "Right-o, Captain!"

"See you at the Alamo!"

He directed several of his fellow gray men to pick up the tail of the Robin and turn it around. I would be taking off into the wind, and expected an easier liftoff. This proved true and in another thirty seconds I was climbing into the night sky, this time without the pesky and dangerous Mipsi trying to bounce around inside my head.

At around six hundred feet I did a one eighty and continued following the road to Alamogordo. I refueled in Taos and again in Albuquerque. The land flattened out and became a desert. And nothing else happened until I actually got to my final destination where, filled with elation and overconfidence, I landed my grandpa's Robin in the middle of a dozing herd of cows that had wandered onto the little hard-packed salt and gypsum strip that was trying its best to pass for a runway. The way I found it was sheer luck and a huge letter "S" for "Spedding" that another squad of Benjamin's gray men had scratched in the dirt surface next to the runway. The gentle bovines started moving around and went into a bit of a panic, and Frank Spedding, who had run out to the landing area to welcome his pellets, sprained an ankle running in the opposite direction to avoid death by hoof.

There was no hangar or even a barn. I wondered how the cows found anything to eat out here. I made my way through a few of the bovine stragglers to a convoy of army trucks and vans.

"You gotta learn to land better," a voice addressed me in heavily New York–accented English.

"What are *you* doin' here?" I said, falling into his New York Italian dialect.

"Ah, you ain't got the accent down. You got to hit the *doin'* a little harder."

It was Hal's dad Charley. He was holding a tommy gun at parade rest. He was so short he nearly did not have to lean it on a handy chunk of stone, but other than that he looked like he knew how to handle his weaponry.

"And what I am *doin'* here is following up on my investments. That means the alcohol import business, which is strictly legal, by the way, plus making sure the goofball over there don't get his balls shot off."

He pointed behind me to where his son Rocco was already helping a squad of GI soldiers unload the heavy lead-lined box from the Robin.

Knowing Regina the way I did, I still could not relax.

"What if Reggie figures out what we did and comes back here?"

Charley grinned and rolled a cold stogie around in his mouth.

"That's sorta what I'm here for. But we don't think that's gonna happen. We're keepin' her busy. We got a couple happy shooters trailing after her. Every now and then somebody lets loose a ping or two just to make sure her and her gang of thugs keep on humping in the direction of the Bay of Mexico."

"Oh."

"Actually, one or two of our guys got a little overenthusiastic and took out a couple of the golden-haired boys. Well, four, actually. We had to pull them back a little. Wouldn't want to take out the whole bunch of frickin' Lugans before they loaded the pooch food on the sub."

"'Lugans'?"

"Hey, they call us 'Dagos' and 'Wops'; we call them 'Krauts' and 'Lugans.'"

Charley shrugged, and then he grinned at me like the wolf moving in on Little Red Riding Hood.

"Now, how about our deal? You promised my firstborn is gonna sign on for *the moo-vies!* So when do I get to see Rocco's name up in the lights?"

"Soon. Seriously. I'll be working on that. I promise."

He pinched my cheek. It was an affectionate gesture, but it did sting a little.

"I know you will," he said.

CHAPTER 30

I was at loose ends, as the expression goes. It is like you are watching a movie and the heroine has completed what she thought was her nearly impossible task, only there is something else out there nagging at the back of her mind, things shouldn't be this easy, and if they were this easy, then where was the cheering and the marching band?

It was hot out there in the middle of nowhere, New Mexico. I sat in the protective shade under the left wing of Grandpa's Robin and watched as the army troopers drove away with his precious cargo. Nothing else changed. There was no tremendous shaker, no grand moment as the timeline reverted to its old self. I could hear the buzz of insects and the *moo* of a distant cow. And then Dark Man resolved himself into my ability to see him.

"Wow. Do not do that!"

He gave me his *Mister Superior* look.

"I tried for a gradual showing so as not to frighten you."

"Try it again so I can get used to it."

He faded to invisible. I concentrated and found that I could make out his faint presence. But I did not mention that as he swam back into my vision. He was barefoot and naked except for a short set of briefs. He ran his skin through a range of tints from cherrywood through ebony before settling on a deep redwood.

"For maximum photonic absorption," he said. He closed his eyes and softly sang a couple of lines from David Bowie's *Space Oddity*.

Ground Control to Major Tom
Take your protein pills and put your helmet on.

He stretched out on the ground as close to me as he could get without being in the shade.

"I declare us the champions, at least the winners of this round."

"How so?"

"The Nazi sub won't get to Hamburg for another few weeks. Your lovely aunt has no idea her prize is dog food."

I glanced at him, lying next to me like a lump of reddish brown wood, wondering if he'd had his way with Regina. I was pretty sure he had. The fellow was like a sexual garbage truck, picking up trampy Earth girls wherever he could find them.

"I am surprised the whole Earth is not populated with witches by now."

"Don't be cruel. I do have my standards."

"Right. If it has a vagina, you poke it. And what is this about 'We are the champions'? You did not really help me except when you had to."

"Don't be a spoilsport. We have to talk."

"What about?" I said.

"You need me. You may be straightening out this little timeline fantasy of your aunt's, but you are in terrible danger."

"Exactly what is my problem?"

"If you'd just let Mipsi in, I could make you understand in a flash."

"That is not going to happen, space pirate o' love."

"I could force you."

I felt a curious push at what I guess the old hippies would call my aura, or my *kirlian presence*.

274

Hell, until a moment before I did not even know I *had* such a presence, but I realized instinctively I could not let him get away with that. I did not understand what was going on, but I knew it was the raw beginning of some sort of a struggle for dominance. I suspected it was going to continue as long as he was hanging around, but I had to do something to get him to back off.

"I'll kill your little sex pal," I said.

Imagine, me threatening to kill anyone! But Zandor clearly thought it might be a possibility.

"You wouldn't," he said. He rolled over and looked up at me.

"Little Mipsi? I would crush her like an ant. Ask her."

The purple-light sprite came fluttering out of his left ear and one look at the expression on her face was enough to tell the story. Since I had batted her around and stuffed her in a bottle, she was afraid of me.

Zandor was a study in controlled fury. I did not know what he was going to do next. He looked like he was considering some seriously unpleasant options when I noticed a trail of dust approaching across the desert. It spun in a circle and did a few loops the way high school kids do to burn off a little adrenaline and in the process waste a lot of tire rubber. It was Hal in his steel-blue Buick Special. I jumped up and started across the dusty runway, as much to escape Zandor as to see him.

"Rocco! You're late!" I lied. "Sorry, Zandor, I have a hot date."

That made him sit up and take notice.

"But wait! We haven't finished our conversation!"

"No, we are finished here. Go put a helmet on your dick, Major Tom."

I came up on the driver's side of Hal's good old Dynaflash.

"Move over, pal. Let a lady show you how to drive!"

I piled in and hit the gas and the good old Dynaflash spit a cloud of dusty gravel in Zandor's direction before I had the steely beast in control, or maybe I was in control all along and just did that for spite. I waved good-bye to Dark Man, who had a big frown pasted all over his demigod-like features.

I drove Rocco back toward civilization, going just about as fast as we could go, only stopping along the road at a place called the Wagon Wheel Café where they had great chicken tacos, and we found a motel just out of town on the way north to Albuquerque. Hal proved to be gentle and understanding of a stunt girl's needs, and when it came to size I think he was every bit as impressive as strutting Zandor, the alien who would be a demigod of love.

Late the next morning, Rocco and I lay together thinking separate thoughts about us and the future. There was so much I could not tell him. One way of looking at it, we were just a young couple who, with a lot of help from his dad's gang, the FBI, some odd gray men, a few elderly ladies who claimed they were witches, and a strange-looking black man alien, had somehow managed to retrieve Frank Spedding's radioactive pellets from the Nazis. Of course, there was that one trip to the future, but

Rocco seemed to have an amazing capacity to accept the strange and the weird.

"How is it you can believe all this crazy stuff?" I said.

"About you being a witch?"

"Well, yeah."

"That's easy. I'm a big Edgar Rice Burroughs fan. *A Princess of Mars*. John Carter. *Tarzan of the Apes*. Ju-Ju Bird, there's stuff out there you can't even imagine."

I had to remind myself we were in the 1930s. Since Rocco was taking things in stride, maybe it was better to leave well enough alone. Chances were that introducing him to the space-time continuum, wormholes, and stellar disruptions might be a bridge too far. It was going to be enough of a challenge to present him with another disruptive form of travel by brooming. And that was looming on our event horizon, because it was the only way I could think of to fulfill my promise to his dad.

"You like me a little, right?" I started, hoping Hal would not spot the note of hesitation in my voice. At least that part seemed okay. He was oblivious that anything might be the slightest bit wrong. Good sex can do that to a person.

"I love you!" he bubbled enthusiastically. "Love you! Love you! Love you!"

Lord love a duck! We have a wild fling in the hay and now he loves me! I was at the deep end of the pool, and me without water wings. How was I going to flounder my way out of this one? Sure, I wanted love and Rocco/Hal certainly had all the right parts, but for me love was still a someday thing. I had so much to learn and to do, just to earn my stripes as a full-fledged mistress of the dark arts, or whatever it was that I was.

"Well, I get a kick out of you too, kiddo," I said, thinking back to what might have been appropriate slang some years before I was born. "But I have a problem."

"Shoot," he said. "Nothing we can't fix."

"Well, you see, I promised your dad I would get you a film gig."

"I don't see the problem. Good old Dynaflash can zoom us out to Hollywood in a day or two."

I knew it, this boy wanted to be a star! And frankly, I believed he had the real goods. He was devastatingly handsome and his voice had that just-right timbre and range for heroic as well as loving declarations in the talkies. Hey, I am a wannabe director; I do know these things.

I patted his hand, the one closest to me that was toying with the soft skin on my left breast.

"Wait. Give me a moment here, lover-boy. I know what to do! I need to drop you off to see an agent named Seymour Blinker. His office will be somewhere in Beverly Hills."

"I should find it in a phone book, go there, and say you sent me?"

"Yes, find it in a phone book. But do not use my name. Seymour does not know me. I know his son, a kid named Sumner."

His face fell. "And just how is this going to work?"

"Do not worry, my dear Rocco. Tell him you know he is casting for a movie called *Fighter Squadron*. Hollywood is a place full of secrets that nobody ever keeps. Nobody is supposed to know about that picture, so he will think you are an insider. He will give you a part in it. Trust me, I know these things."

His expression cleared, and he said, "Well, okay then."

I had to admire his ready spirit of adventure. Hal was the ultimate risk taker; he did have that acting talent going for him, and if a little ride down the river would get him into the movies, he looked primed and ready to take a shot at it.

"Huh. Well, okay, but we've got serious work to finish here before we go on some kind of a frolic."

He leaned over me and discovered my left breast with his lips before moving on to the other one. I felt my nipples harden and a warm flush race through my body.

The boy was right, you know? There was work to be done.

I was thinking there were not too many of God's gifts as wonderful as lazy sex in the late morning. I rolled over, pushing Rocco on his back. As our lips brushed I straddled his thighs and pushed my hips down to gently but firmly wrap myself around him. And then I smoothly shifted us into first gear. I knew how to drive this machine.

CHAPTER 31

Once, a matter of some years before all this mad business with Regina wanting to warp history so she could become queen of the world or whatever, I had a brief fling with a stunt guy named Billy Zip who took me on a weekend date to a far-out nude hippie hot springs place in the Mojave Desert. A few weeks later, Billy headed for Morocco with a starlet whore to work on a flick. He did not get the gig or the girl, but that is not the point. I still remembered the nude hippie hot springs, and as we drove Haliburton (Rocco) Hamilton's sleek Buick west across Arizona, I started to get the idea that remote hot springs location might be useful. The way I saw it, I was going to have to broom him along with me, but it would be complicated because I was going to have to drop him off mid-broom at a specific time in show biz history. He would land a part in *Fighter Squadron* and, unless I blew the broom-drop (or whatever we witchey-poos called it), film history would be on its way.

For all Rocco knew, we were heading for Los Angeles to meet up with an agent to get him in the movie biz. And while that was sort of the idea, the problem was a lot more complicated than what I was telling him. I knew my agent's dad, the famous Seymour Blinker, had supplied some relatively unknown actors for *Fighter Squadron*. That was in 1948. With my newfound skills at brooming, I was hoping to drop Rocco off in Beverly Hills in that fated year, while I was making my way back to my own present.

But you know life has to be more than work, work, work. Rocco and I enjoyed one heck of a lusty night in what was then the small cow town of Las Vegas. He had gotten into a bottle of rum and was sleeping it off as I drove us across the California border.

We left the two-lane blacktop and the road turned into gravel, and then became a little more than a dusty dirt path. The rough passage did finally wake Rocco when he nearly fell out of the car as we navigated a steep and rocky downslope.

"Hell, Juni, where are we?"

"A hot springs place. I have been here before. Hang on!"

That was the wrong choice of words, because at that moment I managed to hang the Buick up on a particularly lumpy boulder in the center of the path, leaving us to spin.

"But I didn't bring my bathing suit," he said as he got out and looked at the problem.

"Not necessary, dear friend. Come on!"

With his help we managed to get his car off the rock. We put the convertible top up and began walking down a steep path. The noonday sun was uncomfortably hot, but fortunately for us, the springs were only a hundred yards away.

When we got there, several nude couples waved a friendly welcome. A breeze was up and the smell of marijuana was in the air.

We climbed over rocks and stood hand in hand, looking down at the clear water thirty feet below.

"You sure this is a good idea?" Rocco said.

"Yep."

A shadow crossed the pond. For a moment I thought it might be a hawk or a vulture, but looking up I saw the shape of Regina's predatory harpies diving toward us. Hal had not noticed.

"You mean we just jump in?"

"Yeah," I said. "Better keep your clothes on."

"Why?"

"You'll see."

I was standing next to him, still with my dress on and Jenny's travel bag over my shoulder. The harpies were in full dive mode. We did not have a moment to spare, but Rocco hesitated.

"You're not going like that?"

Before he could say anything more, I gave his arm a big yank and pulled us over the edge. The theory, of course, was that I could bring him along with me. More than a theory, I had read the instructions in my not-a-prayer book. I was not all that great at Middle English, but the recipe said *Than wheil hald one tigh, thet pilgrim comen weth.* My theory was, that meant Rocco was coming with me.

And I was right. I felt Hal freeze in terror as we slipped from free fall into *free time fall* and the endless flicker of night and day began.

Now came the hard part. We were leaving 1939, and I had set my mind to return to home, my real place and time in the river of my own life. But how was I, a rash novice at the art of brooming, going to know exactly when to let him go so he would arrive at his film star destiny? I tried counting years, desperately doing my best to remember how long it had taken for me to get backward from my normal time to 1939.

282

I heard his yell through the falling winds of time as if we were two skydivers in mid-flight.

"This is crazyyyyy weirrrrd!"

"Roccooooo! Do not forget to change your name!"

"What's my last name?"

1944. 1945. 1946. 1947. By my rough calculations we were out of time.

"Time is a river! You will think of something!"

I kissed his cheek, let go of his arm, and gave him a firm shove.

I got lucky on that one, and know that I was able to keep my promise to Rocco's dad. If you are interested, you can go to imdb.com and look it up for yourself. There's an uncredited player who plays a second lieutenant in *Fighter Squadron* in 1948. And in 1949 you will find a detective in a movie called *Undertow* played by an actor who calls himself Roc Hudson.

CHAPTER 32

I had hoped I was brooming to Jenny's bungalow in the present day. However, my skills being what they were, I ended up a mile or two away, on the corner of Fredonia and Ventura Boulevard, near Hanna-Barbera's animation studio and even closer to my apartment. A *Deutschland Today* newspaper in a street corner stand indicated I had only missed my target by a week or two.

Deutschland Today. That was not reassuring. I had broomed back to my present and it still looked like Regina's plot to change history had succeeded.

It was the middle of the night and the streets were deserted. I slung my travel bag more comfortably over one shoulder and took the short hike up Fredonia to my apartment. I was going to have to be satisfied with the brooming progress I had made. Hell, take the joy; at least I had landed in Southern California. I could only pray that I had done a proper job getting Rocco to his film gig in the late 1940s.

I stopped off briefly at my apartment and picked up my mail. My dismay mounted as I noticed the mail was all stamped with good old red, white, and black Greater German Empire stamps. Were we too late in trying to stop Regina? Was everything we had done for nothing?

I changed into a pair of sweats. Then I unchained Putt-Putt and let the old gal chug me on up the hill to the bungalow.

The scene when I got there was one of unexpected calamity. Jenny's property—mine, now—looked like it had been hit by a firebomb.

The entire cottage, and Benjamin's place behind it, had been burned to the ground, and all that remained were a few blackened beams of charred wood.

A lone fireman was dozing in the driver's seat of his small red Volkswagen pickup truck. He stirred as I knocked on his window.

"Vas is das?"

That was not the language I was hoping to hear. Had everything we had done been a waste? Had Regina somehow managed to get the uranium pellets to Germany? Had John Warner's death been all for nothing?

The fireman would not roll down his window. He just frowned at me and shook his head as if I was the one doing something wrong.

"Iss after curfew," he said, wagging one scolding finger at me.

"What happened here?" I shouted through the glass.

"Who knows? Somebody chust trows the match. Americans are such pigs."

And with that he started his engine and drove away.

Something stirred behind me. I turned to see Benjamin sitting on a rock near where in happier times the hang glider crowd had launched their flights from the hillside cliff. He had a small suitcase and looked ready to leave.

I walked over to him. He was gray as ever, but seemed somehow smaller and shrunken in his spirit.

"Benji."

I gave him a hug and he responded with a tired smile.

"It was Regina," he said. "She was like a living torch. She just stood there and shrieked her crazy laughs while she blasted away like a living flame thrower."

His clothing was scorched.

"You saved some things."

"Yes, some things. Not much. But I'll be okay."

I tried to block the fury I felt mounting inside. *Regina would pay for this!*

But I could not let myself go off half-cocked. My aunt was dangerous and she wanted to kill me. I had to think clearly.

"Benjamin, come stay with me. I have extra room."

"It's no use. Regina has won."

"We do not know that. We do not know how any of this works. I am thinking it may take a while for the river to straighten itself out again. And, you know, why would she pick now to destroy Jenny's place?"

"What do you mean?"

I knew I was going out on a limb, but if my wicked aunt had wanted to burn her mother's bungalow, decades had passed since the war, and she could have done it at any time.

"Something's going on, Benji. I think the future is in a sort of balance. It may not know which way to go, and Regina is getting desperate."

I do not think he entirely believed me, but there was a ray of hope in his expression as he climbed on Putt-Putt behind me.

CHAPTER 33

After some trial and error, I figured out I could call Jenny's old friends on the witch line, a sort of private mental cell phone system.

We gathered for a meeting around the kitchen in my apartment. I sent out for coffee and strudel at the nearest Deutschbucks. Blu, Tillie, and Margotha pulled up chairs while Benjamin stood politely to one side.

"Right now I would like to burn *her* house down!" I said.

I was thinking about Regina's big brick mansion in Winnetka, the one she had laid together brick by brick with such loving care.

Blu shook her head.

"No, babes. That be what the crazy bitch want. She be lookin' for fire for fire."

Tillie nodded.

"Yes. Misdirection. We don't know what is happening, but neither does she. We know Regina delivered the bag of pellets to the submarine, but there was no way she was going to get on that sub."

Blu nodded. Ancient Margotha looked like she was dozing off, but I sensed a glittery awareness about her.

"Yes. She hates confined spaces."

I thought I understood.

"So maybe she thinks her plan is working," I said.

"And why wouldn't she? So far, it seems to be. There haven't been any quakes in a few days," Tillie said.

But just as she spoke, there was a bit of a tremor. We looked at each other and did a group shrug.

"I cannot just sit here and do nothing," I said. "I want to rip her to shreds."

"No," Tillie said.

"Not yet," Blu said.

"You are not ready," Margotha said.

"Well, I have to go anyway."

Benjamin opened his suitcase, and after digging through the charred remains of the few items he had saved, he came up with a tattered black gown. He held it at arm's length and shook the ashes from it.

"Jenny's war dress," he said.

I recognized it, though I had only seen it once before. It was the swirling black robe my grandmother had worn on that long-ago Easter morning when she had saved me from Regina's arrow.

Without a moment's hesitation, I put on the garment. It felt all silky and smooth and fit me like a glove. We stood in a circle and held hands. I wished my friends good luck, and then I jumped off my patio deck.

I was aiming for a time a week or two after I finished my grandfather's task by flying the Robin to Alamogordo. But I did not head for New Mexico. This time, I aimed for the Plaza Hotel in New York. Admittedly, I was still a novice at the difficult craft of brooming, but I guess I managed to come pretty close, this time showing up only a couple months late, in August 1939.

One look around Palm Court with all the Nazi flags and the red, white, and black bunting, and I could see things were looking bad for my *'the river of time takes a while to get back in its original course'* theory.

What a bummer! All our efforts to stop Regina looked to be a dismal failure. The newspapers shouted triumphantly that Hitler had begun his invasion of Poland, and Europe seemed sliding toward the war. Maybe before coming here I should have done a little more checking to see how things actually turned out. No, that would just have delayed my chance to get back at my aunt.

Okay, so she had changed history. The question was, *What could I do to change* her *history?*

And there was one other small detail. There was no news whatsoever about Hitler dropping an atom bomb on London. I had been worrying that maybe Regina had discovered what we had done and returned to Alamogordo to steal Grandpa's precious cargo. But maybe the Nazis did not have the radioactive pellets after all! Maybe the river of time was messy, with a lot of little coves and creeks, and some things just had to work themselves out.

I was here now. I was alive and I had some powers. Maybe I barely understood them, but they were real, and so just possibly all was not hopeless. Maybe it was up to me to help the river get back on its proper path. So I gathered up my resolve and went into a ladies' room where I primped my hair, put on a little dark red lipstick (for drama) and checked my "battle" outfit. And then I returned to Palm Court just in time for tea and afternoon biscuits.

A quartet was playing classical music. The musicians took a short break and then were joined by a teenager wearing what looked like a boy's version of a Nazi stormtrooper's outfit. The musicians struck up a marching beat and the teenager stood and began to sing in a quavering high tenor:

Die StraBe Frei den braunen Batallionen
Die StraBe frei dem Sturmabteilungsmann!

"What the hell is going on?" I whispered under my breath.

The teen boy sang:

Es schau'n aufs Hakenkreuz voll Hoffnung schon Millionen
Der Tag fur Freiheit und fur Brot Bricht an!

"He's singing to the glory of the Nazi movement," Tillie said. "'The day of freedom and bread dawns.'" She gave off a snorting little laugh.

"Tillie!"

Yes, Grandma Jenny's old friend Tillie Noonschnapper was sitting across the table from me, dressed in a black battle gown that looked as battered and worn as my own!

"You didn't think we were going to let you have all the fun, did you?"

"It's dat wicked ol' Horst Wessel song," another voice said. "Trumpeting the joys of the skinhead life."

That last was from Blu Baxter. She slid into a seat next to Tillie. She had her own battle gown, topped off with a tall and rumpled cone hat with a brim around it.

"Like the hat?" she said. "I thought maybe I'd go with the classic witch look."

"I think it is perfect. Where is Margotha?"

"Oh, she be around somewhere," Blu said. "Margo never one to miss a party, particular not this one!" Her smile faded into a grim warning.

A waitress came around and I ordered hot tea and raspberry and blueberry scones for everybody. I was not sure what to do next, but I figured the moment my aunt spotted us, events would take care of themselves.

Regina arrived with her own quartet of male admirers and took over a table near the musicians. I recognized the chubby Baron von Kurtzmark clinging to her side. The rest of her men looked like a mix of German military officers and self-important European diplomats and businessmen. When the young tenor reached the chorus in his song, they turned as one and gave the stiff-armed Hitler salute. I found that bit of *Mein Führer* ritual as unsettling as you might imagine.

Uncle Alfred was nowhere in sight. I hoped my spider-lady aunt had not seen reason to do him in. I knew he was a turncoat and a bad guy, but we had enjoyed a few moments and it was not my nature to stay mad at everybody. I guess bottom line I felt sorry for him, mostly because he had stuck with her through the years.

It was actually the salute that started the fight scene that turned out better than most of the action you pay to see in the movies. Everyone in the room saluted like robots—that is, everyone except the people sitting at our table and one old flower lady in the corner who sat slumped over her wilting wares and looked to have fallen asleep. We attracted attention because we were not giving the stiff-arm gesture, and when Regina was moved to look in our direction, she naturally spotted me.

I tried to calm myself. I had a pair of Grandma Jenny's crafty friends at my side and maybe we all had done better than I knew to set things right. Maybe this was a significant moment, the exact time when the river of time started reverting to its true channel. If so, it had better get going because that Nazi song was getting on my nerves.

I knew I had to concentrate on Regina, but at that moment something else caught my attention. There was an albino gentleman seated at a table on the far side of Regina and her gathering of admirers. This elegantly attired fellow was accompanied by a gorgeous lady dressed in a lavender chiffon gown. Of course I knew the handsome couple. It was my alien buddy and his light-sprite pal.

Blu saw them at the same time as I did and nudged me in the ribs. "There's a sight you not gonna see but once in a lifetime! Zandor figured out the Nazis hate the black folk, so he done put on white face to please the crowd!"

As we watched, Dark Man rose and came over to Regina's table. He bent down and cupped one hand to whisper in her ear. My wicked aunt looked up from her table and her gaze locked on mine. I was not sure what Zandor told her, but her expression became one of thunderous rage.

"That's *my* dress!" she shouted.

The waitress brought a cart with our tea and scones, but I could see we would not be taking refreshments. I stood up and faced Regina, and somehow found the voice to tell her how wrong she was.

292

"No, Regina. It was Jenny's. You were disinherited for—among other things—your lack of humanity. My grandmother gave me *everything*. So now this dress is mine!"

"*My* dress!" she shouted, her voice rising.

At that moment, Dark Man, who had returned to his own table, said something to his lavender companion. She moved toward Regina, and the moment she reached her, something frightful happened. My aunt was transformed into something like a purple windstorm, a ball of fury. She was still herself, but magnified into something monstrous, openly evil and dangerous. She puffed up like a poisonous serpent, and when it seemed she would burst, she hurled a ball of bright purple energy in our direction. That force, whatever it was, knocked Blu, Tillie, and me halfway across the room. We were shocked senseless and lay scattered about at her mercy. And of course, mercy was something she completely lacked. She huffed and puffed, building herself into another fireball of fury.

But before she could send a second burst of energy our way, a blast that was certain to take us out with a killing blow, the flower woman in the corner of the room came to life. The forgotten old hag rose from her sitting position and I heard the sound of groaning joints and snapping tendons as she began to straighten her ancient crippled frame. She grew in height and stature until she appeared to be ten times the size of an ordinary woman, and her form glittered with the colors of the rainbow.

"You—killed—my—beloved—daughter!" she said.

Her voice growled like thunder, and she jabbed a forked finger gesture at my aunt. A bolt of jet-black energy streaked from her fingers, a dark blast that sent Regina flying backward across the room to crash into a far wall. My aunt shook her head and looked around. Her aura of purple power was gone. I saw the flitting image of Mipsi the light-sprite flutter drunkenly across the room to retreat inside Zandor's ear. And Zandor himself stood and started to sneak away.

Margotha had saved us, but in doing so it looked like she had used all her powers. She was now hunched over as before, just a frail old flower lady sitting in the corner again. The rest of it was going to have to be up to us.

I knew my aunt. She had risked everything to become queen of the world. No battle would be over this quickly for her. She stood and slapped her head, trying to clear her thoughts. She called out for help, shouting in German, and a group of her personal troopers, men in dark turtlenecks and shiny black pants, practically oozed out of the walls to form a protective circle around her. At the same time, Zandor stopped in a doorway. He must have been confident of the outcome when he threw in with Regina, but now it looked like he was hedging his bets.

The scene became even more chaotic as several squads of uniformed American soldiers stormed into the room and engaged Regina's thugs. Taking advantage of the confusion, Blu, Tillie, and I moved forward until we surrounded Regina. We did it without thinking. I guess our idea was to keep her from physically running away. But everyone in the room paused whatever they were doing as Regina climbed up on a table in front of her. She flung her hands out in a dramatic gesture and shouted, "Good-bye world that I have known and loved!"

I knew what was coming next.

"Do not let her get away!"

But my wicked aunt was already leaping off the table and beginning to fade into wherever she thought she was going to make her escape.

There was only one thing left that I could try. I jabbed at her with the same forked fingers gesture I had seen Jenny use on that Easter morning when Regina had thought to kill me, the same gesture Margotha had used moments before. I leaned toward my wicked aunt like a predator that was ready to spring and screamed at her in a voice that sounded to my own ears like the cry of a furious hawk.

"You go see Sue!"

She heard me. I am sure she heard me. And the look of sudden fright on her face told me she got it, too.

Another brief moment and she was gone.

And then—and I do not know how or why—but the greater reality, whatever that is, finally began to react to what had happened. Not all at once, but piece by piece and bit by bit. The first thing I noticed was the crowd around the table where Regina had stood began to thin as the Nazis seemed to leave, one by one. I am not sure, but I think they started to disappear from our reality. Everyone seemed to be confused and upset and the fighting actually stopped. Some of Regina's thugs dissolved and some of them popped out of sight and

295

a few of the leftovers pushed their chairs back and ran for the door. The musical quartet hit discordant notes for a moment, and then began to play a familiar tune. I recognized the melody, and the words came to me, words I was afraid I would never hear again:

My country 'tis of thee/sweet land of liberty/of thee I sing

The room was shuddering and shaking, and bits of broken glass were falling on the dance floor. Tillie and Blu looked at each other. Blu shrugged and smiled.

"I know what we gotta do!"

"Oh, yes, my friend! This is an *occasion*! Party, *party!*"

Blu snapped her fingers and the quartet broke into their interpretation of a jazzy old New Orleans song:

Itchy gitchy ya ya ya!
Itchy gitchy ya ya ya!

Tillie retrieved the baron from under a table where he was hiding and after she did a little hocus to repair his bewildered spirits, they managed a few slow dances while working their way up toward a jitterbug. At the same time, Blu moved in on Dark Man to make her own statement on interstellar racial relationships, while a Tinker Bell–size Mipsi cheered from her perch overhead on one of the crystal chandeliers. Even Margotha revived enough to land an old college professor who could perform a decent waltz.

As for me, I came up with the tenor singer. He was older than he looked, actually in his late twenties, so I was not totally robbing the cradle. He turned out to be a fairly decent guy who said he was not really a Nazi but just a journeyman tenor who sang whatever was put on the stand in front of him, and so I decided he was old enough to learn a few things about life, liberty, and the pursuit of happiness.

There was a last shudder or two in the bright room at the Plaza as reality snapped back into its original course. Yes, we were going to have to fight a world war and many would die, but that was the way the river of time actually had been intended to run, and at least this small part of the universe would not be obliterated by one bad witch's foolish ambition and greed.

We danced on, hoping this would be the last of Regina's evil schemes and things would be more or less normal for the rest of our charmed lives. At least, that was the way we were feeling in the brash and bold borough of Manhattan in the good old US of A as time drifted us along into September of the year 1939.

THE END